ALSO BY ROB MURPHY

FICTION
Kingdom Come

ROTTEN
TO THE
CORE

= ROB MURPHY =

authorHOUSE®

AuthorHouse™ UK
1663 Liberty Drive
Bloomington, IN 47403 USA
www.authorhouse.co.uk
Phone: 0800.197.4150

*Rotten to the Core is a work of fiction and the creation of the author's imagination. Any
organisation which exists is referred to in a fictional context and the book is in no way a reflection
on the views of the organisations or their staff. All characters in the book are fictional and any
resemblance or similarity of same to people currently alive is coincidental and not intentional.*

Published by AuthorHouse 10/30/2017

ISBN: 978-1-5462-8299-0 (sc)
ISBN: 978-1-5462-8300-3 (hc)
ISBN: 978-1-5462-8298-3 (e)

Print information available on the last page.

PROLOGUE

1 June 2009
Rue Perronet
Neuilly-sur-Seine
Paris

"Zut!"

François Picard, Secretary-General of the Fédération Internationale de Football Association, better known by its initials, FIFA, was not a happy man. The headline in the sports pages of *Le Monde* read

England to bid for 2018 World Cup

Competition for the right to stage the 2018 World Cup intensified after the English Football Association announced its intention to submit a bid.

Currently, Russia are favourites to win the right to stage the next but one World Cup, with Turkey and Spain running a close second. However, there are several concerns about Russia's fitness to hold the World Cup because of the distance between venues, lack of adequate infrastructure and the overt racism of Russian football fans. In addition, many Western countries have expressed their concern about the increasingly oppressive behaviour by the government led by Dimitriy Ivanov.

England previously bid to stage the 2006 World Cup but was unsuccessful because of widespread concerns about their archaic infrastructure and transport networks and the menace of their notorious football hooligans. However, over the past ten years, the country's transport networks have been improved immeasurably and they have at last brought the hooligan problem under control. The English bid proposes using twelve modern stadiums including the magnificent rebuilt national stadium at Wembley in North London. It is possible to travel between each proposed venue by rail, which will appeal to FIFA delegates concerned about the number of games in Russia requiring air travel. The extreme example will be those games taking place in the Far Eastern city of Vladivostok, which is ten hours flying time from Moscow.

"What's wrong, Darling?" asked Picard's wife, Cècile.
"Nothing, dear" replied Picard. "See you this evening".

The same day
French Football Federation
Boulevard de Grenelle
Paris

François Picard's worst fears were realised when he arrived at his office. There was a message from his PA, Nicole Gachôt. It read "Sergei Lavotchkin rang you at 8am. Please ring him back urgently – it's about the World Cup".

Picard had been Chairman of the French Football Federation between 1989 and 2007 and, as he had been made a Life President, he still had an office. He was well aware that support from a newly independent Russia and supported by other former members of the Soviet Union had been critical to France being awarded the right to stage the World Cup in 1998. At the time, none of the proposed venues had been built and there was strong political pressure for Morocco to be the first African nation to stage the World Cup. The support of Russia was to prove critical in helping France win the vote. Now, Russia wanted their payback in terms of support for their World Cup bid.

There was a personal stake for Picard in Russia's bid being successful. Not only was he tipped to become FIFA's next President after the current incumbent, Joao da Costa, stepped down but Russian oligarchs close to the President, Vladimir Rudakov and the Prime Minister, Dimitriy Ivanov, had promised a kickback worth £30 million in sterling.

If England were to win the right to stage the 2018 World Cup instead of Russia, not only would Picard lose out financially. At best, he would lose Russian support for his bid to become FIFA President. At worst, he had good reason to fear for his life. The Russians were not good losers.

Five minutes later, Picard had Sergei Lavotchkin on the other end of a phone line.

Lavotchkin was not happy that he had found out about the England bid through the internet.

"François, how come you had no knowledge of the England bid? They can't have prepared it overnight".

"The English FA must have kept the bid under wraps for some time, Sergei" replied Picard. "They've obviously learned lessons from their failed bid for 2006."

"Do you realise that they might win the right to stage the World Cup, François? The bid looks highly professional and they'll get support from all the ex-Warsaw Pact nations, the USA and countries that used to be in the British Empire."

"Relax, Sergei" said Picard. "Don't forget the British Government's made a load of enemies over the past ten years. Remember Iraq?"

Picard was referring to the United Kingdom's participation in the Second Gulf War in 2003 where they defied international opinion to join the USA in military action to overthrow the government of Saddam Hussein. He continued.

"What's more, they've not got a good record for managing projects. The Olympics is running at three times the original budget. Russia will win the World Cup, no problem."

"I'm glad you're confident, François" replied Lavotchkin. "Remember we supported your bid for the '98 World Cup. Also, Berezhnikov and Tupitsin are expecting a return on their investment."

Lavotchkin was referring to Alexei Berezhnikov and Vladimir Tupitsin two of the most powerful oligarchs in Russia who had offered a sizeable payment to Picard if Russia won the right to stage the 2018 World Cup.

"I think it might be sensible if you started pulling a few strings, my friend." With that rejoinder, Lavotchkin rang off.

François Picard had arranged to meet Gerard Basquet, France's representative at the Union of European Football Associations, better known as UEFA, for lunch.

L'Auberge Bretagne was a Breton seafood restaurant, and the Coquilles St Jacques starter and the Sole Bonne Femme main course was highly recommended. Picard ordered both.

"I understand you've got trouble with the Russians, François" said Basquet. "Any reason?"

"They backed our bid for the '98 World Cup, Gerard" replied Picard. "Not surprisingly, they want the same from us."

"I thought you were helping them."

"I have been" said Picard. "Until last week, Russia were overwhelming favourites to stage the 2018 World Cup. Until England put in their bid."

"Is that definite?" asked Basquet.

"It is, Gerard. And it looks a very strong bid too. If England get the World Cup instead of Russia, it won't do our relations with them any good. We need Russia's support for other tournaments, such as the Olympics. I assume Russia is supporting our bid for Euro 2016?"

"They are, François. By the way, this might amuse you. Scotland and Wales have also submitted a joint bid."

"Are you serious? Their combined population is only eight million and I don't think either country has qualified for anything in years. Do they really think they'll get it?"

"You are quite right, François" replied Basquet. "Scotland last qualified for a major tournament in 1998. For Wales, it's even longer. They made the quarter-finals of the European Championships in 1976. But they think that, because London's got the Olympics, they'll have a go in staging a major tournament."

"Do they present any threat to our bid, Gerard?" asked Picard.

"None at all" replied Basquet. "They may have four massive stadiums – Hampden Park, Celtic Park and the rugby stadiums in Cardiff and Edinburgh. But they'll need to build at least six more to meet our requirements on capacity, plus they'll need to improve their roads, rail services and airport and hotel provision. In contrast, we've got everything in place from 1998."

"What does the British Government think?"

"Not sure, François. The Government's deeply unpopular at present. If English taxpayers' money is spent on the Scotland and Wales bid – remember that both countries now have home rule – it will go down like a lead balloon with voters. They've got a General Election next year and they need every vote possible. Backing a white elephant won't help them at all."

"Furthermore, there's a good chance that, if Scotland and Wales got Euro 2016, it will all go tits up. Which won't do the England bid for the World Cup any favours."

That afternoon
French Football Federation
Boulevard de Grenelle
Paris

François Picard had enjoyed his lunch, even if it was with a potential rival in the hierarchy of football administration. He had good reason to fear Basquet who carried a lot of support because he had been been a former football international with 50 French caps in the 1980s. Picard was a graduate from the prestigious École National d'Administration and resented the fact that someone with modest educational achievements like Basquet had advanced solely because of his past sporting prowess.

On the way back to his office, Picard had been thinking about what Basquet had said. Particularly about the potential damage that a Scotland/Wales Euro 2016 could do to England's chances of staging the 2018 World Cup if they failed to deliver.

Suddenly, it all became crystal clear. If Scotland and Wales won the right to stage the 2016 European Football Championships, it could wreck England's chances of being successful with their bid for the 2018 World Cup. Particularly if they got into immediate difficulties with the massive programme of work required to satisfy UEFA's requirements. If there were concerns about the ability of Scotland and Wales to stage Euro 2016, FIFA delegates might have doubts that England could do the same for the World Cup. Which would leave the road open for Russia. And there might be an added benefit of France stepping in if Scotland and Wales were unable to deliver the tournament.

The last benefit was that Gerard Basquet's career as a leading football administrator would be finished if France lost the Euro 2016 vote.

Picard picked up the phone and rang Sergei Lavotchkin.

"Sergei, François here. Further developments to report."

"Go ahead."

"Scotland and Wales are bidding for Euro 2016. It's a complete no hoper. They need massive expenditure on new stadiums, roads, railways, airports and hotels. The British Government's unlikely to support it because of the potential cost and the impact on the England World Cup bid. And neither country's a major player in international football. There's a strong chance both hosts would go out at Group stages. Chances are that UEFA will lose money if it's held there."

"Very interesting, François" said Lavotchkin. "What do you want me to do? Back the Scotland and Wales bid?"

"Yes" replied Picard.

There was a silence for a few seconds as Lavotchkin struggled to understand what Picard had asked him to do.

"François, are you serious? Are you asking me to arrange for Russia to support a rival bid for Euro 2016? You realise this would mean us voting against France."

"I'm deadly serious, Sergei. The Scotland and Wales bid is a complete no hoper. But many countries are tiring of what's seen as a closed shop of the major countries staging tournaments. There's a chance they may get a strong sympathy vote."

Picard continued.

"If Scotland and Wales are awarded Euro 2016, there's a good chance it will undermine England's World Cup bid. Particularly if they get behind on the work required or they go over budget. After all, they are part of the United Kingdom like England. That will increase Russia's chances of winning the right to stage the World Cup in 2018."

"What about UEFA's General Council, François?" asked Lavotchkin. "Can you be sure that they will back Scotland and Wales? After all, as you said, it is not a strong bid."

"I'm sure that UEFA can be persuaded, Sergei" replied Picard.

two weeks ago, Gordon Hunter and Alun Williams presented their proposals to UEFA to approve. Unfortunately, UEFA's agreement was not forthcoming and the SFA and FAW have been asked to reconsider their proposals."

"Any reason why, Alex?" asked Rolfe.

"They did not think that the proposed venues did not cover either country widely enough" replied Forsyth.

Richard Morgan, First Minister for Wales, joined the conversation.

"The SFA and FAW proposals focused on sticking to the main urban centres. Two venues each in Cardiff, Edinburgh and Glasgow. One venue each in Aberdeen, Dundee, Newport and Swansea. This would have kept costs to a minimum as there would be no expenditure on roads or railways and only airport facilities for Swansea to worry about. Only one new stadium would have to be built from scratch and all venues have reasonable revenue potential in the future. But UEFA want the tournament more widely spread across both Scotland and Wales."

"Which means using Inverness and Wrexham, Karen" said Forsyth. "The SFA and FAW rightly rejected both venues because of the high infrastructure costs and low revenue forecasts. Substantial expense would be required on improving the A96 and A483, plus rail links. Capacity at Inverness Airport would need expanding to cope. And two new 30,000 capacity stadiums would need to be built. To be used by football teams with average gates of no more than a tenth. I think you'll agree that we'd be spending money unwisely."

"Has this been pointed this out to UEFA?" asked Rolfe.

"Williams and Hunter did, Karen" explained Morgan. "But UEFA has refused to budge. Their line is that other countries who've hosted the Euros have complied, so we should."

"Then how does the SFA and FAW intend to find the money?"

"That's the problem, Karen" said Forsyth. "We're looking to business to step in. Or to do a Private Finance Initiative deal. In the current financial climate, that could be a tall order. If that's not possible, we'll have to consider raising taxes. Unless central Government could step in and help out."

"We're even more constrained" said Morgan. "All our funding is from central Government." The Welsh First Minister was aware that Wales, unlike Scotland, had no tax-raising powers.

"Sorry, guys" replied Rolfe. "I recognise you're both in a bit of a fix. But there's no way that the UK Government can bail you out for Euro 2016. Public finances are very tight at present. There's also a lot of resentment in England at the perception that Scotland and Wales have received preferential treatment in the past. You'll just have to find the money from your own resources."

"You've made yourself clear, Karen" said Forsyth. "As will I. This is a glorious sporting opportunity for Scotland and Wales, and I'm disappointed that the UK Government is not prepared to give it the priority that has been accorded to the Olympics. Even though our eventual aim is for full independence, I have been willing to support bids by both Great Britain and England to hold international sporting events. But no more. Richard?"

"Likewise, Karen" said Morgan. "Don't think our coalition partners will be too pleased at the lack of support from the UK Government." Morgan was referring to the fact that the Welsh Assembly Government was ruled by a coalition between the Labour Party and Plaid Cymru, the Welsh nationalist party.

As the meeting ended, Karen Rolfe's worst fears had been realised. There was now a risk that Scotland and Wales would not back England's World Cup bid. She knew there were Conservative members of the Cabinet who wanted her out. If the World Cup bid failed, Rolfe would be the scapegoat.

"Tell me, Doug, how much extra over the original budget would this new stadium in the docks cost?"

"About £25-30 million at least" replied Irvine.

"Jesus Christ!" exclaimed Forsyth. "We'll never be able to afford that. Can't you cut costs from other parts of the programme?"

"I wish we could, First Minister" said Irvine. "But UEFA have been quite specific about the facilities they want. We wanted a second stadium in Edinburgh and proposed using Tynecastle. But UEFA insisted that we used Inverness as a venue. Which meant building a brand-new stadium and upgrading both the A96 and the airport. If we lose even £25 million from the budget, we will have to cut back on something – either the stadium, the airport or the A96. Could mean losing the right to stage the tournament."

"Don't forget we've got partners in staging Euro 2016, First Minister" said Hunter. "Don't think the Welsh will be too pleased with us if we have to give up the right to hold it".

Forsyth was aware that the following year there were elections to the Scottish Parliament. Losing Euro 2016 would not be a good advertisement for the SNP.

"Look fellas, I want Euro 2016 as much as you do. It's going to be a great opportunity to sell Scotland to the world. But we've got to face reality. Public finances are tight at present. We're not likely to get a sympathetic hearing from the UK Government. What's more, we've got an election next year and I don't think the Scottish taxpayer will welcome being clobbered for more money, even for a cause like this."

"If I find some money in the coffers, I'll be the first to let you know. But in the meantime, you'll have to think how best to meet this challenge."

24 December 2010
The Metropol Hotel
Teatralny Prozd
Moscow

"François, good to see you again."

Sergei Lavotchkin, Russia's FIFA representative and member of the Executive Council, warmly shook the hand of the Secretary-General.

"Come this way. Oleg Grishin and Vladimir Tupitsin are also here. Vodka?"

"Yes please" replied Picard.

Lavotchkin had booked a meeting room in the plush five-star hotel located opposite the Bolshoi Ballet. Grishin, who was Russia's representative at UEFA and Tupitsin, a wealthy oligarch who had made a fortune in buying up state assets following the collapse of the Soviet Union nearly twenty years earlier, were waiting for the two FIFA representatives.

Grishin and Tupitsin shook hands with Picard.

A waiter poured out four glasses of Stolichnaya and brought a tray over.

"Thank you, Gennady" said Lavotchkin.

The four men then started the day's business. Lavotchkin opened the proceedings.

"Oleg, Vladimir, you will be aware that François has been helping us with our attempt to win the right to stage the World Cup in eight years' time. We face a difficult challenge from the bid submitted by England. However, events may be moving in our favour. Earlier this year, as you know, Scotland and Wales won the right to stage the European championships due to take place in 2016. For that, we must thank Oleg. And François for coming up with the idea."

Lavotchkin continued.

"The Scotland/Wales bid must be one of the weakest ever to win the right to stage a major sporting tournament of any kind. They need to build three brand new stadiums, one new airport and expand capacity at another to meet UEFA's requirements. They've also got to expand hotel capacity and improve two major roads. The total bill will come to around £5 billion. Even if all the work is done on time and to budget, there are serious doubts that the two countries can afford it. If there's any delays to this work, we can guarantee there is no chance that Scotland and Wales will be able to stage Euro 2016.

"I do not need to spell out the impact of Scotland and Wales falling behind with their preparations or running out of money. As both countries are still part of the United Kingdom, any shortcomings will impact upon the viability of England's World Cup bid. It is therefore in our interests for Scotland and Wales to fail in delivering the preparations required for Euro 2016. Francois, do you have the latest situation report?"

Picard withdrew a copy of a British newspaper from his briefcase. It was the *Daily Mail*. It had been hostile towards the hosting of Euro 2016 by Scotland and Wales from the start as it considered the tournament to be a costly exercise in political grandstanding by the Scots and the Welsh, with

English taxpayers expected to pay for something they would not benefit from.

On page 4 of the *Daily Mail*, there was the following article.

Euro 2016 in doubt as Scots and Welsh hit planning and finance problems

Barely six months after being awarded the right to host the finals of the European Football Championships in 2016, Scotland and Wales have already run into problems in providing the infrastructure that UEFA has demanded. There are growing doubts about their ability to host Euro 2016 which, in turn, could damage England's bid to host the 2018 World Cup.

The Scottish Football Association's plan for a new stadium in Dundee has been dealt a serious blow by the refusal of Dundee City Council to approve planning permission for a proposed new stadium following considerable local opposition. The SFA's plan was for a stadium to be built in Caird Park, on the northern side of the city. The SFA are now having to consider an alternative site in Dundee's docklands which will require decontamination before construction work can begin. The additional bill is expected to come to £35 million.

Plans to build a new airport for Swansea have also run into difficulties. Proposals for the airport to be built on the northern shore of the Gower Peninsula five miles west of Swansea have been opposed by many local residents, along with farmers and fishermen who will lose their livelihoods. A Department for Transport consultation on the new airport is currently taking place and a decision is expected early next spring.

Any decision not to proceed with the airport may lead UEFA to question the ability of Wales to cope with the expected volumes of supporters who are expected to attend Euro 2016.

There are already rumours circulating that UEFA may reconsider its decision to award Euro 2016 to Scotland and Wales and that the French Football Federation is preparing its own proposals to step in should the tournament be taken away from Scotland and Wales.

"As you can see from this article, it has taken Scotland and Wales just six months to run into difficulties with staging Euro 2016. More will come. If permission is given for Swansea Airport to be built, environmental activists will protest and may resort to direct action. Also, I do not think that construction workers will take kindly to building on previously contaminated land. And this is before we start considering how they are going to improve roads and build hotels.

Scotland and Wales may end up being perfectly capable of staging Euro 2016 and have all the infrastructure in place before the start. But that will be in six years' time. What we must consider is now. If Scotland and Wales fall behind on preparations or go over budget, people will naturally question England's ability to deliver the World Cup in 2018. FIFA vote on the award for the 2018 World Cup in eighteen months' time. Any shortcomings in the preparations for Euro 2016 will surely benefit your bid to stage the World Cup."

Lavotchkin, Grishin and Tupitsin all nodded their agreement.

There was a knock on the door. A tall, hard-faced man walked in.

"May I introduce you to Colonel Grigoriy Tereshkov."

Tereshkov was a colonel in the FSB, Russia's secret service and successor to the notorious KGB from Soviet days. His responsibility was liaison with activists and subversives in other countries.

"Gentlemen, I may be able to help you. I understand you may need assistance to help the Motherland's glorious bid for the 2018 World Cup. I am the man who can help you win this."

Tereshkov continued.

"Great Britain is a divided country. Has been since Mrs Thatcher was Prime Minister. And the current Government's policy of austerity is reopening those old wounds.

"This is what we propose to do. The FSB has maintained links with Britain's trade unions even through Russia is no longer a Communist country. The pay and job security of workers in the construction industry has been reduced over the past two years as employers now have the upper hand. This has increased the sense of grievance amongst workers so it will take little provocation to result in industrial action. The trade unions can deliver this.

"The construction industry will be critical to the delivery of facilities for Euro 2016. All it will take is a few strikes to delay work to bring in question the ability of Scotland and Wales to stage Euro 2016.

"The FSB also have close links with environmental activists in Great Britain. Most are ferociously anti-capitalist in their views and willing to resort to direct action. Their main targets are roads, airports and nuclear power stations. They could be a valuable resource in slowing down major construction projects."

The three football functionaries and the oligarch were smiling at what they heard. With a bit of help from the FSB, England's credibility to hold the next World Cup would be severely undermined by the failure of its Celtic neighbours to deliver the European championships. Russia would be the beneficiary of this.

CHAPTER 3

30 June 2011
City and County of Swansea
Civic Centre
Oystermouth Road
Swansea

The results of the Department for Transport consultation on the planning application for the new airport at Swansea was about to be announced. The Press Suite at the Civic Centre was packed to full capacity.

On the top table were Mr Justice Syrett, the High Court judge who had chaired the consultation panel, Stuart Moriarty, Director-General for aviation policy at the Department for Transport, Bryan Duffy, a consultant engineer from Balfour Beatty, Mark Crossland, a management accountant from PriceWaterhouseCoopers and Catherine Williams, leader of the ruling Labour group on Swansea City and County Council.

Mr Justice Syrett indicated that he was ready to speak.

"Ladies and gentlemen, I am now ready to announce the outcome of the consultation into the planning application by the Civil Aviation Authority to build a new airport for Swansea on the Gower Peninsula.

"The consultation was launched on 2 December 2010 and asked for the views of the public and organisations with an interest to consider proposals for an international standard airport which can accommodate domestic and international flights and jet airliners. Four proposals were submitted for consideration. The first was for a new airport to be built to the east of Penclawdd on the banks of the River Loughor. The second was to use a site to the west of Crofty. The third was to use a site on the coast north of Llanrhydian. The final option was to extend the existing airport at Fairwood Common.

"No less than seven thousand representations have been made in response to this consultation. Three thousand two hundred responses were in favour of building a new airport, while three thousand five hundred were against. Another three hundred responses were non-committal.

"The option of extending the existing airport at Fairwood Common was the first to be considered. Local residents were strongly opposed to this proposal. In addition, the proposal was considered to be the most expensive as people's homes would have to be compulsorily purchased and, in addition, new railway and motorway links would have to be built to connect with the existing Swansea-Carmarthen railway line and the M4. The Inquiry Panel therefore decided not to proceed with this option.

"The Inquiry Panel then considered the three further sites. The first site considered, to the east of Penclawdd, is the closest to Swansea and is also relatively close to existing road and railway connections, so costs would be minimal. However, air safety consultants were concerned about its proximity to a road bridge carrying the A484 over the River Loughor. The Panel concluded that safety concerns could not be addressed and decided against choosing this site.

"This left a choice between the Crofty and Llanrhydian sites. The latter site has the advantage of being in an unpopulated area, although I understand that cockle beds, an important provider of local employment, are nearby. However, the Crofty site is some two miles closer to Swansea and would incur less expenditure to build.

"The Panel has therefore decided that the new airport for Swansea should be built at the Crofty site."

There was immediate uproar as the significant number of the local community from Penclawdd and Crofty leapt to their feet and started shouting.

"Shame on you!" bellowed a large man in his late forties.

Prominent in the throng was the Penclawdd councillor, Ken Davies.

"This decision is a complete travesty of democracy" shouted Davies. "No one wants this airport apart from a few rich businessmen who can't be arsed to drive the forty miles to Cardiff."

Catherine Williams took the microphone in an attempt to pacify the now angry horde.

"Ladies and gentlemen, you are doing yourself no favours by behaving like this. Will you please let Lord Justice Syrett finish..................."

Before Councillor Williams could finish, derisive shouts were coming from the audience.

"Boo!"

"Rubbish!"

"Utter bollocks!"

Ken Davies was now leading a noisy chant.

NEW AIRPORT! NO WAY!

NEW AIRPORT! NO WAY!"

NEW AIRPORT! NO WAY!"

NEW AIRPORT! NO WAY!"

Catherine Williams activated the panic button on the top table, which alerted security staff to the fact the meeting had got out of hand. A call was made to the police who, within three minutes, had arrived to restore order.

Councillor Davies was one of twenty men and women arrested for a breach of the peace.

1 July 2011
Clemence Street
London E14

"Hey fellas, read this."

Ashley King passed a copy of the *Daily Mirror* to Jez Duffield and Ste Nugent who were sitting on a sofa which was close to approaching the end of its life. King and Duffield were scruffily dressed and their long hair was matted into dreadlocks. Nugent sported a crew cut and tight-fitting trousers and a top and, as many people suspected, he was gay. All three men were members of the anarchist Black Bloc group.

The story which had gained King's notice was on page 5 and referred to disorder in Swansea following an announcement of plans to build a new airport in the Gower Peninsula.

"Sounds like the locals in Swansea don't like the idea of a new airport on their doorstep" said Nugent.

"This is an opportunity not to be missed" said Duffield. A lifelong activist who had accompanied his parents on demonstrations since he was a toddler, he had been in the forefront of protests and demonstrations against the austerity policies of the Conservative-Liberal Democrat coalition government since it had taken office the previous year. Duffield had been on the student march the previous November where the Conservative Party headquarters had been broken into and in the occupation outside St Paul's Cathedral.

Duffield continued. "I reckon we can get a mass occupation of the airport site. Activists from not only Britain but Europe too will come in. Also, if we start sabotaging contractors' equipment and digging tunnels, it'll become prohibitively expensive."

Nugent was wary.

"Jez, you'll have seen from previous protests that the Government intends to crack down on all dissent against its policies. The police and courts have been given a free hand against us and the Government's supporting the use of super injunctions to stop us organising. We all risk ending up in jail and for a long time. And how are we going to be able to fund an occupation of the airport site? The St Paul's protest has already run out of money."

"Relax, Ste" said Duffield. "The money's sorted. We could fund an occupation for the next five years if necessary. Don't forget we've got support here and abroad. Geri Singleton's already been engaged to defend us against any court action. We've got support in the European Parliament. All we need to do is to take the matter to the European Court of Human rights and the Government will be forced to back off."

Duffield had indeed spoken to Geri Singleton who had first made her name twenty years earlier when she helped secure acquittals for seven men and two women who had been jailed in the 1970s for terrorist offences at the height of the IRA bombing campaign in Britain. What he did not mention was that he had also met Galina Zhivkova, a Third Secretary at the Russian Embassy and an agent in the FSB. Zhivkova had pledged to provide over £500k in funding for activity to disrupt the construction of the new airport at Swansea.

22 July 2011
Stannergate Road
Dundee
Scotland

Willie Stark steadied the JCB excavator he was driving as he aimed to dig a new section of foundations for the prospective City of Dundee sports stadium that was to be built for Euro 2016. He was in a good mood as the weekend was approaching and the August Bank Holiday was little more than a week away.

Laing plc had started work on building the new stadium earlier that month following completion of work to decontaminate the site which had formerly been a jute mill. This had added over £30 million to the overall cost of building the stadium and, six months earlier, the project had looked dead in the water as the budget for the work did not exist. However, a late intervention by Sir Robert Brewster, a billionaire financier, in which he met the budget shortfall with no questions asked had enabled the docklands stadium project to proceed.

The bucket in Stark's excavator dug into the silty soil and deposited its contents into a container which would be taken away by lorry for use for reclaiming land from the sea. Suddenly, Stark was convulsed by a coughing fit. This alerted his workmates to the fact he was in trouble.

"Hey, Willie, are you alright, man?" Mick Henderson, a tall, ginger-haired man was first at the scene.

"Was a minute ago, Mickey" replied Stark. "Dug into that section over there and......."

Stark started coughing violently again.

Lee Imrie, the Unite shop steward, came over. "What's up, fellas?"

"It's Willie" replied Drew Morton, another excavator driver. "He looks unwell."

"Lee, I reckon the mob who were supposed to decontaminate the site didn't do their job properly" said Tom Geraghty. "There's still a funny smell."

Imrie noticed the smell too. He headed straight to the site office and rapped sharply on the door of the Site Manager, Colin Hay.

"Can I have a word, Colin, now. It's urgent."

Hay, a burly, broad-shouldered man in his late forties, was not happy at having both the work and his Friday afternoon disrupted.

"What's up now, Lee? Demand for an additional tea break?"

Imrie was not impressed at Hay's casual and dismissive attitude.

"If you must know, Colin, one of the workers has been taken ill. Willie Stark. And while you're there, Environmental Solutions didn't properly decontaminate the site. It stinks like a sewer and we reckon Willie's been poisoned."

Hay still felt that Imrie was trying it on.

"Look, Lee, Environmental Solutions have 30 years' experience in this type of work and they have to obtain formal accreditation from Government inspectors that they have properly decontaminated the site. Here's the Scottish Government certificate."

Hay showed the certificate to Imrie.

"Willie's been a good worker here. Tell him I'll sign him off sick and he should go to his doctor. I'll see him back at work, hopefully early next week."

"You don't get it, Colin" replied Imrie. "This site's unfit to work on. Come with me and I'll show you."

Hay reluctantly agreed to accompany Imrie to the location where Stark had been working. He smelt the slightly fetid aroma but his conclusion was different to that of Imrie.

"Lee, that's no' contaminated soil. That's nothing more than marsh gas. Fairly common in riverside locations and harmless."

Imrie was by now in the mood for a confrontation.

"If anything happens to Willie, Unite will be holding you and Laing responsible, Colin. I'm taking this up with the District Convenor."

25 July 2011
Laing plc
Hanover Square
Edinburgh

"Steve, you wanted to see me. Come on through."

Steve Bird, Laing plc's Project Manager for the City of Dundee stadium walked through to the office of Gavin Robertson, the company's Regional Director.

"I've heard there's problems with the Dundee stadium project, Steve. I assume that's why you've come to see me."

"That's right, Gavin" said Bird. "The workers are out on strike. Apparently, one of them was taken ill on Friday. He's in hospital at present and the doctors don't know what's wrong with him. But the workers have got the idea that the site's contaminated and that's why this bloke was taken ill."

"Wasn't the site decontaminated, Steve?"

"It was, Gavin" replied Bird. "By Environmental Solutions. They're a trusted and respected operator in this field and they would not risk their professional reputation by doing anything less than a thorough job. And there's a signed certificate from Scottish Government inspectors to prove it."

"You say Unite are involved. Anyone in particular?"

"The shop steward's a guy called Lee Imrie. A bit of a hothead but, by all accounts, he's otherwise a damn good worker. I suspect the District Convenor for Dundee might be pushing things. Gregor Stevenson. Heard of him?"

"Stevenson? Yes, unfortunately. Ambitious, after a top post in the union, always trying to inflame disputes. By the way, this might interest you."

Robertson showed Bird a press cutting from three years previously. Under a headline of **STORM OVER UNION MILITANT SUPPORT FOR SEPARATISTS**, there was a picture of Stevenson in military fatigues, posing with an AK-47 alongside pro-Russian separatists from South Ossetia who were fighting the Georgian government for the right to join Russia. It was highly controversial as the Russian Air Force was bombing Georgia at the time.

"Jesus Christ!" exclaimed Bird.

"Steve, if we had recruited in Poland and Romania instead, none of this would have happened. They're damn hard workers and they wouldn't down tools over trivial matters."

"We tried that, Gavin. But we were under pressure to hire local workers. The local MSP made an issue of it and browbeat the Department for Employment into giving way. She's a member of SNP and got the Scottish Government to back her. So, Department for Employment advised us to give first refusal to local workers to keep the peace."

"Isn't that illegal? That surely contravenes the principle of free movement of labour enshrined in the Lisbon Treaty. And I thought that employment law was reserved."

"You're right on both counts, Gavin" replied Bird. "But the issue of using immigrant labour for a project which is supposed to regenerate Scotland is an explosive one."

"Steve, if Unite refuse to back down, I think we should reconsider and recruit foreign labour. The Scottish Government can't do diddly squat about it and I reckon the UK Government will back us."

30 August 2011
BBC News

"This is Adam Bell with the latest news on BBC.

"Opposition to the proposed new airport for Swansea has continued to grow. Over the Bank Holiday weekend, the occupation camp set up by local residents on the proposed site

was joined by over 200 environmental activists from across the United Kingdom, and more activists are expected to join the site. A request by the leader of Swansea City and County Council, Catherine Williams, for talks about possible compensation was snubbed by the leaders of the camp, and the lead contractor, Redstone Construction, are now considering legal action.

"Now for further news. The dispute between Unite and Laing plc over safety at the site of the new City of Dundee Stadium has yet to be resolved, despite a further round of talks between the two sides. The dispute over alleged failings in work to decontaminate the stadium site in Dundee's docklands prior to construction work starting has already delayed work on building the new stadium, which is intended to be ready for Euro 2016."

6 September 2011
Cabinet Room
10 Downing Street
London

David Talbot was not best pleased to find out about the occupation camp at Swansea Airport and the Unite strike in Dundee. The first Cabinet meeting of the new Parliamentary session was to have been dedicated to rolling out the next phase of the Coalition Government's policies to address the budget deficit and to transform Britain. Keynote policies were the reform of the police service, the restriction of benefits paid to the unemployed and low earners and the rollout of the "Big Society", under which the voluntary sector would take over responsibility for services previously delivered by central and local Government.

Instead, the Government would have to focus on sorting out an industrial dispute and an illegal occupation. Both were throwbacks to the 1970s and 1980s and were the kind of irritation that the government of Margaret Thatcher had worked hard to eradicate.

Talbot turned to the Secretary of State for Transport, Peter Bridgeman, and the Secretary of State for Employment, Ben Richardson, for explanations.

Peter Bridgeman was first to reply. Of average height but stockily built, Bridgeman was a one-time steelworker from Sheffield who rose to become an HR manager for Corus after taking a degree in psychology at Hull University in his mid-twenties. He was now in his early sixties and was planning to stand down as an MP after the 2015 General Election.

"I'm sorry that I took my eye off the ball over this, Prime Minister. Until the past week, the issue was not a significant one. You know that a few local residents occupied the site a couple of months ago following the decision of Lord Justice Syrett's Inquiry to locate the new airport on the south bank of the Loughor Estuary. My Department and Swansea City and County Council have been in contact with the protestors to negotiate a settlement which would have ended the occupation. Unfortunately, over the Bank Holiday weekend, a whole load of environmental activists moved onto the site to join the occupation. As you will know from previous experience, many of these are professional agitators and troublemakers and they will not be satisfied until they force abandonment of the airport project.

"I get the impression that Swansea City and County Council are hoping that the problem will fade and go away, and they seem reluctant to take action. Rumour has it that the Council leader is related to some of the protestors and that's why they won't do anything. I'm giving them two weeks to persuade the protestors to leave or to take legal action. Otherwise, I'm going to the courts."

"Thank you, Peter" said Talbot. "Keep me informed of progress please. Ben."

Ben Richardson was one of the Conservative Party's rising stars. A former Army officer, now in his late thirties, he was a strong right-winger on both economic and social issues. Although some party members saw him as a potential future leader, others regarded him as too dogmatic and inflexible for the top post.

"The dispute between Laing plc and Unite has been running since the end of July. You will know that Laing were awarded the contract to build the new City of Dundee stadium which will be used for Euro 2016. It's on the site of a former jute mill and the site needed to be decontaminated before construction work could start.

"Apparently, a worker was taken ill and Unite are alleging that decontamination work wasn't done properly. They are now demanding "danger money" from Laing before they will start work again."

"What's Laing's response, Ben?" asked Talbot.

"A fairly robust one, Prime Minister" said Richardson. "I spoke to Gavin Laing a couple of days ago. They are refusing to back down and rightly so. They've got a certificate to prove that the decontamination was done properly. You should know they're thinking of sacking the workers concerned and recruiting replacement labour directly from Poland. And frankly, I'm all in favour of letting them do that. For starters, it will teach Unite a lesson that they can't drag industrial relations back to the 1970s."

"Have you spoken to the Scottish Government about this, Ben?" asked Karen Rolfe, the Secretary of State for the Environment, Communities and

Local Government. "The City of Dundee Stadium is part of a programme designed to regenerate deprived parts of Scotland – hiring foreign labour will hardly look good when unemployment is still high."

"Karen, may I remind you that employment is reserved business. I have no plans to contact the Scottish Government."

Mark Rudge, Secretary of State for Trade and Business intervened.

"I think everyone has forgotten there is a common thread to both the Swansea Airport and City of Dundee Stadium issues. Both are being built as part of the biggest white elephant seen in this country for many a year. I'm talking about Euro 2016. As I've said before, there's no economic benefit to the UK in holding this tournament. It is a giant vanity project for Forsyth and Morgan to strut on the world stage, and the English taxpayer is expected to shell out to make it happen. The Government should have nothing more to do with this tournament and leave the Scottish and Welsh Governments to sort things out."

There was a stunned silence across the room for five seconds as the Cabinet took in the implications of what Rudge had said.

"Mark, do you realise what that would do for England's 2018 World Cup Bid?" shouted Hugh Greville, the Secretary of State for National Heritage. "We need the likes of Scotland and Wales to back our bid."

"Are you seriously suggesting that we sit back and do nothing in the face of organised lawlessness?" said Home Secretary Sarah Crosby.

The discussion was interrupted by the sharp rap of a gavel by the Prime Minister.

"Can I bring this meeting to order" barked Talbot. "We've already wasted 20 minutes arguing about issues which are not part of the Government's core agenda. May I suggest we wrap up the Swansea and Dundee issues now and proceed."

Talbot then turned to Bridgman, Richardson and Rolfe.

"Peter, as I said earlier, can you continue to report on the situation in Swansea and apply for a court order if the protestors won't leave the airport site. Ben, let Laing know they are within their rights to dismiss the workforce and recruit from anywhere in the European Union they think fit if Unite refuse to call off industrial action.

"Karen, you're due to meet Forsyth and Morgan next month. Let them know we expect their co-operation in sorting out these issues. And make it clear that, while the UK Government continues to support Euro 2016 in principle, can cannot provide any bailout for additional commitments."

26 September 2011
Unite Headquarters
Theobald's Road
Holborn
London

Gregor Stevenson was feeling pleased with himself. Having obtained the support of Shona Murray, the Scottish regional representative of Unite, he had secured a meeting with Sean Monaghan, the Executive Council member with responsibility for building, construction and allied trades. Murray accompanied him.

A week earlier, Laing plc had dismissed all the workers on the City of Dundee Stadium who were in dispute with the company over health and safety issues, and were recruiting replacement labour from Eastern Europe. Angry clashes had taken place outside the stadium the previous Wednesday as the sacked workers tried to stop the replacements from gaining access to the site, and no less than 15 demonstrators had been arrested, including the Unite shop steward, Lee Imrie. Stevenson saw an opportunity to escalate the dispute.

Monaghan, a Liverpudlian, was like Stevenson a militant left-winger and keen on direct action to support the union's interests.

Stevenson outlined the details of the dispute, from the day Willie Stark went sick with respiratory problems to Laing sacking the striking workers.

"Shona, Gregor, this sounds very serious" said Monaghan. "We've got plenty of knowledge about Laing. They've been major contributors to Conservative Party funds and, in addition, they have been notorious for endorsing dangerous working practices, for trying to shut out unions and using private investigators to spy on activists. You can be assured that your comrades will receive the support of the Executive Council."

17 October 2011
Department for the Environment,
Communities & Local Government
Eland House
Stag Place
London

The intergovernmental Meeting was the second one to have taken place since the elections for the Scottish Parliament and Welsh Assembly in May.

The Scottish National Party now had an absolute majority and First Minister Alex Forsyth could govern without having to broker agreements with other parties in Holyrood. In contrast, the Welsh Assembly elections had failed to produce an absolute majority so the Labour/Plaid Cymru coalition continued for a second term with Richard Morgan continuing as First Minister.

First item on the agenda was Euro 2016. Karen Rolfe, the Secretary of State for the Environment, Communities & Local Government, opened the proceedings.

"I am afraid the issue of Euro 2016 has had to come up again, gentlemen, because there are serious ongoing issues about the credibility of your plans to host the tournament. I'm talking about the delays to the construction of the new airport for Swansea and the City of Dundee Stadium. I will not bore you with details about which you will be familiar, but I think you will agree it is fair to say that HMG have real concerns about whether Scotland and Wales is capable of staging the tournament in five years' time.

"Richard, there is still no sign of the occupation of the Swansea Airport site ending. You and Swansea City and County Council have had plenty of opportunity to persuade the protestors to leave. I am afraid that Her Majesty's Government's patience has run out. Department for Transport will be seeking a High Court injunction requiring the protestors to vacate the site. What plans do you have to speed up construction work once the site has been cleared?"

"Karen, I think HMG is acting rather hastily" replied Morgan. "Despite what the papers say, most of the protestors are local people. All they want is reasonable compensation for losing their land or livelihood. If we could have an additional £10 million available, we could pay off those farmers, fishermen and property owners. The occupation would then be over."

"I'm sorry, Richard" said Rolfe. "There is no more money available. You will appreciate that the UK Government is already running a large deficit because of the previous Government's reckless spending policies."

Before Rolfe could question the Scottish First Minister, Forsyth fired in his opening question.

"Karen, before you ask me about progress on the City of Dundee Stadium, can you answer this? When Euro 2016 was awarded, it was intended to be an opportunity to regenerate Scotland and Wales. UK Government supported the idea of preference being given to local workers in any construction works and in delivering the tournament. Then why is it that Laing have just dismissed workers with a reasonable grievance about health and safety issues and replaced them with foreign labour?"

Rolfe was determined to hold her ground.

"If you have forgotten, Alex, the work to decontaminate the stadium site was carried out by accredited experts in the field and they produced a certificate which inspectors from *your* Government signed off. I now understand that the worker who went sick had a history of respiratory problems and that he should not have been employed for that reason. Instead, Unite have taken a position of bone-headed opposition and have left Laing with no choice in the matter. And by the way, Her Majesty's Government were not very impressed by the lack of police presence at the site last week."

"And your point is......................."

"Alex, we expect the Scottish police to play their part in enforcing the law of the land. This appears to have been absent."

"Policing in Scotland is a matter for my Government, Karen. Not yours."

"You appear to have forgotten that, under the devolution agreement, Her Majesty's Government can exceptionally take control of policing responsibilities if public order is not being maintained."

Morgan then spoke.

"Karen, remember that England will need the votes of Wales and Scotland if it is going to stand any chance of succeeding with its bid for the 2018 World Cup. It appears that the UK Government has no intention of co-operating with either my Government or the Scottish Government in overcoming the difficulties that have emerged in preparing for Euro 2016. If you continue to impose your solutions on us, I will instruct our FIFA representative to reconsider his support for England's bid."

"And I will be doing the same regarding Scotland" added Forsyth.

23 October 2011
The Royal Mile
Edinburgh

The runners in the Edinburgh Half Marathon had completed the first mile and a half and were now proceeding down the Royal Mile past Canongate Kirk. The three favourites to win, Ben Keino and Wilson Kipregut of Kenya and Johanes Bikile of Ethiopia, had moved to the front of the leading pack to ensure they were in a good position early in the race.

Back at Edinburgh Castle, Chief Inspector Gary Somerville of Lothian and Borders Police gave a sigh of relief. The trouble he had been expected to take place had not happened.

The Half Marathon was being sponsored by Laing plc, a major construction company. They were in dispute with the trade union, Unite, over safety standards at the City of Dundee Stadium, which was being built for Euro 2016 and would thereafter be used as a shared ground for the city's two football teams. A month earlier, they had dismissed all the striking workers and recruited replacements from Eastern Europe.

Unite's response had been combative. There had been clashes outside the stadium site and buses used to transport the replacement workers to the site had been vandalised. Two days earlier, Somerville had attended a briefing in which he was told that Unite intended to disrupt the Half Marathon and that they would be joined by protestors from the Socialist Workers Party, Militant Tendency and Class War. A large police presence was put in place to prevent the demonstrators getting close to the athletes but the turnout was smaller than expected.

Close to the Royal Mile Factory Outlet, a couple of men dressed in singlets and shorts slipped under the barriers and onto the course. The crowd of spectators groaned. A couple of exhibitionists ruining a great day out for everyone else. Like most of the spectators, PC Simon Fletcher thought that the intrusion was from a pair of show-offs. He reached for his radio and called his Sergeant, Alison McKechnie.

"Sarge, a couple of idiots have got onto the course. Shall I nick them now or wait for reinforcements?"

"Hold it for now, Simon" said McKechnie. "We'll arrange to nick them by Holyrood roundabout. Can you get down there as we may need some help."

"Roger that, Sarge."

Within seconds, more runners had sneaked onto the course and, by the time they had reached the Scottish Parliament, some fifty 'athletes' were jogging at a slow speed in front of the leading official runners. They would hold up everyone in the race.

The crowd started booing. They were annoyed that a major showpiece for Scotland's capital city had been disrupted.

Fifty metres before the Holyrood roundabout, the intruding runners stopped and sat down, blocking the road. The leading runners unfurled a

Unite banner as a red-haired man of below average height stood up. It was Lee Imrie, the Unite shop steward who was representing the sacked workers.

"Ladies and gentlemen, I'm sorry for spoiling your afternoon. But this event was sponsored by Laing, who have just sacked a hundred workers because they challenged them over being forced to work in unsafe conditions. Laing has refused to speak to us, so this is the only way we can bring to their attention the fact they have denied the Dundee workers justice."

Later that day
BBC News

Adam Bell was halfway through the 10pm news bulletin when he moved onto the Edinburgh Half Marathon.

"Demonstrators from Unite caused chaos at the Edinburgh Half Marathon this afternoon after they blocked the roadway near the Scottish Parliament. Police made fifty arrests."

"This delayed the race, which was eventually won by Kenyan Ben Keino, for over an hour."

"The trade union, which is in dispute with the race's sponsors, Laing plc, about the dismissal of a hundred workers who were building the City of Dundee Stadium, claims that the company has repeatedly rejected offers of a meeting or arbitration over the dispute which arose over claims that workers were expected to work in unsafe conditions. However, Laing has denied the Union's allegations and, in a statement, a company spokesman condemned the union for gross intimidation."

1 November 2011
Cabinet Room
10 Downing Street
London

The first item on the agenda for the Cabinet meeting was the occupation of the Swansea Airport site.

"Peter, what's the latest position on Swansea Airport?" asked David Talbot.

"Good progress, Prime Minister" replied Peter Bridgeman. "We've secured a Court Order which requires the protestors to leave the proposed airport site by no later than 12 November. That's a week Saturday."

"And what if they don't leave?"

"We'll use the police to arrest anyone who refuses to leave for contempt of court. I've already spoken to Sarah about this."

Bridgeman glanced towards the Home Secretary.

"Well done, Peter" said Talbot.

The next item was the Unite dispute with Laing.

"You will be aware of disturbing developments in this dispute, Prime Minister" said Ben Richardson. "It seems that Unite have taken to harassing and intimidating senior company officials and disrupting sponsored events. The most recent was the Edinburgh Half Marathon a week ago."

"It's an absolute disgrace" said Mark Rudge. "Behaviour more fitting of the Mafia. What's being done?"

"Laing want to take Unite to court. There are two possible routes. One is Section 241 of the Trade Union and Labour Relations (Consolidation) Act 1992, which allows for prosecution for intimidation or annoyance. However, the Act is drafted so it relates to the intimidation of an individual person rather than an organisation. The other is Section 8 of the Protection from Harassment Act 1997 which applies to Scotland, but again it is phrased so it only applies to an individual person rather than an organisation."

"Can't we amend the law to make this illegal?" asked Sarah Crosby.

"That's what we're doing, Sarah" replied Richardson. "We're adding an amendment to the Trade Union and Labour Relations (Consolidation) Act 1992 that will make it an offence to cause intimidation or annoyance to an organisation in pursuance of an industrial dispute. Not only will it carry a maximum sentence of five years imprisonment, it will also allow aggrieved parties to claim compensation up to £1 million. And as employment law is reserved, it will apply to the whole UK."

CHAPTER 4

12 November 2011
Crofty
West Glamorgan
Wales
10am

The blue Ford Mondeo saloon drew up outside the proposed site for the new airport for Swansea. Three High Court officials got out and walked towards the site.

Behind them, no less than forty police vans were parked. All had a full complement of officers dressed in riot gear, mainly from South Wales Police but with support from the Dyfed-Powys, Gloucestershire and Gwent forces.

Malcolm Rogers, the most senior court official, had a megaphone to address the occupation camp.

·"Can everyone here pay attention. We have come to execute a Court Order on behalf of the Department of Transport to reclaim the site earmarked for the construction of the new airport for Swansea. You are therefore required to leave this location with immediate effect. If you do not comply with this order, we will have no option but to enforce your removal."

"Oh yeah – and whose army?" came a shout from the occupation camp.

Rogers conferred with the most senior police officer, Chief Inspector Donna Richards from South Wales Police.

"Chief Inspector, how long should we give them to leave?"

"Half an hour" said Richards. "Then we go in."

There was no sign of anyone moving. At 10:30am, Rogers and Richards spoke again.

"Looks like no one's going to go quietly, Chief Inspector."

Richards pulled out her radio and summoned the six Inspectors in charge of the police detachments.

"OK guys, we're going in."

Within seconds, a huge phalanx of police officers, dressed in body armour and helmets, surged into the site to execute the High Court Order.

An hour later, the site was empty. No less than 300 people, including three councillors from Swansea City and County Council, were in police custody.

16 November 2011
Unite Headquarters
St Theobald's Road
Holborn
London

Unite's Executive Council was meeting to discuss its campaign to oppose the amendment to the Trade Union and Labour Relations (Consolidation) Act 1992. It would make illegal any action in furtherance of an industrial dispute which was regarded as intimidation, harassment or annoyance and was an extension of the 1992 legislation in that action directed against an organisation came within the scope of the Act.

Over the previous three years, Unite had been successful in securing favourable outcomes to industrial disputes by targeting the companies their members were in dispute with. Directors, shareholders and senior managers found hostile demonstrators on their doorstep and events sponsored by those companies had suffered from disruption. Their most recent success had been to hold up the Edinburgh Half Marathon three weeks earlier.

Unite's General Secretary, Rob Calder, opened the meeting. A Scot from Motherwell, he had been in the post for just under two years.

"Comrades, you will have in front of you details of the Government's proposals to introduce yet more anti-Union legislation. If introduced, the Trade Union and Labour Relations (Consolidation) Act 1992 as amended will outlaw the successful campaigns we have run to defend our members' interests. I will agree that our tactics have been somewhat direct at times but this is the only way we can influence the people who run British industry of the error of their ways. Because we have been successful, the Government now wants to outlaw the practice of directly targeting companies who treat our members like serfs.

"You will be aware that the Government is trying to finish off the job started by Mrs Thatcher to cow the working classes into total submission and subservience to the ruling classes. This is why they have dusted off old anti-Union policies. It is therefore essential that we resist this legislation by all means possible.

"There are four members of the Cabinet who are strongly in favour of this legislation. Ben Richardson, Peter Bridgeman, Sarah Crosby and Mark Rudge are all pushing for this legislation to be introduced. I've also identified junior Ministers and backbenchers known to be in favour. See how enthusiastic they are when they've got several of our members on their doorstep."

"Rob, have you thought this through?" asked Damian Wilcocks, the Local Authorities representative. "The Government has already shown an appetite for a tough response to anyone who takes direct action against them. Remember the riots earlier this year?"

In August 2011, riots broke out in both London and in several English cities after a suspected gangster was shot dead by the police in Tottenham. In the space of four days, homes and businesses were burnt down, five lives were lost and an estimated £200 million worth of property damage took place.

The Government's response was swift and draconian. Police forces were told to go out and hunt down offenders and over 3,000 arrests were made. All-night sittings of courts were introduced and defendants were brought to court as soon as they had been charged, and the courts were given the instruction to be robust in sentencing. Nearly 1,300 defendants received custodial sentences.

"And don't forget that the Government is toughening up anti-terror legislation. If we start harassing MPs and Government Ministers, they won't hesitate to use everything they've got in the book against us. And remember that public opinion is still hostile to the unions, even over thirty years since the Winter of Discontent. The Government is likely to have support for this legislation is we start using leverage against MPs."

"We'd get further by lobbying Liberal Democrat Ministers and Cabinet members. If they fail to support the measure, it will go nowhere."

"We can't afford to do nothing, Damian" shouted the Wales representative, Jenni Williams. "Don't forget we've now got links to unions in EU countries. If we can't do anything, they will. And remember the French unions don't take prisoners."

"Forget the Liberal Democrats" said Anwar Khaliq, the Food, Drink and Tobacco representative. "They sold their soul to the devil as soon as they agreed to be the Tories' coalition partners."

Sean Monaghan was next to speak.

"Comrades, there is one area where the Government is very weak. They want to secure the World Cup for England in 2018. You will have seen on the news that David Beckham and Prince William were lobbying abroad to support the FA's bid. In just over two weeks' time, FIFA will vote to decide who gets the World Cup."

"If we were to send FIFA delegates details of the Government's proposed legislation, it wouldn't look too good for the England bid. On top of that, I've seen the footage shot of the police action to remove the occupation of the Swansea Airport site. Not very pretty I can assure you."

"Everyone knows how corrupt FIFA are as an organisation. But they appear to get cold feet about allowing countries with poor human rights credentials to host tournaments. Comrades, we could do more damage by sinking England's World Cup bid than by any leverage against Government Ministers. Let's try it."

17 November 2011
Clemence Street
London E14

Sean Monaghan had little difficulty in finding Jez Duffield's address. He took the Docklands Light Railway to Limehouse and walked the short distance to the run-down terrace house where Duffield and fellow Black Bloc members lived.

Monaghan had grown up in one of the poorest parts of Liverpool but even he was shocked at the squalor that Duffield and his mates lived in. Dirty dishes filled the kitchen sink, old clothes were strewn everywhere and ashtrays full of cigarette butts littered the lounge. A distinct aroma of cannabis filled the air.

Nevertheless, Monaghan recognised that Duffield, behind the unwashed denims and matted dreadlocks, was politically astute. The Black Bloc were well-organised, as shown by their role in the anti-austerity protests, the occupation camp outside St Paul's Cathedral and occupations of vacant buildings. Many of their members had avoided being arrested following the riots earlier in the year. There were rumours of their involvement in drug trafficking and the production and sale of hard-core pornography and that they were collaborating with Al-Q'aida, but nothing had been proved.

Duffield opened the front door a few seconds after Monaghan knocked.

"Hello Sean. Come in. What can I do?"

"Jez, I understand you've got filmed footage of the police action to break up the Swansea Airport occupation."

"I have, Sean" replied Duffield. "Why?"

"Jez, in two weeks' time, FIFA will be voting on who stages the 2018 World Cup. The Government's desperate that England get it. England's not hosted it for nearly fifty years and the Tories are still miffed that it took place and that England won it while a Labour government was in power. You've probably seen that David Beckham and Prince William have been globetrotting, trying to drum up support."

"No, I haven't" replied Duffield.

"You will also have heard that the Government's planning yet more anti-trade union legislation. If it's passed, it will be illegal for unions to lobby Directors or shareholders of employers they are in dispute with or to hold demonstrations at events they sponsor. And employers will have the right to sue the bollocks off us. We will effectively be emasculated if this goes through."

"We've got one last dice to throw, Jez" continued Monaghan. "We're planning to lobby FIFA reps against voting for the England bid. We're going to send them details of the Government's latest anti-union legislation and tell them that Britain's not the pure, whiter than white democracy the Government thinks it is. That should sway quite a few delegates. But I reckon the clincher might be the film of the police in action at Swansea."

"Too fucking right" said Duffield. "That film shows what television coverage did not – the pigs going in like the SS, using long-handled batons against women, kids and pensioners, tear-gassing and Tasering defenceless people. I want the world to see Britain in its true shitty glory, a fascist dictatorship defending the privileges of the rich and powerful and stamping on the rights of the poor and defenceless. I've already let *Russia Today* and *Press TV* have copies."

Russia Today was not the country's official media channel but it was favoured by the Government for taking an aggressively anti-West line in print and on television. *Press TV* was the official Iranian media outlet and was effectively the spokesman for the Islamic Republic. Both stations employed hard-left British journalists who revelled in critical coverage of their own country.

"Jez, if you let us have a copy, that will sink the England World Cup bid below the waterline. FIFA delegates might be corrupt as fuck but they're very precious about human rights. Any sign of repressive laws or police using batons and they get on their high horse about freedom and democracy."

"Consider it done, man" said Duffield.

21 November 2011
Department for National Heritage
Cockspur Street
London

"Mr Calder, may I remind you that what Unite are planning to do is criminal blackmail." The Secretary of State for National Heritage, Hugh Greville, was extremely angry and the terse expression on his face conveyed this.

Rob Calder, Unite's General Secretary, was however in no mood to compromise.

"No Mr Greville, what we're doing is no' criminal. Your Government is proposing to bring in laws which will stop us defending the rights of our members. And if you persist, we will exercise our democratic right to inform the people who will decide on whether England stages the World Cup in 2018 that your Government is denying the right of free collective bargaining. It is their decision on whether England gets to host the World Cup."

"That's complete rubbish" barked Greville. "Your union's definition of 'free collective bargaining' appears to consist of the right to intimidate employers' representatives outside their own homes and to disrupt events they sponsor for the public's benefit. Such tactics belong to the likes of the Mafia."

"Mr Greville, had Laing bothered to open dialogue with us about our concerns over the City of Dundee Stadium, the dispute would have never happened. Instead, they closed their ears to our concerns. All we did was to bring the message home to their Directors, shareholders and chief officers, and to the public, that they were forcing our members to work in unsafe conditions."

"Don't play that broken record again, Mr Calder" said Greville. "A reputable and accredited waste management company decontaminated the

City of Dundee Stadium site before construction work began. Government inspectors signed off the work. The worker who was taken ill had a history of respiratory problems and should not have taken the job. It seems that your local shop stewards and district convenor was spoiling for a fight with Laing, Mr Calder."

"You, like Laing, appear to have no interest in listening" said Calder. "Remember this, Mr Greville. Britannia no longer rules the waves. Foreigners no longer bend to their will. You are completely powerless in influencing the outcome of the World Cup vote. And you are also powerless to stop us telling FIFA delegates that Britain is no' the pure as white democracy where freedom is cherished."

Greville's face had now pulled into a snarl.

"Mr Calder, what you are proposing to do is treason."

"Correction, Mr Greville" snapped Calder. "We're talking about *England's* World Cup bid. No' Britain's. Remember that England hosting the World Cup will do little for Scotland, Wales or Northern Ireland."

1 December 2011
FIFA Headquarters
FIFA-Strasse 20
Zurich
Switzerland

The Press Suite at FIFA's Headquarters was already full to bursting point as the world's media gathered to find out which country would be awarded the right to stage the 2018 World Cup.

There were four bids to be considered. They were from Russia, England, and joint bids by Belgium and the Netherlands, and Portugal and Spain. Despite concerns in some quarters about Russia's human rights record and about their infrastructure, they were favourites to win. The strongest challenge was from England.

At 1:45pm, FIFA's President, Joao da Costa entered the suite and took his place at the top table. Alongside him was the Secretary-General, François Picard.

Da Costa signalled that he was ready to announce the outcome of the bids to stage the 2018 World Cup.

"Ladies and gentlemen, I am now ready to announce the result of the four bids to stage the 2018 World Cup.

"In the first round of voting, the bid from Russia received nine votes, the bid from Portugal and Spain received seven votes, the bid from Belgium and the Netherlands received four votes and the bid from England received two votes. The bid from England was therefore eliminated."

There were gasps of incredulity from the English delegation. They knew it would be tough to secure the World Cup against a very strong Russian bid which had been bankrolled by several oligarchs close to the Government. The problems in preparing for Euro 2016 in Scotland and Wales, which was behind schedule, had not helped. But no one had expected the England bid to be dismissed so peremptorily.

Da Costa continued.

"The bidding process therefore proceeded to a second round. Russia received thirteen votes, Portugal and Spain received seven votes and Belgium and the Netherlands received two votes.

"I therefore declare that FIFA will be inviting Russia to host the 2018 World Cup."

A massive cheer went up from the Russian delegation.

After the Press Corps left, Russia's delegate to FIFA, Sergei Lavotchkin, sought out Picard, who was in deep conversation with Orville McKenzie, Jamaica's representative who had been influential in swinging delegates from Central America and the Caribbean to back Russia. Picard had played a significant role in lobbying delegates to support Russia's bid and had been instrumental in convincing McKenzie to switch his support to Russia. McKenzie had previously been considering backing England's bid and there had been controversy about claims that he had demanded a bribe for supporting England.

"François, I can't say more how grateful I am for your work in convincing delegates to back us. The Russian Football Federation will be eternally grateful."

"If there's anyone to thank, Sergei, it's Orville." Said Picard, pointing to the Jamaican representative.

"Orville, thank you for your support" said Lavotchkin. "Your reward will be on the way."

"Think nothing of it, Sergei" replied McKenzie. "That will teach the arrogant Brits that they can no longer disrespect me and treat me as nothing more than a plantation coolie." McKenzie was still angry by the hostile treatment he received in British newspapers about the allegation that he had asked for a bribe to support England's bid.

Picard then turned to Lavotchkin.

"Sergei, can I ask you a favour. Our Football Federation is planning to submit a bid to step in to stage Euro 2016 if Scotland and Wales pull out. You know the Scots and the Welsh are already six months behind schedule and there's talk that UEFA might pull the plug if they fall further behind. Any help you can give to support us would be appreciated."

"Sorry, François. You'll have to do this one alone. We're going to have our hands full in preparing for the World Cup. And we've already returned the favour for getting you the 1998 World Cup."

CHAPTER 5

22 March 2012
Stannergate Road
Dundee
Scotland

Colin Hay was a happy man. Laing Construction's Site Manager at the emerging City of Dundee Stadium had just received a telephone call from Steve Bird, the Project Manager, thanking him and the workforce for the rapid progress with constructing the new stadium and explaining that he would be receiving a sizeable bonus. Hay already had visions of taking his wife for the holiday of a lifetime to see their younger son, Gavin, who was now living in Australia.

Since the dismissal of the original workforce following a stormy industrial dispute over safety the previous year, Laing had indeed made impressive progress. The foundations of the new stadium were now in place, as were the water and electricity supply, and concrete and steel girders for the stadium structure were on order. They were now barely a month behind the completion schedule demanded by UEFA.

The excellent weather that Scotland and indeed most of the United Kingdom had enjoyed for over two weeks had helped speed up work. The temperature stood at twenty-two degrees Centigrade.

Pawel Nowak was at the controls of a large crane which was moving heavy steel girders to a section of the site where they were going to be set hard in concrete. A mixer was busy preparing the quick-drying concrete which would hold the girders in place. Nowak, a Pole from Gdynia, manoeuvred the levers to lower the girders. Below him, several workmates were ready to guide the girders into a neat pile near the site boundary.

Suddenly, Nowak felt a snatching motion. To his horror, the heavy-duty cables holding the girders in place snapped. He yelled out to the men below to look out.

It was too late. The six workmen standing below the girders, three Poles, two Romanians and a Lithuanian stood no chance as sixteen tons of steel fell on top of them.

The same day
Unite
Blackness Road
Dundee
Scotland

Gregor Stevenson was reading through his day's paperwork when his attention was grabbed by the latest breaking news from the BBC on the television screen in the outer office.

The banner headline read **SIX WORKERS DIE IN STADIUM ACCIDENT**. This was followed by the BBC's description of what happened.

"This is Jane Bell with breaking news on BBC."

"Six construction workers helping to build the new City of Dundee Stadium have been killed in a tragic accident when several tons of steel girders fell and crushed them while they were standing underneath. It is believed that cabling securing the girders broke while they were being lowered to the ground."

"This is the first fatal accident at the stadium, which is being built for Euro 2016 which Scotland is hosting jointly with Wales. However, there have been several previous accidents which have led to accusations that short cuts are being made on safety."

Stevenson smiled. Not because of the deaths of the workers, even if they were non-Union and brought in from abroad. Any fatality was regrettable. But this was an opportunity for revenge on Laing plc.

The previous six months had not been kind to Unite. They had lost out in the dispute they had with Laing over safety the previous year. Not only had all the previous workers been sacked but six Unite members, including the former shop steward at the City of Dundee site, Lee Imrie, were in jail after being convicted for criminal trespass after disrupting the Edinburgh Half Marathon back in October. Finally, Unite's decision to lobby FIFA delegates to oppose England's World Cup bid had backfired.

It strengthened the resolve of the Government to proceed with new legislation to outlaw 'leverage' tactics which Unite had deployed so successfully in previous disputes.

Stevenson reached for the phone in his office. His older brother, Hamish, was a senior official at the Health & Safety Executive and was well-placed to run a full investigation of Laing over their safety practices.

"Hamish Stevenson, HSE."

"Hello, big brother. Got something for you."

"I take it you mean the City of Dundee Stadium, Greg? Very sad what happened there today. A lot of those workers have got wives and kids back home."

"Indeed, I do, Hamish. You know there's been previous complaints about Laing over safety practices. And this from non-unionised workers. Now this. Any chance you can get a formal investigation going?"

"Yes. The Scottish Government's not too pleased with Laing as they've ratted on the deal to give priority to local labour. I'll think they'll be delighted if Laing get done."

"Any chance of a prosecution?"

"If they've found to be negligent, yes."

Gregor Stevenson punched the air as if he'd just scored the winning goal for Dundee United in the Scottish Cup Final. In his mind, he saw Laing executives being led out of court in handcuffs and being taken to Barlinnie Prison."

27 March 2012
Stannergate Road
Dundee
Scotland

Colin Hay heard a sharp rap on the door. "Come in" he said gruffly.

Standing opposite him was a tall, sandy-haired man of 50 dressed in a black suit, a white shirt and purple tie.

"Good morning, sir. Hamish Stevenson, Health and Safety Executive."

"Colin Hay, Site Manager. What can I do for you, Mr Stevenson?"

"HSE are carrying out a statutory investigation into the accident that happened last week and cost the lives of six workers. I trust I will have your full co-operation, Mr Hay."

Stevenson noted that the site was quiet.

"Where is everyone today?"

"I've given the laddies the day off, Mr Stevenson" replied Hay. "The funerals of the dead men are taking place."

"Mr Hay, we now need to discuss the scope of our investigation. Me and my colleagues will need to speak to the men working. We will also need to speak to the foremen and chargehands and to view your company's operating and health and safety procedures. This may cause some disruption to your work, but it is essential if we are going to get to the bottom of what happened last Thursday."

"Mr Stevenson, can I make it clear that we are extremely busy. We're behind schedule on building this stadium because of last year's strike and we need to crack on with the work if we're not to be fined by the Delivery Authority. Therefore, I've got no time for any disruption."

Stevenson was not impressed.

"Do you realise, Mr Hay, that the HSE has statutory authority to carry out an investigation? Six of your men died in an accident last week so this has the same status as a criminal investigation. I expect you, as Site Manager, to offer your full co-operation with us."

Colin Hay's ire was also growing. A hard-nosed Dundonian who had worked his way up from the shop floor to a managerial position, he had little time for interfering busybodies from the public sector whom he felt had never worked in the real world.

"Mr Stevenson, I am fully aware of what happened last week. I had to write letters to the next-of-kin of the dead laddies. I will let you know when I've got time to assist with your investigation. Until then, I should be grateful if you could get your arse out of my office and off these premises so we can continue building this stadium."

The HSE representative was no shrinking violet himself and was in no mood to give way to what he considered to be a bullying boor.

"You, Mr Hay, are obstructing the Health & Safety Executive in carrying out a statutory investigation into an industrial accident. That is a breach of the law. I will be back here in two days with an investigation team. If I do not receive your co-operation, I will put the matter in the hands of the police and the Sheriff Court. Good day."

4 April 2012
Singleton, Baines & Partners
Inverness Street
Camden
London

"Come through Mr Davies. Ms Singleton will see you now."

Mandy Grehan, Geri Singleton's PA, led Ken Davies through to a rather modish office. The furniture was very Scandinavian in appearance. All pine and brushed steel while a large desk in black glass dominated the centre of the room.

Geri Singleton was waiting to meet the Penclawdd councillor who was leading the fight against the proposed airport at Crofty on the Gower Peninsula. She was in her late forties, a still attractive brunette dressed in a black trouser suit and a red top. She had made her reputation as a feisty defence solicitor, initially with Bindmans and subsequently in partnership with Marcus Baines, another well-known defence solicitor, with a client list ranging from celebrities to political activists.

"Good to meet you, Ken" said Singleton. "I understand you've been leading the campaign against the new Swansea Airport."

"Indeed, I have, Ms Singleton."

"Geri please."

"OK Geri. I helped No2 Swansea Airport get going back in 2010 and we made a massive submission to the Department for Transport consultation a year later. Fat lot of good that did."

Singleton opened some of the copious documents that Davies had provided. These included photographs of the proposed airport site, information about the farms and local businesses that would be affected by the new airport, the submission from No2 Swansea Airport to the Department for Transport consultation and a report of the Department for Transport's review of the consultation and decision. Also on Singleton's desk was a DVD of the police operation to clear the occupation camp at the airport site.

"Ken, it appears you're saying that Department for Transport failed to take account of the airport's impact on local farms and businesses."

"That's right, Geri" said the burly cockle fisherman. "No less than eight local farmers will lose grazing lands to the airport. They will not have sufficient pasture to support current livestock levels and will be forced to sell. This will hit their income and, dare I say it, their viability. We've already had farms on the Gower closing due to falling milk prices. This could be the killer blow."

"On top of that, the Crofty and Penclawdd cockle beds will be lost forever. Our part of Wales has had world renown for the quality of our cockles. I will be one of about 20 business owners who will be forced to close down."

"Ken, I think you've got a very strong case against the Department for Transport. I've read their guidance on new infrastructure projects and it makes it clear that they must give regard to the impact on existing communities and businesses. They have appeared to have overlooked this."

"What options are open to us, Geri" asked Davies. "You know they've started work on the airport site."

"A lot, Ken" replied Singleton. "The European Court of Human Rights would be extremely interested in the Government's failure to follow its own guidance. It may be too late to save the livelihoods of the farmers and fishermen involved. But if the Government has been found to have breached their human rights by failing to consider the impact on their livelihood, I think you and fellow residents of Crofty and Penclawdd may be in line for substantial compensation."

Davies smiled. As an Independent councillor, he had been elected on a platform of being tough on law and order. Local people knew him as being opposed to the Human Rights Act which he regarded as a criminals' charter and he was equally vehement about European meddling in domestic affairs. And he was about to take the Government to the European Court on Human Rights.

<h3 style="text-align:center">11 April 2012
Euro 2016 Delivery Authority
Argyle Street
Glasgow</h3>

Gordon Hunter and Alun Williams were not at all happy to learn that Euro 2016 was in danger of being blown off course again. UEFA representatives would be visiting Glasgow and Cardiff the following month to check on progress.

Doug Irvine, the Delivery Authority's Chief Executive, was however confident of their ability to mitigate the two latest difficulties to emerge.

"Gordon, Alun, like you, I was not best pleased to find out after Easter about the accident on the Dundee site and that nutjob councillor taking the Swansea Airport issue to ECHR. I've given the Project Team a stern reprimand about the need to be on the ball about breaking news, and I've assigned a Press Officer to the team to ensure there's no repetition."

"I've got our Legal Department assessing the likelihood of the ECHR ruling against us on Swansea Airport and what the impact might be. In the meantime, work will continue. I spoke to Stuart Moriarty at DfT on Friday and he's assured me work will continue. Probably the worst that will happen is that compensation will have to be paid to people who've lost land or livelihoods."

"Much the same for Dundee. That's not the only site they're working on – they're also building the new Inverness stadium. Again, until HSE have reached a decision on whether they were at fault for the accident, work can continue."

"Doug, when do we expect the HSE's report and the ECHR decision?" asked Williams.

"HSE should report by the autumn" said Irvine. "However, their report will state whether Laing were criminally negligent. The Sheriff's office may take over from then. As for ECHR, this is likely to be in the first part of 2013."

"Have you prepared for a 'worst case' scenario, Doug?" asked Hunter.

"As I said earlier, Gordon, the worst that could happen with Swansea Airport is that compensation will have to be paid. As DfT commissioned the project, I assume the UK Government will be liable. With the Dundee and Inverness sites, I've already prepared for the possibility that we will have to retender for work. But it will be partially completed."

"Doug, the consequences could be far more serious than you've made out" said Hunter. "Can you see the UK Government agreeing to multimillion pound compensation payouts for a project which wouldn't have existed but for Euro 2016? It would be UK taxpayers' money going to Wales. Hardly likely to be popular. They will try to load it onto us."

"And I don't see Laing lying down without a fight, even if they are held to blame for the accident." Hunter knew from previous experience that the company was extremely well-connected with friends in the City of London and the UK Government, and had a reputation of being highly litigious.

51

17 April 2012
Cabinet Room
10 Downing Street
London

Transport was the fifth item on the agenda for the Cabinet meeting. Peter Bridgeman, the Secretary of State had summarised progress on HS2, the proposed railway line that would bring high speed services comparable to those in Europe to the Midlands and the North, Crossrail and extending Thameslink's rail services to Peterborough and Cambridge.

He then thumbed his way to a new page.

"Prime Minister, I am afraid that I have to report an unwelcome development about the new airport being built at Swansea. You will be aware that there was opposition to the airport being built and that we had to use the police to remove protestors from the site last November. The No2 Swansea Airport campaign has just submitted a case to the European Court of Human Rights to argue that the decision to use the Crofty site failed to take account of the impact on local residents and businesses. Singleton Baines are acting for them."

Groans echoed round the Cabinet Room. Geri Singleton was one of the Government's least favourite people because of her tiresome pursuit of human rights issues.

Bridgeman continued. "The Court will issue its verdict in about a year's time but we're braced for the worst."

"What might that be, Peter?" asked the Prime Minister.

"That they rule that Department for Transport failed to take account of the impact on the livelihoods of local residents. Particularly farmers and cockle fishermen, I understand. It's unlikely to be that we have to stop work altogether" said Bridgeman. "But they are more likely to demand that we give swingeing compensation to people who have lost property or livelihoods."

"Meaning that English taxpayers will be bailing out the Welsh for a project designed to enable Wales to host a lucrative international tournament of no benefit to England" said Mark Rudge. "They will never stand for it."

"Mark, you are quite right" said Bridgeman. "Had it not been for Euro 2016, Swansea Airport would never have been built. In these circumstances, I do not see why taxpayers in England should be forced to pay compensation to Welsh property owners. I will be commending to the Cabinet that the

Welsh Assembly Government or the Euro 2016 Delivery Authority should meet such liabilities."

"Peter, I totally agree" said David Talbot. "Keep me informed of developments and make sure that any attempt to make the Government liable for compensation is robustly challenged."

The sixth item for discussion was employment. Ben Richardson opened his file of papers.

"Both good news and bad news, Prime Minister. The good news is that construction work at the Dundee and Inverness stadiums to be used for Euro 2016 has proceeded at impressive pace. I spoke to Gavin Laing yesterday and he said that they are almost on schedule and have made up for work lost due to last year's strike. The bad news is that HSE are going after Laing like a terrier with a bone and Gavin fears they will face prosecution over the deaths of the workers last March."

"Remind me what happened, Ben" said Talbot.

"Six workers were crushed to death when a pile of steel girders fell onto them after cabling securing them snapped. Sounds like an unfortunate accident, but Unite have been making a song and dance about safety standards, as has the local MSP."

"Who is he?" asked Hugh Greville.

"She, actually" replied Richardson. "Amy MacDougall, SNP. Got a gob like a foghorn. Trouble is, she's the Minister for Home and Health in the Scottish Government and is being talked about as a future First Minister."

Richardson then returned to the issue of the accident and HSE's involvement.

"As I said earlier, HSE are going all out for a prosecution. If Laing get done for negligence, you can imagine how the likes of Rob Calder and MacDougall will react."

"Ben, you might be interested to know that HSE's chief investigator is the brother of the local Unite convenor for Dundee. See this."

Philip Madge, Secretary of State for the Cabinet, handed Richardson a copy of the *Scotsman*.

"Bloody hell" said Richardson. "So that's why HSE have gone after Laing. Big brother doing little brother a favour. Thanks, Philip."

"Ben, it's time to read the riot act to HSE" said Rudge. "For too long, they've been obstructing business."

"You've got the power to do something, Ben" said Sarah Crosby. "I wish I did" added the Home Secretary, wistful that her authority for crime and policing did not extend into Scotland.

"Hold on a minute" shouted Talbot. "Mark, Sarah, we've got to be careful about how we approach the HSE. Make it look like politically motivated revenge and we'll get slaughtered. But it's right that we should investigate whether one of their officials is carrying out a vendetta against Laing. Ben, can you please take this matter up with the Chief Executive and ask them to carry out a high-level investigation into the conduct of Mr Stevenson. If it's proven that his grounds for going after Laing are baseless, get him removed from the investigation. Laing have been a highly successful company and we can't have public officials settling personal grievances against them."

22 April 2012
Health and Safety Executive
Belford House
Belford Road
Edinburgh

"Come in Hamish. Take a seat. Tea, coffee?" James Muir, HSE's Regional Director for South and Central Scotland East summoned Hamish Stevenson into his office.

Hamish Stevenson had been somewhat perplexed by the message he had received late the previous Friday to report to the Regional Director. He was now about to find out why.

"Coffee please James."

"You must be wondering why I've asked you to come here at such short notice, Hamish" said Muir. Stevenson nodded.

"Reason is that we're assigning you to a new investigation from tomorrow. Local authority play areas. You'll have the details tomorrow morning."

Stevenson was somewhat taken aback. "James, do you realise it's not normal practice to take someone off an investigation that is incomplete? There is still a long way to go on the Laing case."

"I know, Hamish" replied Muir. "However, when there is a need for an experienced investigator to be reassigned at short notice, we have to make these changes."

"Not for a case of a wee bairn falling off a swing or roundabout, surely" replied Stevenson. "James, is there something I'm no' being told?"

"Hamish, it is known across the HSE that your brother's the local Unite big shot in Dundee. And last year, Unite were involved in a major dispute with Laing."

"Aye, they were, James" replied Stevenson. "But the fact that Greg's the local convenor's got nothing to do with the way I've been running this investigation. And frankly, Unite have got a good case. I've visited Laing, James. Their health and safety procedures are a joke and the fella managing the site should have been prosecuted for obstructing me."

"Hamish, I don't doubt your professionalism" said Muir. "But the fact that your brother's a leading local official with a trade union that was in dispute with the subject of this investigation puts our reputation for impartiality at risk by having you on the investigation. Whitehall's already threatening to cut our budget by a further 20 percent on top of the cuts they imposed last year. We don't want to give the Government more reason to do this."

Stevenson was not convinced or impressed.

"Did someone in high places have words about me, James?" asked Stevenson. "After all, it's well known that Laing are a big contributor to Conservative Party funds."

"You know I cannot comment on that, Hamish" replied Muir. "By the way, not a word about this to anyone. The Official Secrets Act applies."

A disgruntled Hamish Stevenson trudged out of Muir's office.

CHAPTER 6

27 July 2012
The Olympic Stadium
Stratford
London

The opening ceremony of the 2012 Olympic Games was now three hours old. Danny Boyle's extravagant production which depicted British history from when it was an agricultural country, through the Industrial Revolution and the First and Second World Wars, was now proceeding to post-war Britain, with an overriding theme being the creation of the National Health Service.

Inside the VIP Suite, political leaders from the United Kingdom and other countries, leading sportsmen and women, sports officials and celebrities were quaffing fine wines and champagne and eating their way through gourmet canapes. David Talbot, the Prime Minister and Jeremy Greenfield, the Leader of the Labour Party, were both present, as was the Duke of Cambridge and former football star, David Beckham. The Duke and Beckham had been prominent in England's unsuccessful bid to stage the 2018 World Cup.

In one corner of the suite close to the panoramic window which offered a view of the proceedings, Mark Rudge, Secretary of State for Trade and business was deep in conversation with François Picard, FIFA's Secretary-General. Picard was strongly tipped to succeed Joao da Costa when the Brazilian stood down as President. He had known Rudge since the 1980s when they were both working for BNP Paribas.

"What do you think, Mark?"

"Impressive production by Boyle, though a bit too left wing for my tastes. He seems to have forgotten that the wealth created by business during the

Industrial Revolution helped to pay for things like universal education and the National Health Service."

"I wasn't talking about the opening ceremony, Mark" replied Picard. "I meant Euro 2016."

"Euro 2016. François, that is an enormous white elephant that will cost the country loads of money and deliver very little in return."

"But your Government is backing it, Mark" said Picard.

Rudge pointed to the corridor outside the suite where they could continue a more discreet conversation.

"François, I hope you realise the position the Government's in. We had to form a coalition after the last election because we didn't have an overall majority. We're stuck with the Liberal Democrats for another three years as they forced us to bring in a law to have fixed term elections. Therefore, we can't pursue the policies we would like to implement."

Rudge continued.

"Another problem is that David's frightened of the nationalists taking control in Scotland and Wales and ultimately the risk of both countries leaving of the United Kingdom. The SNP's already taken control in Scotland and Plaid Cymru's the main coalition partner in Wales. Understandably, he doesn't want to go down in history as the man responsible for the country's break-up. So, he wants to appease the Scots and the Welsh at every turn."

"And I suppose that means supporting Euro 2016" sighed Picard.

"Tell me, Mark. What prospect has Euro 2016 got of being successful?"

"François, can I explain what needs to be done before the tournament can even start. At present, they've got just four stadiums which meet UEFA's size criteria. Hampden Park, Celtic Park, Murrayfield and the Millennium Stadium. Three new stadiums are being built from scratch and three more are either being rebuilt or extended. Problem is that none of them are likely to receive anything near capacity once Euro 2016 has finished. Here are two examples. Inverness and Wrexham are getting thirty thousand capacity stadiums. The two football teams that will use it get no more than three thousand fans per game."

"I see what you mean by 'white elephant', Mark" said Picard.

Rudge continued.

"On top of that, they're having to spend money on improving infrastructure and accommodation. Scotland and Wales are two hundred miles apart at their nearest points. That means road and rail improvements and additional airport capacity. At present, Wales has just one international airport, in Cardiff. They will have to rely on Manchester for the matches in Wrexham. The main roads from the South to the North of Wales are mainly single carriageway. As is the main road between Aberdeen and Inverness. And there's going to be a need for special train services to get fans between venues. All this on the most congested rail network in Europe.

"Finally, François, there's not nearly enough hotel accommodation in either Scotland or Wales to accommodate all the fans who will attend. A massive hotel building programme is required."

"My God, I didn't realise there was so much to do" said Picard. "What progress has been made?"

"Surprisingly, a lot, François" replied Rudge. "We had a significant delay last year due to a strike at the Dundee stadium site but that's all been resolved. All work on stadiums is largely on schedule. We've got a minor worry with the new Swansea Airport as the protest group has taken us to the European Court of Human Rights. However, I reckon that if we agree a compensation deal with the locals affected, we will reach an out-of-court agreement.

"However, the main concern is whether Scotland and Wales can afford to pay for all the work that's needed to be done. On top of what I've already said, we need to consider security – after all, it's an inviting target for Al-Q'aida and the Real IRA. I've heard that they're facing a financial shortfall already and that neither the Scottish or Welsh Governments have the money to bail them out. I've already made clear that English taxpayers should not be burdened and a lot of the Cabinet agree with me."

"What will happen if Scotland and Wales run out of money?"

"I guess they will have to pull out from staging Euro 2016, François."

Picard smiled at the prospect of France stepping in to stage the tournament.

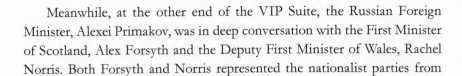

Meanwhile, at the other end of the VIP Suite, the Russian Foreign Minister, Alexei Primakov, was in deep conversation with the First Minister of Scotland, Alex Forsyth and the Deputy First Minister of Wales, Rachel Norris. Both Forsyth and Norris represented the nationalist parties from their respective countries, the Scottish National Party and Plaid Cymru.

"I bet you're both delighted to be staging Euro 2016" said Primakov.

"We are, Alexei" replied Forsyth. "This will be the first real opportunity to project Scotland and Wales onto the world stage." Norris nodded her agreement.

"Unfortunately, the UK Government is showing little enthusiasm for supporting the tournament" continued Forsyth. "We've been told that there's no money coming from the UK Government to support Euro 2016 and that we've got to fund it from our own resources. What grates is that we were expected to show our support for the Olympics because it was a British event. But when it comes to something that will benefit our countries, the Government doesn't want to know."

"Did Scotland and Wales get to stage any events at the Olympics?" asked Primakov.

"Only the football" replied Norris, "and that was limited to a couple of games in Cardiff and Glasgow."

"Team GB is a fucking joke, Alexei" snarled Forsyth. "No players from Scotland or Northern Ireland and just two from Wales. All the rest were English. Might as well have called them 'England'."

"How are things going with preparations for the tournament?" asked Primakov.

"Slower than we would have liked" replied Forsyth. "A strike at the Dundee stadium site last year held things up for a while and there's a row about compensation for the loss of property at the new Swansea Airport which is going to ECHR next year. But the venues are otherwise on track. However, we've also got to provide further infrastructure improvements, including road improvements and additional hotel provision. It's going to be rather tight financially."

"The UK Government spared no expense for the Olympics and the England World Cup bid" said Norris. "They came up with the standard line that the Olympics and the World Cup would inspire people to take up sport and that would in turn promote better health and reductions in crime and anti-social behaviour, as well as being a tonic for the nation that would improve the sense of well-being. Yet when Wales and Scotland are awarded a major sporting tournament, they come up with the lame excuse that we can't organise it, that it is a waste of public money and that the English taxpayer should not be charged a single penny."

"Alexei, what Rachel has just said shows the blinkered, London-centric view of the UK Government" added Forsyth. "We're intending to press on with arrangements for Euro 2016, irrespective of where the money's coming from. Scotland and Wales have been sidelined too often in the past. This time, we're going to have our moment in the sun."

Primakov smiled. He knew that Russia had money to spare and could sense that Forsyth and Norris would be willing recipients.

31 August 2012
Euro 2016 Delivery Authority
Argyle Street
Glasgow

"A fine time to tell me that there's more expense, Robert."

Doug Irvine was not impressed to find out that the Delivery Authority had failed to build into their cashflow reports calculations for road improvements, additional hotel accommodation and extra air, rail and coach services to link the venues. From being within budget, Euro 2016 now faced an unexpected shortfall of £200 million. He knew the difficulty in finding this money. The economy was in recession and business was scaling back on non-essential expenditure across the board. It was unlikely that either the Scottish or Welsh Governments would be able to spare additional resources, and Irvine knew there was likely to be a frosty response from the UK Government.

Irvine was due to meet the SFA and FAW the following week to report on progress, and he knew that Gordon Hunter and Alun Williams would be visiting UEFA the following month for a status update. He was aware that there was support within UEFA for taking Euro 2016 away from Scotland and Wales and handing it to France, and he did not wish to give them an opportunity on a plate.

Robert Shepherd, the Programme Manager for Euro 2016 infrastructure, was lost for words.

"Doug, I'm really sorry for overlooking this. All our attention has been on the venues and big projects like Swansea Airport. I genuinely didn't realise that road improvements and hotels were part of the package as they hadn't been highlighted as priorities when I got the commission."

"Robert, where do you think the fans are going to stay?" said Irvine. "Sleeping on Glasgow Green or in the grounds of Cardiff Castle? I thought someone with your background would have picked this up."

"Is this going to make much difference, Doug?"

"Yes, Robert" replied Irvine. "We've got to find another £200 million. Which in the current climate is like trying to find hen's teeth. We've got UEFA coming over next month. When they find out we've not budgeted for all the work required, we risk having Euro 2016 taken off us. Perhaps now you'll understand what overlooking secondary works means."

6 September 2012
Football Association of Wales
Vanguard Road
Cardiff

"Two hundred million. And where are we going to find that, Doug?"

Alun Williams had a crestfallen look of a man who just realised that he had lost a lottery ticket guaranteeing him to a multi-million pound win. As Chairman of the FAW, he had been used to disappointments, mainly as Wales had missed qualification for a tournament for the past 54 years.

"Alun, I'm really sorry for what happened. Oversight by the Programme Manager of the fact we had to pay for road improvements, additional hotels and transport. I accept full responsibility for what has happened."

"Doug, without you, we wouldn't have got as far as we have" said Gordon Hunter, the SFA Chairman. "Obviously, we've got a difficult challenge ahead in trying to find money when there is none. But I can assure you that there's a lot of goodwill towards Scotland and Wales in the international community. There are many countries which want us to succeed, if only to prove to the bigger countries that countries like ours can successfully stage international tournaments. I'm confident that we can succeed. Don't you agree, Alun?"

"Absolutely" replied the FAW Chairman. "By the way, Doug, we want you to stay on. Are you prepared to continue?"

"I am" replied Irvine.

13 September 2012
Scottish Government
St Andrew's House
Regent Road
Edinburgh

"That's a fine time to tell us that you're short of money, gentlemen. It doesn't exactly grow on trees."

Gordon Hunter and Alun Williams were facing an uncomfortable grilling at the hands of the Scottish First Minister, Alex Forsyth and his Welsh counterpart, Richard Morgan.

"We're really sorry, First Minister" replied Hunter. "Some of the staff at the Delivery Authority made a bit of a cock-up with their figures. Overlooked work needed for improving roads and building hotels. They weren't flagged up as business priorities."

"Two hundred million's a big sum, Gordon. Neither us nor the Welsh Assembly Government are likely to have that sort of money. In case you've noticed, there's a recession on. The UK Government's Autumn Statement is due in a couple of months and we may face more cuts."

"We're targeting businesses, Alex" interjected Williams. "After all, they will benefit from better roads and more hotels so it's in their interest."

"I don't deny that, Alun" replied Morgan. "But they too are cutting back on donations in the current climate. I think you may end up disappointed."

"Alex, Richard, I hope you realise that if we're not able to complete all the works demanded by UEFA, we may lose the right to stage Euro 2016." Hunter was emphatic about the risk to the tournament.

"Gordon" said Forsyth "both Richard and I want this tournament to go ahead. Scotland and Wales have been in England's shadow for too long. This is our opportunity to promote our countries on the world scene. Do what you can to stall UEFA. Richard and I will consider what options are open to plug the gap. Whatever you do, don't sell us out."

"That could be a challenge" said Williams. "Gordon and I are meeting UEFA to report on progress in two weeks' time."

20 September 2012
UEFA Headquarters
Route de Genève 46
Nyon
Switzerland

"Good morning, gentlemen" said Heidi Elsener, PA to the UEFA President, Franz-Josef Sonnenberg. "Follow me."

Elsener led Gordon Hunter and Alun Williams into the UEFA boardroom where the General Council were already seated. The Scottish and Welsh delegation noticed that two new faces were on the Council. Giancarlo Langarotti and Marc Hermans had been replaced by two new members. Henri Marcel from France and Oleg Grishin from Russia had been elected to the General Council earlier that year.

Sonnenberg stood up to greet Hunter and Williams.

"Herr Hunter, Herr Williams, you will know why you've been invited here. As Euro 2016 is being held under our name, it is only reasonable that you give us a summary of progress. From what I've heard, thinks have been a bit quiet of late."

"Mr President, we are actually making decent progress" replied Hunter. "Work's proceeding at pace on the new stadiums at Dundee, Inverness and Wrexham while the Liberty Stadium will be expanded to hold 35,000 people from next year."

"What about Aberdeen?" asked France's representative, Henri Marcel.

"The new stadium's being built by the club, Aberdeen FC" replied Hunter. "They didn't need any outside money as they've got wealthy sponsors. Oil industry."

Williams now stood up to speak.

"Work is also well in hand building the new airport in Swansea and extending the existing airport at Inverness."

Marcel spoke again.

"Monsieur Williams, I recall that the British Government has been taken to the European Court of Human Rights by residents from West Wales who have lost their property and businesses. Isn't that right?"

"It is, Monsieur Marcel" replied Williams. "But we've received indications that the farmers and fishermen affected might be agreeable to an out of court settlement. Even if they don't, it will mean they may get significant compensation from the British Government. But it won't stop the airport being built."

However, Marcel wasn't prepared to let up. He continued to ask probing questions.

"Gentlemen, you appear to have mentioned nothing about roads, railways and accommodation. Can you please explain how far you have got?"

The expression on Hunter's and Williams' faces told everything. It was the question they were dreading.

"Scotrail, Virgin Trains and Arriva Trains Wales have all put in orders for additional trainsets to be delivered prior to Euro 2016 so that they can run additional services between the venues" explained Hunter. "After Euro 2016 has finished, they will replace older stock."

"Roads and hotels, Monsieur Hunter" said Marcel, ominously.

"Rather slower than we would have hoped, Monsieur Marcel" replied Hunter. "On roads, just two are needed. Most critical is the doubling of the A96 between Aberdeen and Inverness. We expect to start early next year. Then there's the A470 and A483 in Wales. As with the A96, we expect to start in 2013. We should finish on time."

"Work on new hotels has also yet to start" added Williams. "But we've got plans to significantly expand hotel availability in all venues and especially in the three largest." He meant Cardiff, Edinburgh and Glasgow.

"But when will they be ready?"

"Monsieur Marcel, I can assure you that all new hotels will be completed in time for Euro 2016" said Hunter.

"And where is the money coming from, Monsieur Hunter?" Marcel was not letting up.

"About fifty per cent will be from the devolved Governments in Scotland and Wales. Matched funding is expected from business as they will benefit from the provision after Euro 2016 is over."

"Really, Monsieur Hunter?" said Marcel. "In the current recessionary climate, I think that may be difficult to achieve. Especially for venues outside London."

The annoyance with the pedantic French representative on the UEFA General Council was clearly showing on the faces of both Hunter and Williams.

"Monsieur Marcel, may I point out that our progress on Euro 2016 is at a more advanced stage than any recent host of either the European Championships or the World Cup" shouted Williams.

Before anyone could respond further, Sonnenberg rapped his gavel on the table for attention.

"Gentlemen, I am grateful to you for your update to the General Council on progress against work in hand. As an Austrian who oversaw the work my country made to stage Euro 2008, I fully appreciate the difficulties that small countries face in staging major international tournaments. I am encouraged that you have overcome some early difficulties in a professional manner. But the concerns that Herr Marcel raised are valid ones. As the governing body for football in Europe, we have a responsibility to all affiliated countries to ensure that any tournament run in our name meets the highest standards. The existence of even the smallest shortcoming in organisation or provision of facilities will tarnish the good name of UEFA.

"Herr Hunter, Herr Williams, the General Council have real concerns about the ability of Scotland and Wales to ensure that provision for transport and accommodation will be in place by June 2016. Work on road improvements and hotels has not yet started and I am afraid that the United Kingdom has not got a good reputation for completing projects on time or within budget. We awarded you the tournament in good faith on the back of an impressive bid which fulfilled all of UEFA's objectives. It would be with great reluctance for us to take the tournament away from you and award it to another country. But we may have to consider this distasteful option if we cannot be satisfied of your capacity to deliver the tournament to the standards we expect.

"For the moment, our decision to award the tournament to Scotland and Wales still stands. But we will be asking you to return in six months' time with, hopefully, better news about progress on setting up her infrastructure for Euro 2016. I sincerely hope that you have made that progress."

Later that day
Hotel Crowne Plaza
Louis-Casai Avenue
Geneva
Switzerland

"François, is that you?"

On the other end of the telephone line was François Picard.

"Yes, Henri. How did the General Council meeting go?"

"Very well, François" replied Marcel. "Scotland and Wales have yet to start work on either the road improvements of additional hotel capacity demanded. Hunter and Williams said that they've got funding for work to start but I didn't believe them. They've overlooked the fact that both Governments and business are reining back expenditure because of the recession. Sonnenberg's given them six months to show progress, otherwise the General Council will consider taking the tournament away and giving it to another country."

"Hopefully, that will be France" replied Picard. "And Henri, if you pull that off, you stand a good chance of succeeding Sonnenberg when he stands down."

CHAPTER 7

8 November 2012
Office of the First Minister for Scotland
Holyrood
Edinburgh

"First Minister, it's Gregor Bannerman for you."

Nicola Glennie, Private Secretary to Scotland's First Minister transferred the call from the Scottish Government's Chief Legal Adviser.

"Thank you, Nicola" replied Alex Forsyth, the First Minister. "Gregor, is it about the EU Regional Development Fund? If so, I hope it's good news."

"First Minister, right on both counts" said Bannerman.

A month earlier, Forsyth had commissioned the Scottish Government's legal advisers to investigate the legality of using money provided to Scotland under its regeneration budget for infrastructure improvements, including road improvements and increased hotel provision. The purpose was to finance the works demanded by UEFA for Euro 2016 which the Delivery Authority had overlooked in its budget plans.

This had been in direct response to UEFA's threat to strip Scotland and Wales of the right to host Euro 2016 because of a lack of progress in providing all the facilities they had demanded and the risk that improvements to roads and accommodation infrastructure might not be in place by the time the tournament started.

Forsyth recognised it was legally questionable to use money provided for economic regeneration to provide facilities that would mainly benefit a sporting tournament rather than regenerate the Scottish economy. However, Forsyth was also aware that there was a strong argument that Euro 2016 would provide Scotland with a significant economic boost and that upgrading the A96 in the Highlands and providing additional hotels would provide benefits for both business and tourism.

"That's excellent news, Gregor. You are confident that infrastructure work for Euro 2016 meets the EU criteria for the regeneration budget. We will almost certainly be challenged once it becomes public knowledge."

"First Minister, we sought advice from Counsel and the Crown Office on this" replied Bannerman. "They both agreed that work in support of Euro 2016 counts as regeneration and that the EU money provided to the Scottish Government for this purpose can be used for infrastructure. Any legal challenge will not have a leg to stand on."

"Sounds like it's all systems go" said Forsyth. "Nicola, can you get me Richard Morgan and Gordon Hunter. I think I've got an early Christmas present for them."

A few minutes later

"Alex, it's great news. But I'm worried that we may lose if the EU mounts a legal challenge. Or the British Government."

Richard Morgan, Wales's First Minister, had doubts about the efficacy of using EU regeneration money to support infrastructure works for Euro 2016.

"Richard, we've got the backing of our Chief Legal Adviser and the Crown Office. There's no way anyone can challenge the legality of us using EU money for Euro 2016."

"I'm not so sure, Alex" replied Morgan. "If the EU finds out, they will refer the matter to their lawyers. They can afford the best and most expensive. And any case against us would be heard in a foreign court. Not only have we got to deal with the EU, we've also got the UK Government. They may see this as going behind their back and we risk having our central grant being cut. For us, that will have a bigger impact as we have no tax raising powers of our own."

Morgan was referring to the fact there were different levels of devolution between Scotland and Wales.

"Richard, do you realise what the consequences of backing out of this commitment are? UEFA have made it clear that they want all roads and hotels promised in place by June 2016 and they've given Hunter and Williams six months to convince them that they will be delivered. If they can't, we'll lose

Euro 2016. You will not only have let down Scotland as a partner nation, you will also have let your own country down, Richard. Am I clear?"

"Alex, I fully appreciate the position" replied Morgan. "Williams told me what happened in Switzerland back in September. But both of us could be taking an expensive gamble which could bankrupt both our countries. And possibly ourselves. The least I can do is to check the legal position at our end."

"Do that, Richard" said Forsyth gruffly. "And make it quick. We want to tell Hunter and Williams to get cracking if it's OK to go ahead."

Forsyth put the phone down and summoned his Private Secretary.

"Nicola, can you get me Rachel Norris."

How urgent is it, First Minister?" asked Glennie.

"Very urgent."

9 November 2012
Office of the First Minister for Wales
Cardiff Bay

"Can I see you, Richard? It's urgent."

Rachel Norris, Deputy First Minister of Wales and the Leader of the Plaid Cymru group in the Senedd entered Richard Morgan's office. An attractive brunette in her early forties, she was the first Plaid Cymru leader from outside the party's Welsh-speaking heartlands in the north and west of the Principality.

"May I ask what it's about, Rachel? I normally expect to have prior notice of requests for meetings."

"It's about Euro 2016. I understand there's an issue over the use of EU regeneration money for infrastructure improvements that UEFA have demanded. Specifically, improving the A470 and A483 between Merthyr Tydfil and Ruabon and increasing hotel capacity."

"Where did you hear this from, Rachel?"

Morgan however had a good idea that Alex Forsyth had spoken to Norris. She confirmed it.

"Rachel, I more than most people would love to see Wales hosting a big international tournament. The last was the Commonwealth Games back in 1958. But we've got to make sure that any expenditure committed is fully legal before we go ahead. The worst thing I fear could happen is that the EU will challenge the use of the regeneration fund and we will have to repay it.

We would have to slash virtually all public spending for at least three years to recoup the losses."

"Richard, Alex got high level legal advice to support the use of EU funding. That must surely count in our favour."

"You've also forgotten the UK Government, Rachel. All our funding comes through them. If they think we've bent the rules and used funding from another source, what's to stop them cutting our grant?"

"Richard, that funding's sitting in our account, waiting to be used. If we leave it there, we risk losing Euro 2016. And letting Scotland down too. If that happens, Plaid Cymru will have to reconsider its position in the Welsh Assembly Government."

Morgan realised that his Deputy was not going to let the matter rest.

"Alright, Rachel, I'll refer the matter to our own legal advisers immediately."

20 November 2012
Office of the First Minister for Wales
Cardiff Bay

"First Minister, Deputy First Minister, here is our advice on the legality of using EU Regional Development Fund for Euro 2016 infrastructure works."

Emyr Rees, the Welsh Assembly Government's Chief Legal Adviser, handed copies of a report to Richard Morgan and Rachel Norris.

Rees then summarised his findings.

"First Minister, I can appreciate your reservations about the use of the EU Regional Development Fund. There is a very fine dividing line between what constitutes regeneration and what does not. Many people will argue that Euro 2016 is nothing more than a sports tournament and, as such, part of the entertainments industry with the motive of delivering a profit for investors. But I had the opportunity of reading the prospectus for the bid that the Football Association of Wales, in partnership with the Scottish Football Association, produced for its bid for Euro 2016. It was made clear that one of the bid's aims was to promote economic regeneration in Wales and Scotland. Furthermore, I am satisfied that the proposed improvement work to the A470 and A483 and the construction of new hotels will, in the longer term, help promote increased economic activity in Wales. That would fulfil the aims of the regeneration budget."

"So Emyr, you are effectively saying that it's OK for us to use this budget as proposed" said Morgan.

"Yes, First Minister" replied Rees.

"And how is the UK Government likely to react?" asked Morgan.

"I'm afraid I cannot advise you on that, First Minister. But I can say that the legality of such a move would be in question. And although I'm not a politician, I suspect that the UK Government would be reluctant to stir up any antipathy by such a move. After all, they are a coalition and the agreement between the Conservative and Liberal Democrat parties would be tested if that did happen."

"Richard, it looks like we've got the green light to go ahead" said Norris.

14 March 2013
UEFA Headquarters
Route de Genève 46
Nyon
Switzerland

Gordon Hunter and Alun Williams were both in a very upbeat mood as they walked into the UEFA boardroom to meet the General Council and give an update on progress with preparations for Euro 2016. Since receiving authority from the devolved Governments in Scotland and Wales to use the EU Regional Development Fund for a road-building programme and new hotels, they had made rapid progress. Planning applications were in hand and work was expected to start in the summer.

"Herr Hunter, Herr Williams, good morning." The greeting from UEFA President, Franz-Josef Sonnenberg was cordial.

Sonnenberg continued.

"Gentlemen, when we last met in September, you will recall that I asked for assurance that work was in hand to provide all the facilities that are necessary to stage a successful tournament in 2016. The floor is yours to explain what has been done over the last six months."

SFA Chairman, Gordon Hunter, was the first to respond.

"Mr President, Council members. May I update you on the latest progress with the infrastructure programme that you raised concerns about."

"Planning applications have been made for two major road improvement programmes. The first is the conversion of the A96 between Aberdeen and Inverness to dual carriageway for its entire length. This work will include by-passes for Keith and Elgin. The second is the improvement of the A470 and A483 between Merthyr Tydfil and Ruabon. Although this road will not be upgraded to dual carriageway status, it will be improved to a wide and straight single carriageway and will include building by-passes for Builth Wells, Llandrindod Wells, Newtown and Welshpool."

"To-date, planning applications have met little opposition. We recognised that the A470 passes through the Brecon Beacons National Park, so we prepared a scheme was sensitive to the environment and has satisfied environmental considerations. We expect to be able to start work during the summer and the new roads should be open for use by late 2015."

"The Delivery Authority has also invited tenders for the provision of up to 10,000 additional hotel rooms in or close to the main match venues. We have received tenders from, Best Western, Hilton, Holiday Inn, Ibis, Jury's, Novotel, Premier Inn and Travelodge. Planning applications have been made and there are not expected to be many obstacles as most of the hotels will be built upon 'brownfield' sites."

"Señor Hunter, it appears that most of these hotels are at the lower price range. Am I right?" asked Jose Maria Canizares.

"That is correct" replied Hunter.

"It is rather surprising that you have not considered providing more luxury hotel accommodation for Euro 2016" continued Canizares.

"Señor Canizares, if I may explain, there is no shortage of top end hotel accommodation in either Scotland or Wales. I think you will find the likes of Gleneagles and Celtic Manor under-used. The main demand is for budget or mid-priced hotels and this is being met."

"Thank you, Herr Hunter" said Sonnenberg.

Alun Williams then stood up to speak.

"Mr President, Council members, may I update you on the rest of the progress. Construction work for the new stadiums at Dundee, Inverness and Wrexham and the expansion of the Liberty Stadium in Swansea continues to be on target and they all should be open by the autumn of 2015. Similarly, the new stadium that Aberdeen FC is building is on course to be completed at the same time."

"Work on the new airport at Swansea is now ahead of target. The main runway is currently being laid down and planning permission for the rail spur and the connecting road to the M4 have been obtained. I recognise some of you have concerns about a possible adverse verdict from the European Court of Human Rights but there have been ongoing discussions with the plaintiffs about the possibility of settling out of court."

"That's not what I heard on today's news, Monsieur Williams" said Henri Marcel. "Did you hear what the lawyer for the plaintiffs had to say?"

"I am aware of Ms Singleton's statement to the Press, Monsieur Marcel" replied Williams. "What counts at the end of the day is not what she wants, it is what her clients want."

Williams then continued with his progress report.

"Work to extend the runway at Inverness Airport will start this summer and is expected to be completed by 2015. Finally, Scotrail, Virgin Trains and Arriva Trains Wales expect to receive delivery of new trainsets by the spring of 2016. All are similar to existing rolling stock so we do not expect there to be any problems with introduction into service. These have been partly financed by the Scottish Government and the Welsh Assembly Government."

Heidi Elsener, Sonnenberg's PA, then led Hunter and Williams to a side room while the General Council discussed progress. Fifteen minutes later, they were invited back into the boardroom.

The UEFA President stood up to address Hunter and Williams.

"Gentlemen, the Council was most grateful for your helpful and comprehensive update of progress. You will be pleased to hear that we have full confidence in the ability of your countries' associations to stage Euro 2016."

A relieved Hunter and Williams thanked the General Council for their time and left to catch their flights home.

22 May 2013
Scottish Exhibition and Conference Centre
Exhibition Way
Glasgow

Mark Rudge, the Secretary of State for Trade and Business had just finished delivering his keynote speech at CBI Scotland's spring conference. The applause from delegates was still echoing round the SECC when he made a beeline to speak to Michelle Rossi. The attractive blonde businesswoman had been appointed as a business champion for Scotland by the UK Government earlier that month.

Business and trade were one of the few areas of government policy that remained reserved and the responsibility of the UK Government.

Nevertheless, the CBI had invited Scotland's First Minister, Alex Forsyth, to speak at the conference and he had done so the previous day.

"Mark, many congratulations on an excellent speech" said Rossi. "As you can see, many of my fellow countrymen appreciate what you are doing to make Scotland a great place to do business."

"Thank you, Michelle" replied Rudge. "By the way, I'm delighted to see that the Scottish Business Development Fund is going so well. I would like to meet some of the people whose businesses have got going – it will get over the point that the Government is doing something to help Scotland."

The Scottish Business Development Fund had been introduced the previous year by the Department of Trade and Business to support business start-ups and expansion in Scotland. It was part of the Government's strategy to promote wealth creation in depressed parts of the United Kingdom. There were similar programmes for the North of England, Wales and Northern Ireland.

"I can certainly arrange that for you, Mark. Some of them are here today."

While on the way to meet some of the business people who had benefited from the Scottish Business Development Fund, Rossi ushered Rudge into one of the breakout rooms.

"Something on your mind, Michelle?" asked Rudge.

"Mark, did you notice the large number of new hotels being built here?"

"Not really, Michelle?"

"You know that Euro 2016 is taking place in three years' time?"

"I do. Don't know how for a minute either Scotland and Wales can afford it. Neither Government has got any money to spare and businesses have been cutting back on corporate donations since the crash in 2008."

"Mark, I've heard that the Scottish Government is using the EU Regional Development Fund to fund infrastructure works for Euro 2016."

Rudge stood open mouthed for a second. In his view, that was a blatant misuse of the Regional Development Fund.

"They're surely not allowed to do that, Michelle. Once again, we're paying the price for Tony Blair's folly in allowing Scotland and Wales to have toytown parliaments."

"I agree, Mark" replied Rossi. "But so much depends on the interpretation of the law these days. I'm sure that Forsyth has done his homework before using the Regional Development Fund – he's not daft. And much depends on whether anyone will challenge the legality of its use for Euro 2016, let alone win."

"Michelle, I am grateful to you for notifying me of this misuse of public money by the Scottish Government. More than some of my Ministerial colleagues or civil servants would do. I'm going to raise this with the Cabinet on my return."

Rudge in fact had no such intention. Relations with the devolved governments was Karen Rolfe's responsibility. She was a Liberal Democrat and unlikely to stand up to Forsyth. Neither was the Prime Minister, David Talbot. In Rudge's view, he was frightened of upsetting the Scots and risking them applying to leave the Union.

He knew just the person who would take the matter on.

25 May 2013
Rue Perronet
Neuilly-sur-Seine
Paris

"Darling, it's Mark Rudge. For you."

Cècile Picard passed the telephone to her husband.

"Mark, what a pleasure to hear from you again. Is it anything important?"

"It is, François" replied the United Kingdom's Secretary of State for Trade and Business. "Are you aware that the Scottish and Welsh Governments are using the EU Regional Development Fund to provide infrastructure for Euro 2016?"

François Picard was stunned into silence for a few seconds. This was news to him.

"I had no idea they were using the ERDF, Mark. Explains why they appear to be on course with the work for Euro 2016. I don't think the EU will be too pleased to see regeneration money being used for a sports tournament."

"Precisely, François. I had our legal advisers look it over this week. What the Scottish and Welsh Governments have done in our opinion is illegal. The ERDF is provided to stimulate economic activity and create jobs in economically-deprived areas. No one can argue that an international football tournament will achieve this."

"I totally agree, Mark" replied Picard. "By the way, what is your Government doing?"

"No point in bothering, François. Remember, we're a coalition and our partners are strong supporters of Scotland and Wales staging Euro 2016. Also, David is frightened of stirring up the nationalists in Scotland and Wales. Both lots are in Government."

Rudge then came to the main point of the conversation.

"François, what can you do? You must have contacts in Government and at the EU."

Picard remembered that an old friend of his from when they were students at the École National d'Administration, nearly forty years previously was now a Commissioner at the EU. If he escalated the matter, Scotland and Wales would be forced to repay the money used for Euro 2016. Moreover, the financial viability of the Scottish and Welsh project to host Euro 2016 would be shattered. There would be only one outcome, and that would be for France to step in and stage the tournament.

He checked his smartphone for the contact details for Gaston Ribôt.

CHAPTER 8

15 July 2013
European Commission
Rue de la Loi
Brussels

"Item 7 on the Agenda. EU Regional Development Fund. Commissioner Ribôt, I believe you asked for this to be included."

The President of the European Commission, Jean-Paul Timmermans, motioned for Gaston Ribôt to take the floor. Ribôt walked over to a lectern equipped with a microphone. Translators were on hand to translate his speech from French into the other EU languages.

Ribôt was now in his early sixties. He had once been a good-looking man but he had put on weight and what was left of his hair had now turned grey. A member of France's main centre-right party, the Mouvement pour la République and a former Minister under the governments of Jacques Chirac and Nicolas Sarkozy, he had been an EU Commissioner since the defeat of Sarkozy in the 2012 Presidential election.

"Mr President, Members of the Commission, thank you for letting me speak.

"The issue I want to draw to your notice is the use of the EU Regional Development Fund – or rather its misuse – by the devolved Governments in Scotland and Wales. You will be aware of this fund. It is paid out to Member states to stimulate economic activity and job creation in areas which have suffered economic and social deprivation. The fund should be used to encourage employers to locate their businesses in economically-deprived areas, to support start-ups of new businesses, to provide training to equip people with the skills required in the modern workplace and to improve infrastructure like road, rail and air connections so that the areas are connected to the main markets.

"During the fund's early days, most of the money went into parts of Europe where there had been little economic development and there had been high levels of emigration. Southern Italy and Ireland were two examples, and they were joined by Greece and Spain when they became full EU members. However, over the past twenty years, the fund has been used increasingly in parts of Europe which have suffered from deindustrialisation after heavy industries like coalmining, steelmaking, shipbuilding, chemicals and textiles declined from the 1980s. The United Kingdom is a significant recipient of grant from the Regional Development Fund because of the decline of heavy industries in Northern England, Scotland and Wales.

"The UK Government manages the fund for the programmes in the North of England. However, the programmes supported in Scotland and Wales are managed instead by the two countries' devolved Governments which you will recall were set up back in 1999."

This provoked a scowl from one of the Spanish Commissioners, Eleña Vazquez. She did not regard the British Government's decision to allow devolution in Scotland and Wales with any favour. Spain was facing noisy demands from the Basque provinces and Catalonia for greater autonomy and blamed the British for letting the genie of separatism out of the bottle.

Ribôt continued.

"It is not the UK Government with whom I have issue although I think Commissioner Vazquez may take issue about their decision to grant regional autonomy to Scotland and Wales. It is the devolved governments in Scotland and Wales with whom I take issue. Two years ago, Scotland and Wales were awarded the right to stage the European Football Championships to be held in the summer of 2016. Their Football Associations assured the Union of European Football Associations that they had the resources to provide all the facilities required to stage the Championships. It appears they got their sums wrong and to meet the shortfall, they have used the EU Regional Development Fund in a blatant breach of its terms and conditions."

"I'm afraid I must disagree with you, Commissioner Ribôt." Marcus Silverman, one of the United Kingdom's Commissioners and a former Minister in Tony Blair's government a decade earlier, was on his feet.

"You appear to have forgotten that, when the Scottish Football Association and the Football Association of Wales made their joint bid back in 2009, they clearly stated that one of the aims of hosting Euro 2016 was to promote business and stimulate regeneration in de-industrialised areas of which both countries sadly have a lot of. Although the bid's original plans did not envisage using resources from the Regional Development Fund, I would strongly argue that they were entitled to have done this because of the clearly stated aims to use Euro 2016 as a tool to attract economic activity. I therefore do not consider that the Scottish Government and Welsh Assembly Government have breached the terms and conditions of the Regional Development Fund."

Ribôt was dumbfounded at the brass neck of the British Commissioner.

"Commissioner Silverman, are you seriously expecting the Commission to believe that a prestige event like Euro 2016 meets the terms of a fund designed to tackle deprivation?"

Laughter echoed round the Commission chamber before the President, Jean-Paul Timmermans, called for order.

Timmermans, a Belgian, then spoke.

"Commissioner Ribôt, I am grateful for you bringing this matter to the Commission's notice. Our reputation has suffered in recent years for allowing financial profligacy to take place with the funds we provide. To restore our reputation, it is essential that this matter is investigated further."

"Commissioner Silverman, I am not unfamiliar with the bids for Euro 2016 and I fully acknowledge your point about Scotland and Wales using it to promote their countries' economies and to tackle the scourge of worklessness. But Commissioner Ribôt has made a valid point about Euro 2016 being a prestigious sporting tournament and one which is hardly in line with the aims of the Regional Development Fund."

"Members of the Commission, I propose that we seek counsel from our legal advisers before arriving at a final decision."

12 September 2013
European Court of Human Rights
Council of Europe
Strasbourg

"Mademoiselle Singleton, will you please take the stand."

Geri Singleton made her way to the stand to give her case on behalf of Councillor Ken Davies and fifty other plaintiffs who were pursuing a case against the British Government for compensation. They were farmers and cockle fishermen from the Welsh villages of Crofty and Penclawdd and their land had been subject to compulsory purchase so that a new airport for Swansea could be built. Consequently, their farms and businesses would be shut down.

The villagers had been offered compensation by the Department for Transport but it was considered inadequate. The Department had made several offers to settle out of court but a dogged Councillor Davies was unwilling to accept this compromise.

Singleton outlined her case.

"Your Honours, may I describe the case I have presented for you today.

"My clients are cattle and sheep farmers and cockle fishermen whose families have lived on the Gower Peninsula for centuries. They have carried on the way of life established by their forefathers and, even in hard times, they have not sought outside assistance. It is fair to describe them as the backbone of their local community.

"Three years ago, the Department for Transport in London published proposals to build an airport to serve the city of Swansea, along with a railway link and an access road. As you know, Swansea is Wales's second largest city with a population of over 270,000 but it is not served by an international airport. There has been pressure from business interests for some time to provide the city with an international airport and that campaign received a boost when Wales, along with Scotland, was awarded the right to stage the European Football Championships in 2016.

"The Department for Transport conducted a consultation on four sets of proposals and announced its decision in June 2011. Unfortunately, the site they selected was the one affecting my clients' farms and businesses. I accept that the Department offered my clients compensation for the loss of their farms and businesses but my clients considered that the amount offered was totally inadequate. I was unaware that the Department had tried to settle with my clients out of court until Councillor Davies notified me two months ago. Ten of the plaintiffs named on my original petition have had their names withdrawn because they agreed to settle out of court.

"I am making the case for compensation for my clients for the following reasons. Firstly, the Department of Transport failed to give due regard to alternative proposals to increase air capacity in advance of Euro 2016. There is strong evidence that an expansion of capacity at Cardiff International Airport would have been sufficient to cope with the additional capacity needs for Euro 2016. It is little more than forty miles away from Swansea and road and rail connections are excellent. Even if it had been necessary to provide an airport nearer to Swansea, a more satisfactory option would have been to have extend the runway and terminal at the existing airport at Fairwood Common. This option would have had far less impact on properties and businesses than the option chosen."

"Secondly, the compensation offered to my clients by the Department for Transport was derisory. Many of my clients have spent a lifetime building up their farms and businesses. Cockles from the Burry Inlet now have international renown and the cockle harvests have enabled many of my clients to run profitable businesses. Saltmarsh lamb from the north side of the Gower Peninsula is also internationally renowned and farmers got good prices for their meat. The level of compensation offered to them would have been appropriate for a struggling subsistence farm, not for the profitable businesses my clients ran."

"In arriving at its decision, the Department for Transport failed to carry out a business impact analysis of its proposals. I consider this to be a serious shortcoming on their part. I therefore lay the argument that the Department for Transport should offer my clients compensation equivalent to the real economic value of their farms and businesses."

Roland Mountford, the Crown Solicitor that the British Government had sent to defend its position, got to his feet.

"Ms Singleton, I would like to thank you for your testimony on behalf of the residents of Crofty and Penclawdd."

"In your testimony, you alleged that the Department for Transport did not give due regard to alternative proposals. Is that correct?"

"It is, Mr Mountford" replied Singleton.

"Ms Singleton, I think it is you who has overlooked some key facts. Firstly, the option for extending Cardiff Airport does not exist. The Union of European Football Associations made it clear from the start that each tournament venue had to have an airport nearby."

Singleton grimaced. She realised that Mountford might be right.

"Secondly, you say that an extension at Fairwood Common was an option. May I remind you that it is close to an Area of Outstanding Natural Beauty and a Site of Specific Scientific Interest. Expanding Fairwood Common would have encroached into these areas and would have breached European law."

"I was aware of that, Mr Mountford" replied Singleton. "May I remind you that the proposals to extend Fairwood Common specifically avoided these areas."

"All the same, Ms Singleton, you appear to be advocating the building of an airport on the Gower Peninsula. I put it to you that the real reason that you were in favour of extending Fairwood Common was that it was located close to a relatively wealthy area which you wanted to inconvenience for political reasons."

"That is complete rubbish, Mr Mountford" replied Singleton.

"If I may continue, Ms Singleton, the compensation offered by the Department for Transport to local residents was significantly higher than that offered to other people whose property has been subject to compulsory purchase. Indeed, no less than 450 local residents have accepted the terms of compensation offered and another 300 are considering joining them. I put it to you that the motivation for this case is not fair play. It is more about greed and the political ambitions of Councillor Davies and some of his colleagues."

"That is an outrageous slur on my clients" shouted Singleton.

"Objection upheld" said the Chief Justice of the Court, Jean-Marie Marchais. "Mr Mountford, please stick to the point and avoid making allegations about the character of the plaintiffs."

Mountford had the feeling that the Court was not going to be sympathetic towards the British Government's views.

2 October 2013
MEN Arena
Manchester

"The last three years have been difficult. There are still further battles to fight. But outside this hall, there are millions of hardworking people who have helped put the "great" in Great Britain. These are the people who take great pride in their work and in their families. These are the people who are fighting with us to help us finish the job we started. And together with us help build a land of opportunity and hope."

As David Talbot finished his speech, moved away from the lectern and embraced his wife, Jane, the audience at the Conservative Party Conference was up on its feet applauding. For Talbot, this was vindication of both his decision to stand for the Party leadership eight years earlier and of the policies his Government had adopted over the previous three years.

Talbot had been far from popular with all sections of the Conservative Party when he became its leader in 2005. As the first Party leader who had been educated at a public school since Alec Douglas-Home in the 1960s, he was seen by many as a dilettante, an out-of-touch posh boy and a lightweight. During the early years of his leadership, he adopted several policies that were quite left-wing and many of the Party faithful felt he was trying to copy the policies of the then Labour Government. But in 2008, Talbot at last had the opportunity to return to traditional Conservative policies after public trust in Labour collapsed following the economic slump.

This was however not enough to give the Conservatives a clear majority at the 2010 General Election and they were forced to enter a coalition with the Liberal Democrats. The early years were tough as the Government's austerity policies faced considerable opposition. Industrial action, protests and riots all tested the Government's resolve. But a successful Olympic Games the previous year proved a morale booster for the nation and there were signs of economic revival. Moreover, the Labour Party had failed to take advantage of the economic downturn and squeeze on people's living standards under the uninspiring leadership of Jeremy Greenfield.

Applause was still rippling through the MEN Arena ten minutes later when Talbot finally left the stage. All around, people were congratulating him.

"That was a marvellous speech, David" said Party Chairman George Turner. "I think you've got the next General Election in the bag."

Before Talbot could take his seat to listen to the closing speech from Turner, an aide rushed up to him.

"Sorry to disturb you Prime Minister, your PPS is on the phone. Says it's urgent."

Talbot was ushered into a side room to take the call. On the other end was Charlotte Drinkwater, his Principal Private Secretary.

"Prime Minister here. Hello Charlotte."

"Thank goodness I've found you, Prime Minister. Bad news."

"What bad news, Charlotte and where from?" asked Talbot.

"The European Court of Human Rights" replied Drinkwater. "About Swansea Airport. Remember the compensation claim by local villagers who have lost land and businesses. Geri Singleton was representing them."

Talbot groaned. Geri Singleton was a solicitor who specialised in human rights and miscarriage of justice cases and was a thorn in the side of the British Government.

Drinkwater continued.

"ECHR have just ruled in favour of the local residents' claim for compensation, Prime Minister."

"Oh my God" exclaimed Talbot. "Do you know how much we've been stung for, Charlotte?"

"Thirty million pounds."

22 October 2013
European Commission
Rue de la Loi
Brussels

Item 3 on the Agenda was the EU Regional Development Fund. Or more specifically the Commission's decision on the complaint that Commissioner Gaston Ribôt had raised about the use of the fund by the devolved Governments in Scotland and Wales to fund infrastructure works for Euro 2016.

The President of the European Commission, Jean-Paul Timmermans, signalled that he was about to speak.

"Members of the Commission, you will recall that, on 15 July, in response to a point of order raised by Commissioner Ribôt about the legality of the use of the EU Regional Development Fund by the Scottish Government and the Welsh Assembly Government to fund works associated with the staging of the European Football Championships in 2016, it was agreed to seek legal counsel. I have with me the report of Maître Jean-Jacques Rousseau, Chief Legal Counsel for the Commission and you also have copies.

"Maître Rousseau has given a very thorough legal analysis of the purpose of the Development Fund and of the activities it is intended to support. He has also addressed the points raised by you, Commissioner Ribôt, and of the counter-arguments that you, Commissioner Silverman, put forward. However, the central thrust of Maître Rousseau's findings was that the Development Fund is a grant specifically designed to stimulate economic activity in areas where there is none because of either the absence of such activity or where it has declined because of changed circumstances. It was not specific about what the Development Fund could be spent on and Maître Rousseau accepted that it could be used for anything ranging from road, rail and air facilities, incentives for employers to create new jobs, grants for business start-ups and retraining of workers with new skills.

"Maître Rousseau was however most specific about the use of the Development Fund to support works that were not wholly or mainly designed to regenerate areas of high unemployment and deprivation. He said that the use of the Development Fund for sporting or cultural events was not consistent with its purpose and was therefore an incorrect use of the Fund. He acknowledged that the organisers of Euro 2016 intend to use the tournament as an opportunity to stimulate trade and business and to generate employment and, through this, address the loss of employment that has affected both Scotland and Wales over the last thirty years. In that respect, he understands why the two devolved administrations have sought to use the Development Fund to support Euro 2016 and he has every sympathy with them. But Maître Rousseau was asked to give a legal opinion, not a political one. His view is that the devolved administrations in Scotland and Wales have made an unauthorised use of the Development Fund that failed to meet the purpose of the programme.

"Members of the Commission, the final decision is yours."

24 October 2013
10 Downing Street
London

Karen Rolfe had a feeling that bad news was on the way. Earlier that morning, she had received an urgent summons for a meeting with the Prime Minister.

The previous two days had been a nightmare. Following the European Commission's decision that the Scottish Government and Welsh Assembly Government had misused the EU Regional Development Fund and that the monies spent on Euro 2016 were to be clawed back, she had been on the receiving end of angry phone calls from the two First Ministers along with demands for press statements. Media coverage had been hostile, blaming her for not having her eye on the ball, and there was speculation that she was going to be dismissed from the Cabinet.

"Good morning, Karen" said David Talbot. "I think you will know about why I've asked you to come here."

"I suppose it's about Euro 2016, Prime Minister" replied Rolfe.

"That is right, Karen. Or, more specifically about the EU Regional Development Fund, which your Department manages. Or is supposed to manage."

"Prime Minister, you surely know that under the devolution arrangements, the devolved administrations are responsible for managing grants like the EU

Regional Development Fund. It is not our business to stick our nose in how they manage it."

"That's not the point, Karen" replied the Prime Minister. "It is your responsibility as Secretary of State for the Environment, Communities and Local Government to ensure that the three devolved administrations discharge their functions in compliance with British and international law. You hold quarterly intergovernmental meetings with the three First Ministers. You should have been aware of what was going on and counselled Forsyth and Morgan against taking such a reckless step. Because you didn't, we face losing Euro 2016 which will do wonders for our relations with the Scottish and Welsh Governments, as well as being a major embarrassment for the United Kingdom."

Talbot continued.

"I'm afraid that your Cabinet colleagues have lost confidence in you, Karen. As has your Party leader. I regret I've got no option but to ask for your resignation from the Cabinet."

25 October 2013
Russian Foreign Ministry
The Kremlin
Moscow

Russia's Foreign Minister, Alexei Primakov, had invited five men back to his office for a meeting. They were Sergei Lavotchkin and Oleg Grishin, Russia's delegates to FIFA and UEFA, Grigoriy Tereschkov, a colonel in the FSB, Russia's state security agency and Vladimir Tupitsin, an oligarch close to the President, Dimitriy Ivanov.

Earlier that day, all five men had been seated on the official podium in Red Square to view the military parade celebrating the anniversary of the October Revolution. Russia's latest tank, the T80, armoured personnel carriers and missile launchers had rumbled across Red Square while Su35 fighters and Tu160 bombers from the Air Force overflew St Basil's Cathedral. The Ivanov government was sending signal to the rest of the world that Russia meant business.

Primakov opened the meeting.

"Gentlemen, thank you for agreeing to this meeting at such short notice. Vodka?"

No one declined the offer.

Primakov then pulled out of his briefcase a bundle of newspapers. One was *Russia Today*, which was now virtually the mouthpiece of the government. The other was the *Daily Mail*, a British paper. Both papers were turned to articles about Euro 2016 and the prospect of Scotland and Wales having to give up the tournament for financial reasons after being banned from using the EU Regional Development Fund for building infrastructure for the tournament.

"You will have read about Euro 2016 and the fact that Scotland and Wales face losing the tournament because they have run out of money. For us, the EU decision is an opportunity."

"Any reason why?" asked Lavotchkin.

"Remember what I said at our meeting at the Metropol nearly three years ago" said Tereschkov. "Great Britain is a divided country and the policy of economic austerity has only made those divisions greater during this period. Both Scotland and Wales have suffered from the policy of austerity, both under the governments of Mrs Thatcher and Mr Talbot. A nationalist and separatist party now runs the devolved government in Scotland and their Welsh counterpart is the main coalition partner there. Foreign Minister, I believe you have met the two First Ministers."

"You are right, Grigoriy" replied Primakov. "I met Alex Forsyth, the First Minister for Scotland when I attended the opening ceremony of the Olympics last year. I have not met the First Minister for Wales but I did meet the Deputy First Minister, Rachel Norris, who is the leader of Plaid Cymru. Both Mr Forsyth and Ms Norris are passionate about promoting their countries on the world scene and feel that the British Government has held them back."

"Sorry to butt in, Foreign Minister" said Lavotchkin "but, if I remember correctly, the only reason we supported the Scotland and Wales bid for Euro 2016 was that it was a no hoper bid that would, and eventually did, undermine England's bid for the 2018 World Cup. Why the sudden enthusiasm for Scotland and Wales now?"

"Sergei, you must realise what the United Kingdom stands for" replied Primakov. "They are not only one of the West's leading powers and a potential adversary for us, both politically and militarily. They are also the United States' most reliable ally in the North Atlantic Treaty Organisation. But, as Grigoriy said earlier, their domestic divisions offer us with an opportunity. If Russia was to step in and offer to make up the financial shortfall for Euro 2016, we would have a foothold on their doorstep. It is possible that, in future years, Scotland and Wales might seek full independence from the United Kingdom. Just think of the benefit to Russia of having allies on the doorstep of one of the West's key economic and military powers."

CHAPTER 9

9 January 2014
Charlie Hebdo
Rue Nicolas-Appert
11th Arrondisment
Paris

Danielle Erbani was an angry woman. Until the previous month, she had been working as a secretary at the French Football Federation but, the week before Christmas, she was summarily told that she had been dismissed from her job. No specific reason was given but the Human Resources officer said that her recent work had not been up to the expected standards and that her attitude left something to be desired.

Erbani had reason to suspect the real cause of her dismissal. A month earlier, she had fallen out with Sylvie Bouchard, who was Personal Assistant to François Picard. She had little time for Bouchard who she considered to be nothing more than a blonde bimbo who had progressed her career through the numbers of the Federation hierarchy she had slept with. It was obvious that, after the row, she had words with Picard who had then engineered her dismissal.

Losing her job was a personal disaster for Erbani and capped a bad year which started with the death of her father in April and continued when she and her fiancé split up at the start of September. The secretarial post at the Football Federation was quite well paid and enabled her to afford a small apartment on the outskirts of Paris. She was now thirty-three years old and would have to compete with younger and prettier candidates to find work as a secretary. And the pay was unlikely to be as good.

A week earlier, Erbani had taken her revenge. Her swarthy, Mediterranean looks which she inherited from her Italian grandparents, enabled her to disguise herself as a North African. She donned a headscarf and managed to gain access to the Federation headquarters in the Boulevard de Grenelle by joining a team of Algerian and Moroccan women working as cleaners. During a period when the team was unsupervised, she went into Picard's office and broke into his computer and downloaded several documents that incriminated Picard in bribery and corruption.

There was no point in taking it to the police or local examining magistrate, or to the mainstream media. Picard was one of the establishment and the documents would be conveniently lost. *Charlie Hebdo*, an irreverent and very left-wing satirical magazine was a far more promising option.

Erbani was invited to take a seat in the office of Max Broussard, the magazine's Managing Editor.

"So, Ms Erbani, you say you have evidence of corruption within the French Football Federation. By the way, what's your first name?"

"Danielle."

"That's fine Danielle. And please call me Max" replied Broussard.

"Max, what I've got is more than evidence of internal corruption within the Football Federation. This goes a lot further. Both FIFA and UEFA are involved. And the hand of François Picard is involved in it all."

"Ah, François Picard. Pillar of the French Establishment. Former Secretary of the Football Federation, now aiming for the top job as President of FIFA. Now tell me Danielle, what has Monsieur Picard been up to?"

"Have you got a computer, Max?" asked Erbani.

Broussard indicated that he did. He took the USB stick from Erbani and plugged it in to his computer.

Erbani guided him to the first document on the USB stick. It was a letter dated 2 June 2009 from Picard to the Russian FIFA representative, Sergei Lavotchkin. It read:-

My Dear Sergei

I was most grateful for the opportunity to speak to you yesterday about Russia's bid to stage the World Cup in 2018. The French Football Federation is eternally grateful for the support that Russia gave to its successful bid to stage the World Cup in 1998 and I would like to wish you every success with your bid.

You are right to be concerned that England has submitted a rival bid for the World Cup. I am most sorry for not putting you in the picture about it earlier.

At first sight, it looks a very strong bid. More than seventy-five per cent of the venues are already in existence and road and rail links, which were a cause for concern before, have significantly improved over the past ten years. More importantly, England appears to have eradicated the menace of football hooliganism. However, the strength of their bid will almost certainly be undermined by the problems they are facing with preparations for the 2012 Olympics. As I said yesterday, the costs are now more than three times what was originally estimated. The United Kingdom does not have a good record to delivering major projects on time or within budget. The rebuilding of Wembley Stadium, which opened over four years later than planned, is but one example.

Another factor that will weigh heavily with some delegates is that the United Kingdom's Government defied international opinion by joining the USA in invading Iraq back in 2003 and is still unpopular with many countries because of that. You may find delegates from Middle Eastern and other Third World countries may, consequently, be more sympathetic to Russia's bid.

Finally, I can confirm that Scotland and Wales will be submitting a joint bid to stage the European Football Championships in 2016. Neither country has either the financial resources nor the infrastructure to stage a tournament of this size and it does not pose a realistic threat to the bid that France is preparing. However, there is increasing sympathy within UEFA for joint bids from small countries. If the bid from Scotland and Wales was by chance to succeed, there is no question of doubt that it would have an adverse impact upon England's bid for the 2018 World Cup. Once it became apparent that neither Scotland nor Wales would be able to meet UEFA's requirements to stage the tournament, it would cast doubt on England's ability to stage the 2018 World Cup. Most FIFA delegates are aware that Scotland and Wales are, like England, part of the same country and will judge the strength of England's bid on what happens in Scotland and Wales.

FIFA is due to make its decision about the 2018 World Cup in December 2011. This will be 18 months after UEFA's decision on Euro 2016. That is sufficient time for Scotland and Wales to undermine the credibility of England's bid.

Yours ever

François

"Good god, Danielle. It appears to be suggesting that Picard undermined France's bid."

"There's more to come, Max" said Erbani. "And I can assure you it gets much worse."

4 February 2014
Vannier et Roux
Rue Montalivet
8th Arrondisement
Paris

A furious François Picard was sitting in the office of Paul Vannier, one of Paris's most prestigious law advocates. On the table was a copy of the previous day's edition of *Charlie Hebdo*.

"These allegations are scurrilous, Paul. Suggesting that I supported a rival bid to our own for Euro 2016 and was paid by the Russians to do so. It's about time that bloody rag was closed for good. It's more than claiming damages, Paul. I want *Charlie Hebdo* prosecuted."

Vannier, a tall, elegantly-dressed man in his late fifties, drew out a copy of France's legal code.

"François, there is no doubt that there is a strong case for prosecuting *Charlie Hebdo*. Whoever provided them with the information must have stolen it from the offices of the Football Federation. If *Charlie Hebdo* did not organise this, they would appear to be culpable for receiving stolen goods. And they may have also breached France's privacy laws. However...................."

"What do you mean by 'however', Paul?" shouted an agitated Picard.

"François, I am afraid that the decision whether to prosecute lies with the Minister of Justice. You are a prominent member of Les Republicains I recall. Somehow, I do not see the Socialist administration lifting a finger to investigate allegations about a leading political rival. I fear that the Government will use *Charlie Hebdo's* allegations to try and smear Les Republicains to gain political benefit. That's how politics works."

"However, if you wish to proceed with a civil action for defamation, I am more than happy to assist you. I think you will have a very strong case."

Later that day
French Football Federation
Boulevard de Grenelle
Paris

François Picard had summoned the Federation's Chief Press Officer, Robert Cantillon, to his office. The telephone lines had been red hot since the *Charlie Hebdo* story had broken.

Cantillon had prepared a press statement to rebut the allegations of corruption. A former journalist on *Le Monde*, he thought that the lines prepared would satisfy Picard. He was to find out otherwise.

"Robert, what kind of crap is this?" raged Picard. "I told you before, I want a no holds barred rebuttal of any allegations of corruption."

"I thought I had done this, Monsieur Picard" replied Cantillon.

"Robert, do you realise that *Charlie Hebdo* has broken the law? Someone stole confidential documents from this office and passed them to *Charlie Hebdo*. At the very least, that constitutes receiving stolen goods."

"We have to be very careful, Monsieur Picard" said Cantillon. "If we allege that *Charlie Hebdo* has committed an offence and it is not proven, they could sue us."

"Horseshit" shouted Picard. "Who will believe a scurrilous rag against one of the country's leading institutions?"

"Very well, Monsieur Picard. I will redraft the statement to make it stronger and more forceful. When do you need it done?"

"Now!" said Picard.

After Cantillon left the office, Picard reached for his telephone. He rang the number of Maurice Lemaître, Head of the Police National.

"Maurice, François here. How are you doing? Haven't heard from you for a long time."

"Probably a lot better than you, François" replied Lemaître. "The allegations made by *Charlie Hebdo* are all over the papers."

"Maurice, do you realise that someone broke into the Federation's offices and stole confidential documents? That's how *Charlie Hebdo* got them. Surely, they are guilty of receiving stolen goods at the very least?"

"We have to tread very carefully with *Charlie Hebdo*, François. They've got friends in the Government. And the Government will want to make political capital from this because of your involvement with the Opposition."

"Maurice, *Charlie Hebdo* are no friends of the police. Remember some of the scurrilous allegations they've made in the past? Your guys must be itching for an opportunity to bust them. Well here it is."

"I've got to admit you've got a point, François" replied Lemaître.

"Don't worry about the Government, Maurice. The Socialists will lose the next election. When we are back in power, I'll ensure you are rewarded."

Barely a minute after Picard had finished his telephone conversation with the Head of the Police National, he received another call. It was Sergei Lavotchkin, Russia's representative on FIFA.

"François, what the hell is going on? Don't you realise that the corruption allegations will impact upon us staging the World Cup?"

"Relax, Sergei" replied Picard. "*Charlie Hebdo* is nothing more than a scurrilous, lowlife rag. The allegations will not be proven; moreover, they are likely to face prosecution."

"For what? Libel?"

"Burglary and theft at least, Sergei. Possibly espionage too. In less than a year's time, *Charlie Hebdo* will be history."

7 February 2014
Charlie Hebdo
Rue Nicolas-Appert
11th Arrondisment
Paris

No less than eight Renault Trafic vans of the Police Nationale pulled up outside *Charlie Hebdo's* offices, escorted by four Peugeot 407 squad cars. With Rue Nicolas-Appert sealed off at both ends, over sixty heavily-armed, black-clad police officers leapt out of the vans and burst into the offices of *Charlie Hebdo.*

Max Broussard was reviewing the drafts for the following week's edition of *Charlie Hebdo* with the editorial team when six armed policemen burst in to his office.

"Freeze" shouted the lead officer. "Everyone put their hands up and no funny business."

"Is this some kind of joke?" shouted Isabelle Martini, the Deputy Managing Editor.

"Silence!" roared a large, burly policeman."

The lead officer, Captain Gaston Rousseau, then explained the reason for the raid.

"Monsieur Broussard, we have reason to believe that *Charlie Hebdo* has illegally obtained commercially confidential documents belonging to the Football Federation of France which had previously been stolen from there. Under the law, we are entitled to search your premises, including any computers or mobile telephony for evidence. Your co-operation I this exercise is required. Failure to comply is a criminal offence. Sergeant Bonneval, search the ground and first floors. Sergeant Estève, search this floor and the second."

The two sergeants led their teams downstairs to search the rest of the offices for evidence that *Charlie Hebdo* had committed an offence or, worse, had organised the theft.

Broussard was outraged at what he saw as an infringement of the freedom of the press.

"Monsieur, you appear to have forgotten that France is a free and democratic country and that the freedom of expression is one of our most cherished rights. This morning, you have trampled over that right. You'll hear more about this."

Rousseau was not impressed with Broussard's arguments. He had carried out numerous raids on subversive and extremist organisations before and had heard the same excuses.

"Monsieur Broussard, I have a job to do" he replied curtly. "Allegations have been made that your magazine was complicit in the theft of confidential documents belonging to the country's Football Federation and has made damaging claims that harm the country's national and commercial interests. That is a serious matter which requires us to investigate. If I remember, your magazine has sailed close to the wind on several occasions in the past. You should not therefore be surprised that you have attracted our attention."

11 February 2014
Interior Ministry of France
Place Beauvau
Paris

Maurice Lemaître knew he was in line for an uncomfortable grilling as he entered the office of France's Minister of the Interior, Manuel Betancourt. It was no secret that Betancourt was highly critical of the police for their perceived reluctance to investigate corruption allegations against *les notables*, the highly placed businessmen, officials and politicians from the Union pour un Mouvement Populaire, France's main centre-right political party.

"Sit down, Maurice" said the Interior Minister curtly. "You will have a good idea why I've asked you to come here today."

"*Charlie Hebdo*?" asked the Director-General of the Police Nationale. "Yes."

Lemaître was an imposing looking man who towered over the dimunitive Interior Minister by more than a foot. But Betancourt, Spanish by birth, was highly articulate and had a razor-sharp brain, and many people were tipping him as a future President. He also had a fierce temper and both allies and adversaries knew better than to get the wrong side of him.

"Maurice, explain why you thought it necessary to stage a raid upon *Charlie Hebdo*."

"Minister, intelligence sources had told us that *Charlie Hebdo* had illegally obtained confidential documents from the Football Federation and that they even organised a break-in to obtain them. Several of those documents concerned discussions about France's stance on the bidding for the 2018 World Cup and, in the wrong hands, were potentially extremely damaging to the country's interests."

"Did that really require eight vans, four squad cars and sixty odd policemen, Maurice? *Charlie Hebdo* is hardly a terrorist organisation. All that was needed was for two officers to have interviewed the Editor and staff under caution and referred the issue to the Examining Magistrate. Instead, you have wasted god knows how much taxpayers' money and made France look like a banana republic internationally."

Lemaître was however not prepared to give way.

"Minister, I accept that *Charlie Hebdo* is not an organisation which promotes violence. But they are mischief-makers and, on this occasion, have damaged French interests."

Betancourt was by now struggling to hold his temper.

"Damage French interests? How? By exposing corruption at the Football Federation? I'll tell you what has damaged French interests, Maurice. Our national representative on FIFA undermining his own country's bid to stage the European Football Championships in return for a bribe. Why aren't the police investigating those allegations?

"Frankly, Maurice, I'm more than disappointed with the shocking performance of the police. Some of you have forgotten that the world has moved on since the days of Chirac and Sarkozy. From now on, I am taking control of the agenda. I decide what the police's priorities are and if you want to start staging major raids, you notify me first. While I'm Interior Minister, I want to see a police force that serves the people and does not suck up to the rich and powerful. If I don't see an improvement, Maurice, I'll be looking for someone else to head up the Police Nationale. Do I make myself clear?"

"Yes, Minister."

3 March 2014
10 Downing Street
London

David Talbot was somewhat perplexed by the request from the MI5 Director-General, Toby Birkett, for an urgent meeting. However, Talbot was aware that any business raised by the Security Services had to be dealt with promptly. Failure to act on what could be a life-threatening incident could spell the end of his political career.

"Good morning, Toby. I understand you have something for my attention."

"Indeed, I do, Prime Minister" replied Birkett. The MI5 Director-General was a short, wiry, athletic-looking man in his late forties and had served in the Diplomatic Corps and GCHQ previously.

"Prime Minister, the Scottish Government and Welsh Assembly Government have been in discussions with the Russian Government about getting financial support for Euro 2016. Here is the evidence."

Talbot went white in the face. The devolved administrations were effectively trading with a hostile state.

"Tell me it's all just a bad dream, Toby."

"I'm afraid not, Prime Minister. The photographs here clearly show First Minister Forsyth and Deputy First Minister Norris in Moscow meeting Russia's Foreign Minister, Alexei Primakov and the Chairman of Gazprom, Mikhail Voronin. I've also got intercepts of the conversations that went on. Do you want to listen?"

"I better do" replied Talbot.

Birkett plugged an MP3 stick into the portable player he had in his briefcase and pressed PLAY.

PRIMAKOV: "Alex, Rachel, good morning to both of you. I'm delighted that you have been able to come to see us. I understand you are having some difficulty with funding Euro 2016."

FORSYTH: "That's an understatement, Alexei. The Scottish Government and our Welsh counterparts were going to use the EU Regional Development Fund to build the infrastructure for Euro 2016 that UEFA had demanded. You know, improvements to air, road and rail transport and additional hotel capacity. Both our Governments took legal advice on using the Regional Development Fund and we were advised that it met the Fund's regeneration objectives. However, the French lodged an objection and the EU have upheld it. We're facing having to repay the Regional Development Fund monies we used for Euro 2016."

NORRIS: "Neither of our Governments has the resources either to pay back the monies demanded by the EU or to fund continued improvements to our infrastructure. We will have to give up the right to stage Euro 2016 at the very least."

PRIMAKOV: "Won't the British Government help out?"

FORSYTH: "Not a chance in hell. They consider Euro 2016 to be a vanity project – unlike the Olympics."

PRIMAKOV: "Is there any chance that the EU may change its mind?"

NORRIS: "We've lodged an appeal to the European Court of Justice. The hearing won't take place until the summer at the earliest."

PRIMAKOV: "Now for the reason I've invited you. With me today is Mikhail Voronin, Chairman of Gazprom. You may have heard of them. They are Russia's largest company in the field of natural gas extraction, transport and sales. Gazprom have been trying to enter the energy markets in the West but have faced continued obstruction from Western Governments. Mikhail, may I invite you to describe your offer to Alex and Rachel."

VORONIN: "As Foreign Minister Primakov has said, Gazprom are the largest company involved in the extraction, production, transport and sale of natural gas in Russia. We would like to extend our business into the West but have been denied opportunities for what I consider to be political reasons. However, I believe you may wish to consider inviting investment from Gazprom."

"The offer I would like to make is for Gazprom to become a sponsor for Euro 2016. We will put in sufficient resources to make good the money being clawed back by the European Union and enable you to continue to improve your countries' infrastructure. How much do you need?"

FORSYTH: "Two hundred million pounds."

VORONIN: "That is no problem, Mr Forsyth. A pleasure to be of assistance."

Talbot looked a little more relieved.

"So, Toby, it appears that it is Gazprom who are going to underwrite the costs of Euro 2016 rather than the Russian Government. They're a private company?"

"Prime Minister, may I warn you that Gazprom is as good as being part of the Russian Government. Anyone working for them effectively has the blessing of President Ivanov. If you allow the Scottish and Welsh Governments to accept sponsorship from Gazprom, that will be the first step towards Russia building client states on your doorstep. Political influence will follow economic influence. Our NATO allies will be concerned at such a move. And the USA will be particularly concerned about the potential for espionage, bearing in mind the location of the nuclear submarine bases at Faslane and Holy Loch and the drones testing site at Abersoch."

"It looks like I've got no choice but to act on this, Toby" said Talbot.

"That is right, Prime Minister."

10 March 2014
10 Downing Street
London

"Come this way, gentlemen."

Sarah Reeves, an Assistant Private Secretary on the Prime Minister's staff, led Alex Forsyth and Richard Morgan into the Prime Minister's office.

"Can I offer you tea or coffee?"

"Tea, no sugar" replied Forsyth.

"White coffee, no sugar" replied Morgan.

Less than half a minute later, David Talbot walked in.

"Good morning, gentlemen. Thank you for coming down here at such short notice."

"What is the reason for asking myself and First Minister Morgan to come here?" asked the Scottish First Minister.

"Gentlemen, I understand that the Scottish Government and Welsh Assembly Government has been holding discussions with Gazprom about obtaining sponsorship for the European Football Championships due to take place in two years' time."

"That is right, Prime Minister" replied Forsyth.

"First Minister Forsyth, do you realise what Gazprom represents? They are all but another arm of the Russian Government. Several of their employees are in the pay of the FSB. You and the Welsh Assembly Government will effectively be explicit in aiding hostile foreign interests."

Alex Forsyth's face visibly darkened.

"You, Prime Minister, appear to have forgotten the failure of your Government to support Euro 2016. We've had no support for infrastructure works, unlike the Olympics. And I haven't seen much support for our battle with the EU over the EU Regional Development Fund."

"I recognise you're in a difficult position, First Minister" replied Talbot. "But getting financial support from a company with close links to a potentially hostile country is hardly the way to go about."

"Then I expect the UK Government to make up the shortfall."

"That is completely out of the question, First Minister. You know that taxpayers in England would never stand for it."

"Then the Scottish and Welsh Governments will continue to negotiate with Gazprom."

"I've already made it clear that my Government is not prepared to tolerate such dealings with a potential adversary" said Talbot. "Persist and I will have to consider the future of devolved Governments and their powers."

"Try that, Prime Minister and we'll be pushing for independence a lot sooner than you think" snapped back Forsyth.

23 March 2014
Chequers
near Aylesbury
Buckinghamshire
England

David Talbot mainly used Chequers for meetings with foreign Heads of State or Government. It was a remote and secure location where he could speak candidly without the fear of sensitive matters being leaked to Cabinet colleagues or opposition MPs. But this weekend, he had invited three of his Cabinet for a cosy fireside chat.

Jeremy Tomlinson, Liberal Democrat MP for North Devon and Secretary of State for the Environment, Communities and Local Government since taking over from Karen Rolfe the previous October, was one of the attendees. Forty-five years old and of average height, he had red hair and a bushy beard. He had however impressed his Cabinet colleagues with his grasp of the portfolio since taking office.

Caroline Russell, the Foreign Secretary, was also present. A slim and still attractive blonde of fifty years old and Conservative MP for East Hampshire, she was the first female incumbent of the post.

Finally, Bob Anderson, the Attorney-General was the last of Talbot's guests. He was far from a typical Conservative, being a Mancunian and educated at a comprehensive school, from which he gained a place at Oxford University to read law. Stockily-built and greying, he still retained his northern accent.

"Caroline, Jeremy, Bob, thank you for giving up your weekend and coming here at such short notice. You're all probably wondering why I've asked you to come."

"EU?" asked Russell.

"Scotland?" asked Tomlinson.

"Both actually" replied Talbot. "You will remember that the Scottish Government and the Welsh Assembly Government are facing a financial clawback by the EU for breaching the terms and conditions of the EU Regional Development Fund."

"I can't forget it, Prime Minister" said Tomlinson. "First thing I had to deal with after taking office."

"Remind me what they did" asked Russell.

"Caroline, they used the ERDF to fund infrastructure improvements required for the staging of the European Football Championships being held in two years' time. They were stretching the description of 'regeneration' somewhat. Well, one of the French Commissioners got wind of it and raised an objection which the EU upheld. The Scots and the Welsh face having to repay £200 million, which is money they haven't got. Potentially, they will have to give up the right to stage Euro 2016."

"Can't see Forsyth being too happy with that" said Anderson.

"An understatement, Bob. I had a very difficult meeting with him and Richard Morgan just under two weeks ago. Apparently, they've been approached by Gazprom for sponsorship."

There were gasps across the room.

"How did you find out, Prime Minister?" asked Russell.

"Toby Birkett told me. That's why I called them in."

"You could have let me know, Prime Minister" shouted Tomlinson.

"Jeremy, I was going to. Unfortunately, you were in New York that weekend."

"How did the meeting go?" asked Anderson.

"Not well at all. Forsyth's refusing to back down over Gazprom."

"How about Morgan?" asked Russell.

"He had very little to say, Caroline. I don't think he wanted to get involved with this charade but was pushed by his deputy. Rachel Norris, the Plaid Cymru leader."

"What's happening next, Prime Minister?" asked Russell.

"The Scottish Government and Welsh Assembly Government have appealed to the European Court of Justice. The appeal's due to be heard in the summer. Which is why I've asked you here today."

"Prime Minister, we've got to support the Scots and Welsh on this" said Tomlinson. "They were rightfully awarded Euro 2016 and have made excellent efforts to deliver the tournament at minimal cost. We can't afford to piss off Forsyth any more. The Scottish Government's planning to apply for a referendum on independence later this year."

"Jeremy, I'm aware of this. I think Euro 2016 would be good for both Scotland and Wales. But they've got to abide by the laws of not only this country but the EU. And I can't accept them taking sponsorship from a potentially hostile country."

Talbot then asked the Foreign Secretary and Attorney-General for their opinion.

"Prime Minister, it is very significant that the issue was brought up by Gaston Ribôt. He's one of France's Commissioners and if Scotland and Wales are forced to give up Euro 2016, France are strong favourites to step in and replace them. Therefore, he's got a clear interest in stopping Scotland and Wales using the ERDF. Another thing about Ribôt. He's close friends with François Picard, FIFA's Secretary-General. You know there's been serious allegations of bribery and corruption against Picard."

"What are they, Caroline?" asked Tomlinson.

"That he took a bribe to arrange for Russia to get the 2018 World Cup. And not only that, Jeremy. That he bribed UEFA delegates to vote for the Scotland and Wales bid against France's own bid."

There was ten seconds of stunned silence.

"What would Picard gain through that?" asked Tomlinson.

"Undermining England's credentials to stage the World Cup. It seems to have worked." Talbot was referring to England's unsuccessful bid to stage the 2018 World Cup.

"Don't think the EU will be too pleased to see a stooge of Picard getting his way" said Anderson.

"Precisely, Bob" replied Talbot. "Which brings me to your part. Do you think the appeal by the Scots and the Welsh stands a chance from a legal perspective?"

"Yes, I do, Prime Minister" replied Anderson. "The bid from Scotland and Wales made it clear from the start that one of the objectives of staging Euro 2016 was to promote regeneration. The bid categorically stated that the tournament would be an opportunity to attract inward investment to Scotland and Wales, to promote exports and tourism and to encourage positive and healthy lifestyles. From my understanding of the EU Regional Development Fund, the work to improve air, rail and road infrastructure and increase hotel capacity would facilitate more than just a football tournament. It will be a long-term investment that will help make Scotland and Wales a good place to do business with."

"I think the appeal stands an excellent chance of succeeding."

"I assume that, if they are successful, they will no longer pursue the idea of sponsorship from Gazprom" said Tomlinson.

12 June 2014
European Court of Justice
Kirchberg
Luxembourg

The five judges who had considered the appeal of the Scottish Government and Welsh Assembly Government against the EU's decision to claw back monies paid from the EU Regional Development Fund walked back into the main courtroom. At the head of the procession was the President of the Chamber, Martin Trautmann, a German judge from Cologne.

Most cases heard by the European Court of Justice were heard in chambers of three to five judges who elected their own President. Trautmann was in the second year of a three-year term. A full sitting of the Court was very rare and reserved for business of exceptional importance.

Trautmann sat in the middle of the panel of five judges, drawn from Belgium, Greece, Poland and Spain and indicated he was ready to deliver the verdict of the chamber. Sitting in the court were Gregor Bannerman and Emyr Rees, Chief Legal Advisers for the two devolved Governments and Melanie Goldsmith, a barrister who was an expert in EU law and hired to fight their case in the European Court. A few feet away sat France's Commissioner, Gaston Ribôt, and further along were the EU's legal team headed by Enrique Santana.

"Ladies and gentlemen, the chamber of which I preside is ready to deliver its verdict in the appeal brought by the Scottish Government and Welsh Assembly Government against the decision of the European Union to reclaim payments of the EU Regional Development Fund for alleged breach of the terms and conditions of issue.

"The basis of the case brought by Herr Ribôt was that the Scottish Government and Welsh Assembly Government had used the Regional Development Fund for activities not covered under its terms and conditions. To recap, this was to support the building of airport facilities, improvements to rail and road transport and the provision of additional hotel space, to meet the requirements laid down by the Union of European Football Associations for hosting the European Football Championships in 2016.

"The purpose of the EU Regional Development Fund is to stimulate economic activity and job creation in areas which have suffered economic and social deprivation. The fund should be used to encourage employers to locate their businesses in economically-deprived areas, to support start-ups of new businesses, to provide training to equip people with the skills required in the modern workplace and to improve infrastructure like road, rail and air connections so that the areas are connected to the main markets. Both Scotland and Wales qualified for the Fund because their economy has suffered considerable contraction over the past thirty years as heavy industries such as coalmining, steel manufacture and heavy engineering such as shipbuilding have declined.

"The case that you, Herr Bannerman, Herr Rees and Fraulein Goldsmith, made in support of your appeal was a persuasive one. You emphasised most strongly that the award of the European Football Championships was an opportunity to attract inward business investment into Scotland and Wales, to promote exports from your country and to encourage tourism, and that the success of those Championships would help generate increased employment and economic activity. You also explained most eloquently that one of the main barriers to encouraging new investment is the under-developed infrastructure in Scotland and Wales and that improvements to airport facilities, roads and railways and the provision of additional hotel space was necessary to encourage businesses to invest and tourists to visit.

"Herr Santana, you also made a well-presented case to defend the decision of the European Union. At first sight, it does not appear that a sporting tournament fulfils the objectives of regeneration. As you have said, many people rightly see it as a prestige event and the opportunity to make money. That is clearly the case with the Olympic Games and the World Cup. However, what should be taken into consideration is that the original bid in 2009 by the Scottish Football Association and the Football Association of Wales made it clear that one of the principal objectives of the tournament would be to regenerate economies which had suffered contraction due to global economics in recent years and thereby increase job opportunities and reduce the level of deprivation in Scotland and Wales, something which the EU recognises exists."

"The Chamber accepts that the Scottish Government and Welsh Assembly Government could have handled the issue with a bit more tact and sensitivity rather than drive forward with an approach which could be described as cavalier. However, we all agreed that the purpose to which the Regional Development Fund was put was consistent with its purpose and aims. The appeal is therefore allowed."

CHAPTER 10

10 July 2014
Palais de Justice
Île de la Cité
Paris

"Monsieur Picard, try and answer the question, please."

Amèlie Bouchon, the Examining Magistrate for Paris, was becoming increasingly exasperated at what she regarded as deliberate stonewalling by François Picard.

"Mademoiselle, I have made myself perfectly clear. The allegations about me taking a bribe are ludicrous to say the least. But to say that I conspired to defeat a bid by my own country, one I have faithfully served for over thirty years, is beyond contempt.

"May I remind you that the allegations have been made by a scurrilous, pro-Communist rag that's been funded by criminals, drug dealers and France's enemies overseas and has had a past record of supporting terrorists. And I've got good reason to believe that the source of the information was a former employee who was sacked for her poor work and bad attitude. And *you* believe that?"

Bouchon was in her late thirties but had made a reputation for having a steely nerve. She was far from intimidated by the bluster of the man sitting opposite who was old enough to be her father.

"Monsieur Picard, we have documentary evidence of correspondence with Russia's representative on FIFA in which you specifically stated that a successful bid by Scotland and Wales for Euro 2016 would undermine England's bid for the 2018 World Cup. And that, if you ensured that the Scotland and Wales bid succeeded, you would be in line for a reward. Your involvement in high level corruption cannot be denied."

"How do you know that those documents are genuine, Mademoiselle Bouchon? That little slut who I sacked could have doctored the evidence. It is she that you should be investigating – for burglary and theft of private property and for making a false instrument."

"I'm starting to lose patience with you, Monsieur Picard" said a terse Bouchon. "May I point out that obstructing a criminal investigation is an offence. I will have no hesitation in adding it to the charge sheet."

11 July 2014
Headquarters of the Police Judiciare
Quai des Orfèvres
Paris

"Maurice, you've got to do something. That bitch Bouchon is trying to get me up before the courts."

François Picard and Maurice Lemaître had known each other for several years. Picard had served as Secretary of the French Football Federation between 1989 and 2007 before taking over as Secretary-General of FIFA. Lemaître had progressed from being a Commandant back in 1995 to becoming Director-General for the Police Nationale in 2009 due to enthusiastically carrying out the demands of his political masters.

"I would like to help, François" replied Lemaître. "But there's little I can do. Since the *Charlie Hebdo* raid, Betancourt has taken full control of policing. He's micro-managing every aspect of our work. I can't so much as fart without his permission now."

"Betancourt!" spat Picard. "That greasy little spic who came here with his parents on a donkey".

"My very thoughts about him, François. A foreigner. Unfortunately, he's very popular and many people think he will run for President in 2017."

Picard cursed under his breath. Lemaître continued.

"I know you're in a tight spot, François. But so am I. If I piss off Betancourt, I'll be out of a job. The police has been my life, François. If I'm forced out, I'm finished. Hope you understand."

"I do, Maurice. What has this once great country come to?"

6 August 2014
Le Café de Rèunion
Rue Victor Massé
9th Arrondisement
Paris

The Café de Rèunion was one of Paris's more seedy bars. Close to the red-light district of the Pigalle, it was a haunt of criminals, prostitutes and drug dealers. François Picard looked totally out of place.

Benoît Dominici emerged from the back of the bar. A small, stocky man in his late forties, he had once served in the Foreign Legion before returning to his native Paris. He had been responsible for several contract assassinations but had never been brought to justice. Some of his 'hits' had been at the request of the French Secret Service, the DGSE so they had ensured no action was ever taken against him.

He shook Picard's hand but not with much enthusiasm.

"So, Monsieur Picard, you want to use my services."

"That is right, Monsieur Dominici."

"Okay, tell me the details."

"Firstly, *Charlie Hebdo*. Then I.................."

Dominici cut off Picard.

"*Charlie Hebdo*? Are you having a laugh?

Picard was stunned at Dominici's directness.

"Yes, Monsieur Dominici. *Charlie Hebdo*. You know, that muckraking commie rag."

"Monsieur Picard. Forget it. I'm not interested."

"Why?"

"Everyone in France knows what you've been up to, Monsieur Picard. Taking backhanders from the Russians to get them the World Cup and shafting dear old France in the bargain. Charlie Hebdo's rather popular at present. If I took that job, I'd be spending the rest of my life on the Île de Ré."

Dominici was referring to the feared maximum-security prison off France's west coast which was used to house France's most dangerous criminals.

"Monsieur Dominici, I am ready to offer five hundred thousand Euros to you if you take this job on. And I'll ensure there are no comebacks."

"You're wasting your time, Monsieur. Goodbye."

28 October 2014
French Football Federation
Boulevard de Grenelle
Paris

"François, come and have a read of this."

Laurent Michalak, the Secretary to the French Football Federation, was on the other end of the line of Picard's internal phone which was reserved for members of the Federation's governing board.

When Picard walked into Michalak's office, he was appalled to see Michalak reading a copy of *Charlie Hebdo*.

"Laurent, I hope this is not some kind of practical joke. I've had a bellyful of Charlie bloody Hebdo as you know."

"It's not, François. Looks like Charlie Hebdo has gone and well and truly shot themselves in the foot this time. Have a look."

Picard picked up the copy of *Charlie Hebdo*. Michalak was right. The front page contained a series of highly offensive caricatures of the Prophet Mohammed. It was more than a case of giving offence to a faith. Many Muslims considered that any slight against the Prophet was punishable by death and there had already been several instances in the previous quarter century where people had paid the ultimate penalty for offending Islam. Furthermore, France had six million Muslims resident in the country and had already been on the receiving end of attacks by terrorists claiming to be acting in the name of Islam.

"*Charlie Hebdo* must have a death wish, Laurent" said Picard.

Over the next half hour, Picard took stock of the situation and saw an opportunity. His solicitors had managed to obtain an adjournment to the judicial proceedings against him over the claims that he had taken bribes to ensure Russia won the right to stage the 2018 World Cup. He next had to report back to the Examining Magistrate at the end of November.

He then thought about the impact of a terrorist attack on the offices of *Charlie Hebdo*. It would be a win-win situation for him. There would be no journalists form *Charlie Hebdo* to testify against him in court. But more importantly the political landscape would change. An assault by Muslim terrorists on a newspaper would be seen across France as an assault upon French values. There would be demands for a crackdown on Muslim radicals and the police and judiciary would put the issue of football corruption on the back burner. Hopefully for ever. And the credibility of the Socialist government, which had been recovering over the previous six months, would be undermined as frightened voters turned to the parties of the Right in the belief they would be more robust in defending French citizens from terrorist acts.

He phoned the Café de Rèunion and asked to see Benoît Dominici.

That evening
Le Café de Rèunion
Rue Victor Massé
9th Arrondisement
Paris

"Monsieur Picard, didn't I make myself clear last time? I'm not interested in being your personal executioner. Why don't you go and shoot *Charlie Hebdo* yourself?"

"Have a look at this, Monsieur Dominici." Picard slammed down a copy of *Charlie Hebdo* on the table. "Now are you interested?"

"I hardly need to bother" replied Dominici. "It looks like some ragheads will top them first."

"I'm prepared to increase my price. Seven hundred and fifty thousand Euros."

"No dice."

"A million Euros, Monsieur Dominici."

"That's better. But if I do it, I'll stand out like a sore thumb. I hardly look like an Arab."

"What I want, Monsieur Dominici, is for you and any accomplices to disguise yourselves as Muslims. A few shouts of *'Allahu Akbar'* as you carry out the hit and no one's the wiser. And if you claim the killings were by a fictitious Islamic group in revenge for insulting the Prophet, most people will believe you. The police and DGSE will be hunting down every known Muslim radical in France, not you."

"Let me think about it for a few minutes."

Ten minutes later, Dominici had made up his mind.

"Okay, Monsieur Picard, I'll do it. Just make sure I'm safe."

"I'll guarantee that" replied Picard.

3 November 2014
Charlie Hebdo
Rue Nicolas-Appert
11ᵗʰ Arrondisment
Paris

No one reacted with any surprise when a white Citroen Berlingo van pulled up outside the offices of *Charlie Hebdo* in Rue Nicolas-Appert. Deliveries to shops and offices in the centre of Paris were common.

Six men dressed in black slipped out of the back of the van. Led by Benoît Dominici, they calmly walked into the reception area of *Charlie Hebdo*. All were carrying concealed AK-47 assault rifles.

"Good morning, gentlemen, can I help you in any way?" Monique Lessieur, the attractive receptionist, asked Dominici and his men the nature of their business.

"We've come to see *Charlie Hebdo*, mademoiselle" replied Dominici. Before Lessieur could continue her enquiries, Dominici nodded to his secondman, Robert Belascain. Belascain pulled out his AK-47 and opened fire. She stood no chance.

The assailants then swarmed upstairs and burst into the offices of *Charlie Hebdo*.

Max Broussard had just finished a meeting with his editorial team when they were confronted by Dominici's team of assassins. Before anyone could take evasive action, a volley of shots rang out. Three minutes later, there was no member of the *Charlie Hebdo* staff left alive.

Later that day
BBC News

"This is Guy Newberry with the latest national and international news on BBC.

"France is once again coping with the impact of the latest terrorist atrocity to hit the country. Earlier today, terrorists from a little-known organisation called Jihade Islamique de France carried out an armed assault upon the offices of the satirical magazine, Charlie Hebdo, in revenge for what they stated was an insult to their religion. Latest reports suggest that fourteen members of staff were shot dead, including the Editor and Deputy Editor.

"The attack appears to have been provoked by a series of controversial cartoons that the magazine published a week ago which mocked the Islamic faith. This is the tenth occasion in

the past twenty years when journalists and publishers have been targeted by Islamic radicals for perceived insults to their faith.

"Already, there has been a great outpouring of public sympathy for Charlie Hebdo with members of the public laying flowers outside their offices in Paris. It has also reopened the debate about the integration of Muslims into French society and their acceptance of Western values.

"These latest attacks will be a blow to the already beleaguered government of François Mignolet as opposition politicians claim that they are incapable of protecting their citizens. Already, the interior spokesman for the main centre-right party, Les Republicains, has criticised the Government for failing to keep the country safe while the Deputy Leader of the far-right Front Nationale has called for the introduction of internment for Muslims, the summary deportation of extremists and the reintroduction of the death penalty for terrorists."

CHAPTER 11

26 January 2015
Federal Bureau of Investigation
J Edgar Hoover Building
Pennsylvania Avenue
Washington DC

"Come in, Mike. Take a seat."

Special Agent Mike Dempsey had wondered why his Section Head, Special Agent-in-Charge Joe Fiorentino, had asked him to report for a meeting. At twenty-seven, he was one of the FBI's younger agents and had made an impressive start to his career. The son of a Boston police officer, he had been the first member of his family to obtain a university education and had applied to join the FBI after graduating.

"Hope I haven't done anything wrong, Joe" said Dempsey.

"Far from it, Mike. Now for the reason I've asked to see you. You know we've been investigating FIFA, the world soccer body, for corruption?"

"I do. I thought that was nearly finished."

"Unfortunately, it's not, Mike. The guys in the field have already uncovered enough evidence to indict their President and half of the governing council of both FIFA and CONCACAF – that's the Central American soccer federation – for bribery and corruption involving the award of Copa America for next year. But we're still only halfway there regarding our investigation into the award of the 2018 World Cup."

"Joe, I've got to apologise for by ignorance about soccer. Not my game. Can you explain what happened?"

"Sure, Mike" replied Fiorentino. "The 2018 World Cup was awarded to Russia after two ballots. There were rival bids from England, Belgium and the Netherlands and Spain and Portugal. Everyone thought England would provide the strongest opposition but they were eliminated at the first ballot. There have been allegations that the Russians had bribed several delegates, not just to vote in their favour but, more importantly, to vote tactically to eliminate England's bid."

"We are currently investigating the role that three men had to play. The first is Joao da Costa, FIFA's president. Brazilian. The second is Orville McKenzie. Jamaican and a former President of CONCACAF. The third is François Picard. French. Currently Secretary-General of FIFA. A former Chairman of the French Football Federation and a former Minister in the government of Jacques Chirac. From what I've head, very close to the Russians."

"What about Russia's delegate to FIFA, Joe? Aren't we investigating him?"

"We are, Mike. Sergei Lavotchkin. Unfortunately, he's rather close to the President so, even if we indict him, there's virtually no chance he will be extradited.

"Which now brings us to the reason why I've asked you to come here, Mike. We want you to take forward the investigation of Picard. Special Agents Ansell and Robertson have already done a lot of work and have proved that Picard was working closely with Lavotchkin. Unfortunately, we've had to detach them for other duties as they are needed on the investigations of da Costa, McKenzie and the other Central and South American delegates. In addition, Picard's had his fingers in a few more pies than originally thought. I think you're the right man for this job, Mike. Are you ready to take it on?"

"Count me in, Joe" replied Dempsey.

6 February 2015
Federal Bureau of Investigation
J Edgar Hoover Building
Pennsylvania Avenue
Washington DC

Special Agent Mike Dempsey had spent the previous two weeks reading into the intelligence gathered by Jennifer Ansell and Chris Robertson on François Picard. Wiretaps revealed the details of telephone calls between Picard and Sergei Lavotchkin between 2006 and 2011.

Already, there was enough evidence to indict Picard for taking bribes as it was clear that Russian oligarchs had offered Picard £30 million to fix the award of the World Cup in Russia's favour. But there were several unanswered questions. The first was how an apparently impressive World Cup bid by England failed so miserably. The second was whether Picard's malfeasance went beyond FIFA.

He called into the office of Deborah Richardson, an intelligence analyst.

"Hey Mike, how you're doing?" asked Richardson. An attractive redhead, she was a year younger than Dempsey.

"Bogged down with this Picard case, Debbie. It's a miracle that Jen and Chris got as far as they did. Half of the possible evidence is either encrypted or has been wiped."

"Why?"

"Picard used to be a Government Minister. He's probably got close links with DGSE and got them to cover his tracks. Don't suppose you've got anything of interest?"

"Actually, I do, Mike" replied Richardson. "A satirical magazine published allegations a year ago that Picard deliberately sabotaged his own country's bid to stage the European Football Championships due to take place next year to undermine England's bid for the 2018 World Cup."

"Jesus Christ, Debbie, are you serious? Tell me more."

"There were three bids, Mike. France, Scotland and Wales and Greece and Turkey. Everyone thought that France's bid would win by a mile but, against all expectations, Scotland and Wales won. They soon got into trouble when carrying out the infrastructure works demanded by the Union of European Football Associations. A strike held up the building of a new stadium while environmental protestors delayed the construction of an airport. When FIFA came to decide on the 2018 World Cup, preparations for the 2016 European Championships were in a mess. Consequently, many delegates doubted whether England would be capable of staging the World Cup."

"Have you found any evidence of bribery relating to the 2016 European bid, Debbie?" asked Dempsey.

"Not yet. But further allegations have been made that delegates were bribed to vote for the Scottish and Welsh bid and that Picard used money provided by the Russians to achieve this."

"By the way, what was the name of the magazine?"

"*Charlie Hebdo*" replied Richardson.

"Hey, Debbie, wasn't that the one which got whacked by Islamic extremists three months ago?"

"I think you're right, Mike."

13 April 2015
United States Embassy
Avenue Gabriel
Paris

"Come in, Mike." Bob Lavigne, the FBI Station Chief in Paris, summoned Mike Dempsey into his office.

Special Agent Dempsey had spent the previous two months researching into the bidding rounds of both the 2016 European Football Championships and the 2018 World Cup and the role that François Picard had played in securing the awards of the right to hold both tournaments. Having exhausted the services of the intelligence analysts in the J Edgar Hoover Building, he had finally secured the permission of his immediate boss, Joe Fiorentino and Deputy Assistant Director Katherine Bruckner, to travel to the United Kingdom and France to make further enquiries. The previous week, he had been in Glasgow and Cardiff meeting Gordon Hunter and Alun Williams, the General Secretaries of the Scottish and Welsh football federations. Both Hunter and Williams knew nothing about the machinations that had resulted in Scotland and Wales being awarded Euro 2016 and were genuinely shocked to learn that corruption had been involved.

Lavigne had been selected for the Paris job because of his French ancestry. His great-great grandfather had emigrated from the south-west of France to California in the early years of the twentieth century. This had proved helpful in establishing good working relationships with the Police Nationale which was essential in enabling the FBI to pursue extra-territorial investigations.

Dempsey shook Lavigne's hand and accepted the offer of a coffee.

"I understand you are working on the investigation into corruption at FIFA, Mike."

"That's right, Bob. For the last two months."

"What's your reason for coming to Paris?"

"The investigation into corruption at FIFA goes wider than FIFA itself, Bob" replied Dempsey. "I've found evidence to suggest that the European Soccer Federation, UEFA, is also involved."

"How come?"

"About eighteen months before FIFA awarded the World Cup for 2018, UEFA made its award for the European Football Championships taking place next year. France put in a bid and were by far the strongest of the three bids. However, UEFA awarded Euro 2016 to a joint bid from Scotland and Wales."

"Doesn't the United Kingdom have a single team?"

"Apparently not. The four countries all have separate associations and field separate teams. No one's bothered to challenge them over it."

"There was a lot of enthusiasm in the Scotland and Wales bid but not much thought about how they would deliver the tournament. Within the first year, they got into terrible difficulties with providing the infrastructure required by UEFA because of a building workers' strike and environmental protests over a new airport. By the time FIFA decided on the 2018 World Cup, it looked like Scotland and Wales were in danger of having to give up their bid. The Russians had little trouble in persuading delegates that England's bid for the World Cup would encounter the same problems."

"Anything more, Mike?" asked Lavigne.

"Plenty more. A satirical magazine over here published claims that François Picard, FIFA's Secretary-General, took a £30 million sterling bribe from the Russians to secure the World Cup. He's not the only FIFA delegate being investigated – we're currently examining the role of Joao da Costa, the FIFA President and several of the Central and South American and Caribbean delegates. However, I'm working on Picard."

"It's also been claimed that Picard bribed delegates on UEFA to vote for the bid from Scotland and Wales for Euro 2016 using money supplied by the Russians."

"Mike, are you being serious?" shouted an incredulous Lavigne. "Picard's his country's representative on FIFA and you're telling me that he arranged for his own country's bid to stage a major tournament to be canned?"

"I know it seems unreal, Bob, but that's what my investigation has uncovered. Which brings me to my reason for coming to France."

"Okay, Mike. Let's have it."

"I want to interview three people, Bob. Firstly, Gerard Basquet. He was the former French delegate to UEFA until he was forced to resign after France failed to win Euro 2016. He's an ex-soccer international and lives up near Calais. He might be able to give some insight to who was working with Picard. Secondly, Paul Jauzion, the Managing Editor of *Charlie Hebdo*. They are the magazine which published the allegations about Picard. And finally, Danielle Erbani, the whistleblower who exposed the claims about Picard's involvement."

"There should be no difficulty in interviewing Basquet" replied Lavigne. "He's been quite vocal in his criticism of Picard. You will need an officer from the Police Nationale to accompany you, Mike. Remember, you are in a foreign country. However, you stand no chance of interviewing either Jauzion or Erbani. Both are deeply traumatised following the terrorist attack on *Charlie Hebdo* last November. Jauzion lost several colleagues who were life-long friends in that attack. To this day, he's under police protection. And Danielle Erbani had a mental breakdown following the attack. Sorry."

Dempsey swore under his breath but he knew Lavigne was right. Unfortunately, it meant that his investigation would be incomplete and the risk was that Department of Justice would be unable to launch a prosecution against Picard.

"Bob, I realise that things are difficult for Jauzion and Erbani. But can you keep your lines of communication open with the Police Nationale. I suspect their dislike of Picard may eventually get the better of them and lead them to talk. When and if they're ready, I would like to come back."

"One more thing, Bob. Any chance you can get the CIA to run a check on the following organisation? Jihade Islamique de France."

"Weren't they the lot responsible for the *Charlie Hebdo* murders?"

"Yes. But no one's heard of them either before or since."

16 April 2015
Gare de Calais Ville
Boulevard Jacquard
Calais
France

The *Train Grande Vitesse* pulled into Calais's main station one hour and forty-five minutes after leaving Gare du Nord in Paris. Special Agent Mike Dempsey was in a good mood, having enjoyed an on-board breakfast of croissants, an excellent baguette and a black coffee.

As Dempsey walked through the barriers into the station concourse, he noticed a heavily--built, balding man wearing a dark blue windbreak and with a sign marked "Monsieur Dempsey". It was Commandant Robert Vacherin of the Police Nationale, who was detailed to accompany him to the interview with Gerard Basquet.

"Monsieur Dempsey, good morning." The big French policeman shook Dempsey's hand and motioned him towards the car park where his car, a Citroen C5, was parked.

"So, you have come to interview Gerard Basquet. For what reason?"

"Commandant, the FBI is investigating claims that certain international soccer federations have been involved in corruption. That is an offence under US law, no matter where it takes place. I understand that Mr Basquet was France's representative on the Union of European Football Associations when they awarded the right to stage next year's European Championships. He may have information that could help our investigation."

"Special Agent Dempsey, I should explain that Gerard Basquet is a highly respected man in these parts. He represented his country on fifty occasions."

"I'm not denying what Mr Basquet has done in the past, Commandant. But I need to interview him to find out why an apparent no-hoper bid was awarded Euro 2016. This may help me find out the connection with the award of the 2018 World Cup. As I've said, all I'm after is information. Mr Basquet should have nothing to worry about."

An hour later
Rue Motte du Moulin
Campagne-lès-Wardrecques
St Omer
France

"Monsieur Basquet?"

A short, stocky man in his mid-fifties opened the door of his substantial villa on the outskirts of St Omer. Gerard Basquet had put on some weight and his blond hair was thinning fast but he was still recognisable as the energetic holding midfielder of the great French football team of the early 1980s.

"Monsieur Dempsey, good morning. Who is the gentleman with you?"

"May I introduce myself" said Vacherin. "I am Commandant Robert Vacherin of the Police Nationale. I have to accompany Mr Dempsey while he interviews you."

"Please come through and make yourselves comfortable."

Dempsey and Vacherin sat down on the large sofa in the lounge as Basquet joined them. A minute later, Basquet's wife, Helène, brought through a pot of coffee.

Dempsey then explained the purpose of his visit.

"Monsieur Basquet, firstly, I would like to explain why I am here." He pulled out his FBI warrant card and showed it to Basquet.

"I am a Special Agent in the Federal Bureau of Investigation in the United States of America and I am investigating allegations of corruption in several of the international soccer federations, including the Fédération Internationale de Football and its decision to award the 2018 World Cup to Russia. There is evidence to suggest that some delegates received financial inducements to support Russia's bid. Under US law, bribery and corruption are felonies, no matter where they took place."

"Monsieur Dempsey, I had no involvement with FIFA" protested Basquet. "I was France's representative on the European Football governing body, UEFA and a Vice-President on their Executive Council."

"I am aware of that, Monsieur Basquet" replied the US Special Agent. "I am trying to establish whether there was a link between the award of the European Soccer Championships, due to take place next year, and the World Cup. Can you explain what happened with the bids for the European Soccer Championships."

"Sure, Monsieur Dempsey. Three bids were submitted, one from France and two joint bids, one from Scotland and Wales and one from Greece and Turkey. The French bid was much stronger than the other two. We still had the stadiums from the 1998 World Cup plus excellent air, rail and road links and plenty of hotel rooms available. We should have won easily."

"What happened?"

"In the first round of voting, France and the joint Scotland andWales bid dead-heated. I thought it was nothing more than a sympathy vote for small countries. It meant going to a second round. I thought that common sense would prevail. I was wrong. To my horror, the bid from Scotland and Wales beat ours."

"I can understand you must have been disappointed, Monsieur Basquet" said Dempsey.

"Disappointed? I was furious. Two countries which had a smaller population combined than Paris, with no common land boundary and only four stadiums which met UEFA criteria had beaten us. What's worse, I got the blame for losing the bid and I had to resign as France's representative on UEFA."

"Did the Scotland and Wales bid have any particular merits that the French bid lacked?"

"None at all" replied Basquet. "Neither country has a strong playing record. They've had to build six new stadiums from scratch. There are just four international airports in Scotland and one in Wales. The roads and railways are like something out of the Ark and there's a serious shortage of hotel rooms. I heard they were in trouble barely a year after being awarded Euro 2016."

About the time the 2018 World Cup was awarded to Russia, thought Dempsey.

"Why do you think the bid from Scotland and Wales was successful, Monsieur Basquet?"

"Several delegates were bribed, Monsieur Dempsey."

"Have you got any evidence to substantiate this?"

"Let me tell you this, Monsieur Dempsey. Five months after UEFA's decision, I was in Geneva on a business trip. Three of UEFA's delegates were staying in the same hotel. They turned up in flash new cars. Franz-Josef Sonnenberg, the President, had a Bugatti Veyron. That's the most expensive car in the world. They were escorting women who were clearly not their wives and they spent a fortune in the casino. You don't make that money by serving on a football federation alone. They had received a kickback from someone."

"Any ideas who?"

"Only one possibility. The Russians. They had a motive – to get the World Cup at any cost."

"Was anyone else involved, Monsieur Basquet?" asked Dempsey.

"Yes, there was. François Picard, our FIFA representative. He's currently Secretary-General."

"Tell me more."

"Picard's always been chummy with the Russians. There's some history behind it. You know France staged the 1998 World Cup. What helped us get it was the support of Russia and the Confederation of Independent States – remember, after the Soviet Union collapsed. Well, the Russians wanted France to return the favour with their bid for the 2018 World Cup. They were faced with a very strong bid from England. From what I heard, Picard arranged for UEFA Executive Committee to be bribed to support the Scotland and Wales bid against our own. He knew they would have great difficulty in staging Euro 2016 and that would undermine the credibility of England's World Cup bid. Which it did. It also meant that the Russians could spend less in bribing FIFA delegates."

"Are you seriously telling me that France's FIFA delegate bribed UEFA to back a bid from rival countries over his own?"

"I am, Monsieur Dempsey. I remember having lunch with Picard six years ago when we discussed the World Cup and Euro 2016 bids. I always remember what Picard said that day when I mentioned about the bid from Scotland and Wales – *if Scotland and Wales got Euro 2016, it will all go tits up. Which won't do the England bid for the World Cup any favours.* Furthermore, *Charlie Hebdo* made the same allegations last year."

"Sounds like you don't like Monsieur Picard."

"Don't like him? That's an understatement. He's a privileged posh boy who went to the ENA and has had an easy ride to the top. He always resented me. I'm a docker's son who's pulled himself up by his bootstraps. What Picard can't stand is that I was a national sporting hero. Played fifty times for France and captained them seventeen times. Have a look at this photo."

Basquet took down from a bookcase a photograph of the French team that won the European championships in 1984. Seated third from right amongst a team that was mainly dark haired and olive skinned was a short, blond-haired man. It was a much younger Gerard Basquet. Hailing from Calais, he was the odd man out in a side dominated by players from the south of France. But his team mates recognised the value of the industry that the little man from the north brought to the national side.

"Have you got what you need, Special Agent Dempsey?" asked Vacherin.

"I have. Monsieur Basquet, many thanks for giving us your time."

"A pleasure, Monsieur Dempsey" replied the former French football international.

17 April 2015
United States Embassy
Avenue Gabriel
Paris

Mike Dempsey was ready to depart for Charles de Gaulle Airport to catch a flight back to Washington DC when Bob Lavigne called him in.

"Mike, got some news about Jihade Islamique de France. Remember you asked for a CIA check?"

"Do they exist, Bob?"

"No. They never have and probably never will."

"So, they were an entirely fictitious organisation."

"Yup. By all accounts, one of our informants told us they were nothing more than a bunch of common criminals who had been paid to do a hit."

Dempsey had in mind who could be responsible.

"Bob, one last favour. Can you keep plugging away at Police Nationale to get Jauzion and Erbani to talk. I think they can help me complete this investigation."

CHAPTER 12

8 May 2015
BBC News

"This is Adam Smith with the latest news from the BBC.

"The Conservative Party have been confirmed as winners of the General Election. With the results in five seats still to be declared, they have an overall majority of ten. Party leader David Talbot will be on the way to Buckingham Palace to meet the Queen later today and be sworn in for a second term as Prime Minister.

"The Election was a disaster for the Labour Party. Despite polls which had Labour level with the Conservatives right up to polling day, they only managed to win 225 seats and their share of the vote was the worst since 1983. Although they managed to win back six seats off the Conservatives, mainly in London, they lost eight more to the Conservatives elsewhere in the country and they suffered humiliation at the hands of the Scottish National Party and Plaid Cymru in their heartlands of Scotland and Wales. There is now speculation that the Labour leader, Jeremy Greenfield, will resign.

"The Liberal Democrats also had a night to forget, losing fifty of their fifty-seven seats. The former Deputy Prime Minister Peter Russell managed to survive in his Sheffield constituency but they are now left with just seven seats, their worst result for almost fifty years.

"The nationalist parties in Scotland and Wales had memorable nights, mainly at the expense of Labour. The Scottish National Party won fifty of the fifty-nine seats in Scotland and party leader Amy MacDougall has claimed the results are a vindication of the party's calls for a second referendum on independence. In Wales, Plaid Cymru increased their number of seats from three to eleven, which now means they hold over a quarter of the Parliamentary seats in the Principality. Party leader Rachel Norris stated that Plaid Cymru are now a mainstream party in Wales and are now looking to follow their Scottish counterparts by taking power in the Welsh Assembly elections next year.

"*Sinn Fein also made advances in Northern Ireland, winning Foyle and South Down from the Social Democratic and Labour Party. This will concern the new Government because of its implications for the peace process in Northern Ireland.*

"*The General Election was a disappointing one for the United Kingdom Independence Party. Despite winning almost four million votes, they failed to win any of their target seats and lost one of the two constituencies they held. Party leader Geoffrey Tilt has already stated his intention to resign.*"

20 May 2015
Cabinet Room
10 Downing Street
London

The Cabinet was in a buoyant mood. Today had marked the first Cabinet meeting since the Conservatives' victory in the General Election nearly two weeks earlier and, more importantly, the first Cabinet meeting of an entirely Conservative government for eighteen years. Free of the shackles of their Liberal Democrat coalition partners, they were now at liberty to pursue a genuinely Conservative agenda.

Prime Minister David Talbot had entered the room to a round of applause from the new Cabinet and, during the previous two hours, Ministers had been outlining their policy plans. Chancellor of the Exchequer James Hamilton had outlined his programme to reduce public expenditure over the next five years which would bring it down to a proportion of Gross Domestic Product not seen since before World War II. Hamilton argued that this tough medicine was necessary to clear the deficit and restore overseas confidence in the pound.

Sarah Crosby, the Home Secretary, outlined her plans for continuing reform of the police, for tightening immigration controls and for increasing surveillance of terrorists and political extremists. Hugh Greville, who had taken up the transport portfolio, outlined plans for a high-speed rail link from London to the Midlands and the North and for a review of the need for a new airport hub in London and the South East. Angela Lawrence, newly promoted to Secretary of State for National Heritage, outlined plans for a review of the governance of the British Broadcasting Corporation. Ben Richardson, Secretary of State for Employment, outlined plans for further workplace reform that would remove the automatic check-off of trade union contributions and require trade unions to provide advance notification of the use of social media to promote disputes. Philip Madge, the Cabinet Secretary, outlined plans for reform of the Civil Service. Last to speak was the new Secretary of State for the Environment, Communities and Local Government, Jason Berry. David Talbot invited him to outline his Departmental plans.

"Can we move to Item 14. Euro 2016. Jason, congratulations on joining the Cabinet."

Other Cabinet members gave Berry a round of applause. Once that had finished, Talbot continued.

"Can you please summarise where we are and what actions you have planned."

Berry was 41 years old, an entrant to Parliament in 2010 and had previously been a Minister of State for Crime and Policing at the Home Office.

"Thank you, Prime Minister.

"Prime Minister, fellow Ministers, you will be aware that next year Scotland and Wales will be hosting the European Football Championships. This decade has truly been a glorious one for British sport as my Right Honourable colleague, the Secretary of State for National Heritage, will confirm. Over the past four years, the United Kingdom has staged one of the best Olympic Games ever, it held a successful Commonwealth Games in 2014 and next year the European Football Championships come back to Britain after twenty years.

"When Scotland and Wales were awarded the right to stage these championships, many people questioned whether they had the capacity and resources to take this forward. Back in 2010, Scotland and Wales had only four stadiums with a capacity over 30,000. They had only three international standard airports between them and rail and road links outside the main population centres were particularly thin. Both countries also had a lack of hotel capacity to accommodate the expected number of supporters likely to attend.

"Since then, both countries have made impressive progress in improving their infrastructure. Extensions to the Liberty Stadium in Swansea have just been completed, Aberdeen FC's new ground, the Aberdeen Asset Management Stadium, will open in August 2015 and the new stadiums in Dundee, Inverness and Wrexham will be ready for opening before the tournament starts in June 2016. The new airport at Swansea is due to open next month, as will be the dual carriageway section of the A93 between Aberdeen and Inverness and the widened and straightened single carriageway section of the A470 and A483 between Merthyr Tydfil and Ruabon. Over thirty new hotels have already opened in the main population centres and another twenty will be open before the tournament starts.

"Unfortunately, the issue of security has reared its ugly head. You do not need to be told about the threat posed to public safety by Al-Q'aida and Islamic State. What is worrying is the increase in the numbers of refugees entering the European Union through the land borders with Greece and by sea over the Mediterranean. As my Right Honourable colleague, the Home Secretary said earlier, there is a real threat of terrorists from Al-Q'aida and Islamic State hiding themselves amongst these refugees. The European Union stubbornly refuses to close national borders which means that terrorists could travel to Calais and try and enter the country via the Channel Tunnel or by sea.

"There is also a threat from home grown terrorists to contend with. The 7/7 bombers all came from this country, as did the murderers of Lee Rigby. In addition, intelligence reports indicate there is significant bodies of terrorist activity in both France and Belgium. Many of the suspects hold French or Belgian nationality, which means we are powerless to prevent them from entering the country.

"Finally, there is also a renewed threat from the Real IRA to contend with.

"The cost of ensuring that Euro 2016 passes without incident is rising daily. This will only be achieved by increasing our presence at points of entry to the country. It will involve greater deployment of the police during the tournament. The security services and secret intelligence services will need to increase their surveillance. You will agree with me that protecting the safety of those supporters attending Euro 2016 is a national responsibility. The bad guys are not going to enter Scotland or Wales alone. They will almost certainly try to enter through England. It is for this reason that I will be asking the devolved Governments in Scotland and Wales to contribute a share of the costs of strengthening security, policing and immigration control for the duration or Euro 2016.

"Best of luck with that, Jason" said Sarah Crosby. "Both Karen Rolfe and Jeremy Tomlinson had enormous difficulty in getting any co-operation from the Scots and the Welsh." She was referring to Berry's two predecessors in the post, both from the former Liberal Democrat coalition partners.

"I think I've got one trump card, Sarah" replied Berry. "If the Scots and Welsh refuse to increase their share of the security costs, we could theoretically refuse to allow the tournament to go ahead on safety grounds."

"That's rather extreme, Jason" said Talbot. "But if that's the price of getting the Scots and Welsh to play ball, we may have to go with it."

"I'm meeting First Ministers MacDougall and Morgan at the intergovernmental meeting in six weeks' time. I'll bring this up then."

2 July 2015
Department for the Environment,
Communities & Local Government
Eland House
Stag Place
London

"Secretary of State, your visitors have arrived." Jason Berry's Principal Private Secretary, Andrew Jemson, had advised that the delegates for the quarterly Inter-Governmental meeting were waiting in the outer office.

Berry, newly promoted to the Cabinet, was keen to make an impression. A good performance on the Environment, Communities and Local Government portfolio, could be a gateway to one of the leading Ministries. However, he knew he would have a hard time with Amy MacDougall. Leader of the Scottish National Party since the resignation of Alex Forsyth following the vote to remain part of the United Kingdom the previous year, Berry had encountered her in the two previous Inter-Governmental meetings. At the best of times, MacDougall could be waspish and combative, and she was on a high following her party's impressive showing in the General Election.

What Berry had not been expecting was for the First Minister for Wales, Richard Morgan, to drop out for health reasons. In his place was the Deputy First Minister, Rachel Norris, who was from the coalition partner in the Welsh Assembly Government, Plaid Cymru. Like MacDougall, Norris had a reputation for being feisty.

"Andrew, please bring them through."

Jemson, a fast stream civil servant in his early thirties led through MacDougall, Norris and the First Minister for Northern Ireland, Peter Henderson.

MacDougall and Norris had been relatively restrained through the early agenda items and the fireworks had come from Henderson, leader of the

Democratic Unionist Party, who was not pleased that arrangements were being made for senior officers from An Garda Siochána, the Republic of Ireland's police force, to act as observers in policing of parades in Northern Ireland. The traditional "marching season" in Northern Ireland, where members of the province's Protestant community staged marches to celebrate the victory at the Battle of the Boyne in 1690 which ended Roman Catholic rule in the United Kingdom, had just started. The marches were a source of conflict between the Protestant and Catholic communities in Northern Ireland and a test of the co-operations between the Democratic Unionists and Sinn Fein, who made up the governing coalition in the province.

Berry had just about managed to assure Henderson that the Garda's role was to observe and involved nothing more.

He then moved to Item 5. Euro 2016 and the cost of providing security.

"May I now turn to Euro 2016. The cost of providing security for the tournament and ensuring the safety of football supporters attending has unfortunately risen. The strongest threat is from Islamic extremists. The threat from Al-Q'aida has not diminished and has been joined by the growing threat of Islamic State. What happened in Paris last November is a chilling reminder of what can happen if we are complacent. There is compelling evidence that terrorists are hiding amongst refugees who are travelling to Western Europe and we do not need reminding that many of the perpetrators of atrocities are citizens of European Union countries, unfortunately including our own.

"This threat has been compounded by an increase in violent activity by Irish republicans who have not accepted the Good Friday agreement. The Real IRA has carried out several murders over the past year and we have reliable intelligence reports which suggest they are planning a major attack on the mainland this year. Finally, there is a continuing threat of hooliganism. Not only from domestic supporters but now from several of the countries taking part. In particular, Russia, Poland and Turkey have a bad reputation.

"To keep the tournament safe from these combined threats, we have had to increase the budgets of the police, the armed forces and MI5, as well as contracting with G4S for additional security. The estimated additional cost is £60 million."

MacDougall and Norris gasped with shock. They had a premonition of what Berry was going to say next.

"Scotland and Wales are going to benefit from staging Euro 2016, both in terms of national prestige and financially in attracting visitors. I think it is therefore reasonable that the Scottish Government and the Welsh Assembly Government pay half of the additional security and policing costs. Say £18 million from Scotland and £12 million from Wales."

MacDougall's face had visibly darkened. Although a small woman, she had a fiery temper and Berry had just ignited it.

"Excuse me, Mr Berry. Did I hear you correctly? You want *my* Government to cough up extra money to pay for something that's *your* responsibility?"

"Ms MacDougall, may I repeat myself. Your country is about to benefit financially from a prestigious sporting event. England will receive no benefit whatsoever, yet its taxpayers are having to fork out to pay for the cost of staging it. The least I can expect is that Scotland and Wales both pay their way towards the additional costs of keeping this event safe. After all, you are now able to raise taxes by yourself and, in addition, you are responsible for your own policing."

MacDougall refused to give way.

"No, Mr Berry, you appear to have forgotten something. National security is reserved business. My Government has no say in how it is run. And Scottish taxpayers are already paying towards it through taxes paid to your Government."

Norris then joined the argument.

"And Wales doesn't even have control over its own police forces." She was referring to the fact that policing in Wales, unlike Scotland, was still the responsibility of the Home Office.

MacDougall then brought up the issue of the 2012 Olympic Games.

"Remember the Olympics, Mr Berry? Scottish and Welsh taxpayers had to pay for the costs of running an event which almost entirely took place in England. All we got was a couple of football matches."

Berry was now getting annoyed with the chippiness of the Scottish First Minister.

"Ms MacDougall, your attitude confirms what I and my colleagues have always thought about you and your party. That England is to blame for all your misfortunes and that you see us as a giant cash cow. Well the party's over. My Government has supported Euro 2016 all the way but I'm now expecting you to pay a reasonable share of the security and policing costs. It is outrageous that you are expecting English taxpayers to pay for the costs of keeping your tournament safe."

"And what if we don't?" said a defiant Norris.

"The UK Government will have to pull the plug on supporting Euro 2016."

"Do that and I'll see you in court" said MacDougall slowly and menacingly.

7 July 2015
Cabinet Room
10 Downing Street
London

David Talbot had asked six members of the Cabinet to stay behind after the regular Tuesday meeting had finished. Bob Anderson, Jason Berry, Sarah Crosby, Angela Lawrence, Mark Rudge and Caroline Russell were slightly perplexed about the reason. The new Cabinet had only just been appointed so a reshuffle was unlikely.

Talbot re-entered the room and closed the door.

"Ladies and gentlemen, thank you for staying behind. What I am going to tell you has considerable national significance and will affect all your portfolios. However, it is to remain secret and I don't want this discussed with other Ministers, officials or even other Cabinet members.

"Yesterday, I took a call from US Secretary of State Oliver Norbury. The US Department of Justice, along with the FBI, are carrying out a criminal investigation into the conduct of four major football federations. For alleged bribery and corruption. One of them is the Fédération Internationale de Football Association, better known as FIFA. Another is the Union of European Football Associations – UEFA. The remaining two are the Central and South American Federations.

"The investigation primarily concerns the award of the 2018 World Cup which, as you know, was awarded to Russia. However, there are other awards of tournaments under investigation, including the award of next year's European football championships to Scotland and Wales."

There were gasps around the room.

"Are you telling us that the Scots and Welsh bribed their way to getting Euro 2016, Prime Minister?" asked Anderson.

"Actually, no Bob" replied Talbot. "From what Norbury said, the only reason they were awarded Euro 2016 was to undermine England's bid for the 2018 World Cup."

"What are the implications of the Americans' investigations?" asked Rudge.

"I was coming to that, Mark" replied Talbot. "If Department of Justice lay charges against FIFA and its Executive Council, they may have to reconsider their decision to award the World Cup to Russia. There is now a real prospect that England might be asked to stage the next World Cup. This means starting preparations now. That is why I've asked you to stay on."

"The next World Cup!" exclaimed Anderson. "I was only a kid when it happened last time." He was referring to the 1966 World Cup.

Talbot turned to Berry.

"Jason, can you get back to First Ministers MacDougall and Morgan to advise them that the UK Government will meet the additional policing and security costs in full."

"Prime Minister, are you serious?" asked Berry. "Only a week ago, you said we were right to demand that the Scots and Welsh paid a fair share of the additional costs."

"I know, Jason" replied Talbot. "But the big picture has changed. We need the support of Scotland and Wales to stand a chance of getting the World Cup. We've got to be nice to the devolved Governments."

Mark Rudge rolled his eyes. Once again, the UK Government had capitulated to pressure from the devolved Governments in Edinburgh and Cardiff. The English taxpayer faced additional bills to meet the cost of this jolly which would offer them no benefit.

As he sat in the back of his official car taking him back to the Department of Trade and Business's Victoria Street headquarters, he had time to think. There was still time to undermine Euro 2016. Other Ministers were unhappy that English taxpayers were having to pay for the costs of staging the tournament in Scotland and Wales. If the Scots and Welsh had to drop out, there was one leading candidate to stage it. France. The only problem was that François Picard was facing potential extradition to the USA to face corruption charges. But what if the investigation was compromised?

CHAPTER 13

3 September 2015
Federal Bureau of Investigation
J Edgar Hoover Building
Pennsylvania Avenue
Washington DC

"Mike, I've got some good news for you. Glad you were around."

Ten minutes earlier, Special Agent Mike Dempsey had received a call on his mobile phone from his boss, Special Agent-in-Charge Joe Fiorentino, asking him to report to Headquarters. At the time, he had been planning to take some leave and travel back to his hometown of Boston. His older brother, Pat, a sergeant in the city police force, was holding a party to celebrate his engagement and he was also intending to see the opening NFL game between New England Patriots and Atlanta Falcons.

"Lucky you caught me when you did, Joe. Another five minutes and I would have booked a flight to Boston."

"Mike, the reason I've asked you to come in is that there's been some important developments in the Picard investigation. I've just had Interpol on the line. Apparently, the two guys you wanted to interview are ready to talk."

"You mean Jauzion and Erbani, Joe?" asked Dempsey.

"Correct, Mike" replied Fiorentino.

"When do I need to go?" asked Dempsey. "My brother's just got engaged and I was planning to go up to Boston to see him next week."

"Mike, I'm afraid I've got to spoil your plans" said Fiorentino. "You need to be in Paris Monday sharp. Bob Lavigne will fill you in with the details. The two guys you want to interview are still afraid they'll get topped. Any delay and they'll refuse to speak again. Apparently, Interpol has heard rumours that members of the Paris underworld has been offered a contract to waste them."

"Shit, sounds like there's no time to lose. Joe, tell Lavigne that I'll be in Paris this weekend. If we lose Jauzion and Erbani, the investigation into Picard is stuffed."

"Mike, thanks" said Fiorentino as Dempsey left the office.

4 September 2015
Three Chimneys Farm
near Heathfield
East Sussex

Mark Rudge had driven from his Pimlico flat earlier that day to the substantial flint and brick farmhouse which he shared with his wife, Fiona, and his two children, Oliver and Emily. He was preparing for his constituency surgery which he was supposed to hold every week but which, with his duties as Secretary of State for Trade and Business, had slipped to more like once a month. His constituency was one of the safest in the country – in the General Election four months previously, he had obtained a majority of 25,000. Nevertheless, he felt he needed to make the effort to show his face in the constituency. He could not afford to be complacent – he was aware that the UK Independence Party was making some ground in articulating dissatisfaction with the European Union and that five senior members of the local Conservative Association had left to join UKIP over the past year.

The house was empty as Fiona Rudge and her children were visiting her parents and would not be back until the late afternoon. For Mark Rudge, this presented the opportunity to contact François Picard and tip him off that he was under investigation by the FBI.

Rudge entered his study on the first floor of the house. All round was photographic evidence that he was a high flier. Pictures of him as a school prefect, in the rugby and cricket teams at his school, graduation day at Oxford University, as a high-flying banker with BNP Paribas and Morgan Stanley, his wedding to Fiona sixteen years earlier and of his children. Like him, destined for success.

One glittering prize had avoided Rudge. Becoming leader of the Conservative Party and Prime Minister. He had become an MP for the first time ten years previously. He hadn't even had time to make his maiden speech when the party leader, Michael Howard, resigned. The Conservative Party had lost its third General Election in succession and there was little prospect of their fortunes changing.

Against this backdrop, the party turned to David Talbot, then a relatively new MP, to restore its fortunes. Talbot had the advantages of relative youth against his main rivals, as well as being good looking and an excellent communicator. Rudge had been a contemporary of Talbot at university and considered him something of a lightweight. He felt that Talbot lacked resolution in the face of challenges and that the Government had made too many compromises during its term of office. Everything from abandoned privatisations through to compromises with the European Union and the devolved governments in Scotland, Wales and Northern Ireland. Rudge was certain he could have done a better job.

The only difficulty was that Talbot had won a majority for the Conservatives at the General Election and was starting his second term as Prime Minister. The Conservative Party did not get rid of successful leaders.

He reached for his telephone. Picard's telephone number was in a personal organiser and he dialled the number.

To his delight, Picard answered it.

"Hello, François. How are you keeping?"

"Mark, I'm delighted to hear from you. What's the reason for your call?"

"François, there's something you need to be aware of. The FBI's currently investigating FIFA for suspected corruption regarding the award of Copa America and the World Cup. You are one of the FIFA officials under investigation."

"*Sacre bleu!*" exclaimed Picard. "FIFA is an international federation. The Americans have no right to meddle in our affairs, Mark. We have not broken their domestic law, in fact, we have almost nothing to do with the USA."

"Unfortunately, François, they do" replied Rudge. "Their legal system allows for extraterritorial prosecutions. Not only for terrorism and espionage but for corruption too. Apparently, the FBI are investigating da Costa, Lavotchkin, McKenzie and yourself and are now extending the investigation to cover UEFA's award of Euro 2016. They are now going after Sonnenberg and Langarotti."

"Mark, I can't thank you enough for warning me about this" replied Picard.

As Picard rang off, Rudge punched the air. Picard was the one man who could deliver Euro 2016 for France if the Scotland and Wales bid faltered. Nine months was a long time in politics as well as football. He knew that if Scotland and Wales failed to deliver Euro 2016, it would damage the political credibility of both the Scottish National Party and Plaid Cymru and finish all the talk about seeking independence from the United Kingdom. A successful tournament would only be a platform for further grandstanding by Amy MacDougall and Rachel Norris.

However, any talk of someone stepping in to take their place was dead in the water without a credible alternative. If François Picard was sitting in a US prison rather than in the offices of FIFA or the French Football Federation, this wasn't going to happen.

7 September 2015
Charlie Hebdo
Rue Nicolas-Appert
11ᵗʰ Arrondisment
Paris

"Monsieur Jauzion. Special Agent Mike Dempsey from the Federal Bureau of Investigation to see you."

Nathalie Vannier, Charlie Hebdo's receptionist, led the tall American through to the office of the magazine's Managing Editor. With him was Jean-Paul Robilliard, a Commandant from Police Nationale in Paris, who was accompanying him while he was interviewing French nationals.

Jauzion was a short, slimly-built man in his late forties. His shoulder-length black hair was starting to thin and his complexion betrayed too many late nights and Gauloises.

"Good morning, Monsieur Jauzion. Delighted to meet you at last. I believe you have some information about François Picard."

"I most certainly do, Monsieur Dempsey" replied Jauzion. "I understand you are investigating Monsieur Picard."

"And several other members of FIFA and UEFA, Monsieur Jauzion. Which I believe you can help with."

"Come this way." Jauzion motioned for Dempsey and Robilliard to a back office where there was a desktop computer installed. He inserted a USB stick.

Once Jauzion had started the computer, he used the mouse to move the cursor to a folder marked 'Investigation: FP' and pressed 'Open'.

The first file pulled up was a letter that Sergei Lavotchkin had sent to Picard on 16 June 2009

My dear François

I was grateful to your prompt response following our telephone conversation on 1 June regarding Russia's bid to stage the World Cup in 2018.

I totally agree with you that England's bid may face opposition from Middle Eastern and Third World countries because of the United Kingdom's role in the Iraq war in 2003. However, we should not underestimate the strength of England's bid. Most of the facilities demanded are either in place or are on order, so the cost to FIFA is likely to be minimal. In addition, the United Kingdom appears to be less affected by the current recession than many other countries. If England was to host the World Cup, the potential cost to FIFA will be less that if it was staged elsewhere. This may sway members of the Executive Committee.

The Russian Football Federation has close links with many of the African delegates and I believe many of them can be persuaded to support our bid. Da Costa has been enthusiastic about Russia staging the World Cup in 2018 and should be able to bring the South American delegates with him. Central America and the Caribbean is more difficult. Can you please lobby Orville McKenzie as he carries a lot of clout with CONCACAF.

I like your suggestion for backing the Scotland and Wales bid to stage Euro 2016. They may get a significant sympathy vote before UEFA realises their lack of capacity to stage such a tournament. I agree with your view that an award of Euro 2016 to Scotland and Wales would undermine England's World Cup bid. Can you approach Sonnenberg, Canizares and Langarotti to swing them in favour of a bid from Scotland and Wales.

Many leading businessmen and investors close to the President have a large financial stake in Russia succeeding with its bid to stage the World Cup. I will ensure that you are suitably rewarded if this outcome happens.

Yours ever

Sergei

"Seems like Lavotchkin was up front with his offer to bribe Picard" said Dempsey.

"There is more to come, Monsieur" said Jauzion, as he moved to the next file.

Later that day
United States Embassy
Avenue Gabriel
Paris

"How did it go, Mike?"

Special Agent Mike Dempsey was sitting in Bob Lavigne's office.

"Bob, couldn't have gone much better. Jauzion had a whole load of files on Picard. There's some pretty hard evidence that Picard not only took bribes from the Russians to ensure they got the 2018 World Cup. It appears that Picard also used Russian money to bribe the UEFA President and at least five members of UEFA's General Council. On top of that, I've got pretty reliable evidence that old man da Costa took a backhander off the Russians to swing the vote."

"Are you finished then, Mike?" asked Lavigne.

"Not yet, Bob. I still need to interview Danielle Erbani. Understand she's got access to financial transactions that could nail Picard. Without them, DoJ won't have enough evidence to prosecute."

"I'll get onto the Elysee and find out when they can set this up or you."

8 September 2015
Rue Perronet
Neuilly-sur-Seine
Paris

"Monsieur Picard."

François Picard recognised the voice on the other end of the phone. It was Patrick Rovin, a Major in the Police Nationale. Rovin was in his mid-forties and was resentful that what he considered to be less capable officers had been promoted to the higher ranks. He was therefore open to corruption and made a lot of his income through taking bribes in return for information.

"What do you want, Major Rovin?"

"Got some information that might be of use."

"Go ahead, Major."

"An FBI agent is in town, Monsieur Picard. Making enquiries about you."

That certainly woke Picard up. He remembered Mark Rudge's telephone call the previous week.

"FBI? Who is it, Major? Who has he asked? Where is he staying?"

"For a small reward, I can tell you, Monsieur."

Picard despised Rovin. A low -ranking *flic* with low morals. But useful all the same.

"Alright, Major Rovin, how much are you asking for?"

"Five thousand Euros."

"Done. I will arrange for a transfer to your bank. Now let me have the details."

"His name is Mike Dempsey. A Special Agent. Height 1.90 metres, short reddish hair. He was interviewing the editor of *Charlie Hebdo* today."

"*Charlie Hebdo*! Why didn't you tell me earlier?" The name of the satirical magazine threw Picard into a panic as he knew they still had documents that could incriminate him.

"I didn't know until after the interview happened" replied Rovin. "However, Dempsey is staying on. He will be interviewing Danielle Erbani later this week. Most probably Saturday or Sunday."

The mention of the former secretary at the French Football Federation, whom Picard had got sacked, saw the hackles rise.

"Major, get me Erbani's current address" shouted Picard.

"For another two thousand Euros, Monsieur Picard."

Picard knew he had no choice but to comply with the demands of the bent *flic*.

"One final word. Be careful before you think about causing any harm to Special Agent Dempsey. The Yanks will hang you out to dry if anything happens to him. Also, he's got an escort from Police Nationale. One of our high-flyers. Anything happens to him and we'll be after you."

That evening
Le Café de Rèunion
Rue Victor Massé
9th Arrondisement
Paris

"Another Kronenbourg, Marie."

Benoît Dominici was about to settle down for his second beer of the evening when his smartphone rang. On the other end was François Picard. He groaned. If one man was destined to spoil his evening, it was the Secretary-General of FIFA.

"What now, Monsieur Picard?" drawled an unenthusiastic Dominici.

"I've got more work for you, my friend. And a job that will pay well."

"I've told you before, Monsieur" snapped Dominici. "The *Charlie Hebdo* job was the last I do for you. Find some other mug to carry out your dirty work."

"Come on, Monsieur Dominici" replied Picard. "*Charlie Hebdo* was a success. You got a million Euros for that job and you haven't had to flee France. I got that commie rag off my back and the muzzies got the blame. Support for Monsieur Flanby, which was pretty low to start with, has fallen through the floor and the public's calling for a crackdown on immigration."

Picard was referring to President Mignolet by his disparaging nickname.

"And your point is…" said Dominici.

"That no one is giving a flying fuck about alleged misdeeds in high places."

"So, Monsieur Picard, tell me what you want done."

"Danielle Erbani. Early thirties, Mediterranean looking. Lives at 30 Residence de L'Ermitage, Avenue Maurice Thorez, Saint Denis. Two jobs I want done, Monsieur Dominici. Firstly, I want that bitch taken out. Secondly, I want any computers, remote hard drives, USB sticks found there destroyed."

"Okay, Monsieur Picard, I'll take the job. To you, a million and a half Euros." Picard gagged at the price but he knew the alternative was an FBI prosecution.

"Very well, Monsieur Dominici. A million and a half Euros. How soon can you start?"

"This weekend."

"Not soon enough. No later than 11 September. An FBI agent is due to interview her over the weekend."

138

11 September 2015
Residence de L'Ermitage
Avenue Maurice Thorez
Saint Denis
Paris

Mike Dempsey was delighted that Danielle Erbani was prepared to meet him earlier than planned. It meant he could obtain the evidence of corrupt financial transactions he was looking for.

The previous two hours had been highly productive for Dempsey. Erbani had shown him evidence that not only Picard, but also Joao da Costa, FIFA's President, and no less than six members of the Executive Council had taken financial inducements from a consortium of Russian oligarchs in return for support for Russia's World Cup bid. In addition, Erbani had evidence that Picard had in turn used Russian money to bribe Franz-Josef Sonnenberg, UEFA's President and four members of UEFA's Executive Council to vote for Scotland and Wales's bid to stage Euro 2016. In all cases, the money had been paid into numbered bank accounts in the Cayman Islands.

This was what Dempsey needed. It was now up to his FBI superiors to decide whether to seek prosecutions.

It was now 8pm and was dark outside. Dempsey and Commandant Jean-Paul Robilliard of Police Nationale, started to pack their bags and get ready to leave.

"Mademoiselle Erbani, I cannot thank you enough for your co-operation" said the FBI agent. "I will ensure you receive an appropriate reward."

"Thank you, Monsieur" replied Erbani. "I've got one question. What will be done to make sure I'm safe? I'm worried what Picard might do."

"Don't worry, my dear" replied Robilliard. "Police Nationale takes its responsibilities towards witnesses very seriously."

Benoît Dominici had taken the Metro to Saint Denis and had decided to walk to Avenue Maurice Thorez. It was the rush hour and he would look inconspicuous amongst all the other commuters heading home. It was much less risky than driving to Saint Denis or taking a taxi. CCTV cameras would pick up his numberplate of his car and he was already well-known to the police. And a taxi driver would recognise him.

Dominici walked through the entrance doors of the Residence de L'Ermitage and found the lift. The doors opened and he took it to the third floor.

Erbani's flat was one of five on the landing. He reached in the pocket of his leather jacket and pulled out a bent hairpin. Security in the municipal flats wasn't great and opening the lock was a job he had done countless times before. He started to work on the lock.

Suddenly, Dominici's concentration was broken by the sound of a door opening. It was Flat 32 on the other side of the landing. A tall African man came out.

"Bon soir, Monsieur" said the African.

"Bon soir" replied Dominici. He was relieved to see that the African headed for the lift and did not stop to ask further questions. He got back to work on the lock. After a minute, it opened.

Dempsey and Robilliard were about to leave when Dempsey heard a slight sound.

"Commandant, I think we have company."

Dominici was a seasoned assassin and was extremely stealthy when breaking into premises. Most people would not have noticed him breaking in and their last split second of life would have been seeing Dominici opening fire on them. But Dempsey had learned a lot in the five years he had been in the FBI. On top of that, he was highly alert and sensed there was danger. Both Dempsey and Robilliard started to reach for their guns.

The sight of a shadowy figure at the entrance to the lounge confirmed Dempsey's fears. As Dominici burst into the lounge, Dempsey grabbed Erbani and pulled her to the floor.

"Get down, Danielle" screamed the FBI agent as Dominici opened fire. His shot missed his intended target and hit the television set instead. It exploded with a loud bang.

Barely a split second later, Dempsey returned fire. One shot penetrated vital organs in Dominici's body, the other went straight through his brain. Dominici was already dead when he fell to the ground.

Dempsey suddenly realised what he had done. He had shot dead a French national in his own country. Surely this would risk a major diplomatic incident between the USA and France.

"Commandant, I am deeply sorry for………….."

Robilliard cut him off. "No need for apologies, Monsieur Dempsey. You have done Police Nationale a huge favour."

23 October 2015
Federal Bureau of Investigation
J Edgar Hoover Building
Pennsylvania Avenue
Washington DC

"Ms Bruckner is ready to see you now." Diane Lovato, PA to the FBI's Deputy Assistant Director, directed Special Agent Mike Dempsey into Katherine Bruckner's office.

"Good morning Mike. Please take a seat."

Bruckner was fifty years old, blonde haired and still quite attractive. However, she had earned a reputation as a tough and demanding boss and was tipped to be a future Director of the FBI.

On the table was Mike Dempsey's report on his investigation into corruption within FIFA and UEFA.

"Good morning, Ma'am."

"Please call me Katherine" replied Bruckner.

"Mike, I have just read your report on your investigation into FIFA. Sounds like you've uncovered more misdeeds than was originally anticipated."

"Indeed, I have, Katherine. I found out that Picard's malfeasance went beyond the 2018 World Cup. He was also responsible for fixing the award of the European Soccer Championships in 2016."

"Against his own country, I believe. What on earth possessed him to do that?"

"Picard reckoned that, if Scotland and Wales were given the right to stage the European Championships in 2016, they would undermine England's bid for the 2018 World Cup. So, he got the Russians to bribe some of the leading lights in UEFA so they would agree to Scotland and Wales being allowed to stage them."

"Why would Scotland and Wales staging a soccer tournament undermine England's World Cup bid, Mike?"

"Picard reckoned that Scotland and Wales would be incapable of staging such a prestigious tournament. Both are small countries with low GDP and were faced with sizeable capital expenditure on infrastructure to satisfy

UEFA's requirements. Not only that, both countries are still part of the United Kingdom. So, any failure on their part to be on schedule for the European Championships, it would cast doubt on England's ability to stage the 2018 World Cup. Which would benefit Russia's rival bid."

"Now I see the connection between the European Championships and the World Cup. Out of interest, how have Scotland and Wales fared, Mike?"

"Better than everyone thought" replied Dempsey. "They have completed all the infrastructure works and are on course to run the tournament."

"Sounds like Picard borrowed the script from *The Producers* for this scam."

"What was *The Producers*, Katherine?" asked Dempsey.

"Mel Brooks' first film. Made in 1967. It was about a fraud in which the perpetrators staged a musical which they thought would be a complete flop and intended to cash in on an insurance payout. Instead, it became a roaring success and they tried to sabotage it."

"What's the likely outcome following my investigation, Katherine?"

"Good news, Mike" replied Bruckner. "I will be recommending to the Director that we seek authority from the Department of Justice for prosecutions against not only Picard, but also da Costa, Sonnenberg and several other leading members of both FIFA and UEFA. We have already referred separate investigations on the Central and South American Federations to Department of Justice."

"One thing further, Mike. You have impressed a lot of people here with the professional and determined way you have carried out his investigation. In particular, Joe Fiorentino and Bob Lavigne were impressed with your work. I will be recommending you for both a commendation and promotion to Special Agent-in-Charge."

"Thank you very much, Katherine."

"Mike, you will be pleased to learn that you can take the leave you planned for last month. You have more than earned it."

CHAPTER 14

3 December 2015
FIFA Headquarters
FIFA-Strasse 20
Zurich
Switzerland

For Joao da Costa, announcing the award of the right to stage the 2022 World Cup would be his last act as President of FIFA before he stood down. He had reached his 90th birthday two months earlier and he felt that thirty-five years at the head of the world's football federation was enough.

Da Costa felt proud of his record as President of FIFA. When he took over, the organisation was still Euro-centric. He had done a lot to expand the game of football to Africa and Asia and, during his time in office, countries from Asia and Africa had staged the World Cup. He was however personally affronted by claims of corruption within FIFA which he felt primarily came from the media in the USA and the United Kingdom. Da Costa regarded both countries as hankering for a past when their imperial power dominated the world and took the view that they would have to take their place under what he regarded as the "New World Order".

At 2pm, the FIFA Council took their place in the Press Suite. At the centre of the table sat da Costa, while Secretary-General and favourite to succeed him, François Picard, sat alongside him. Either side of them sat the six FIFA Vice-Presidents.

Five countries had bid to stage the 2022 World Cup. Favourites were Australia who already had most of the required infrastructure in place. The only concern was that it was necessary to fly between most of the venues, but that had been managed by the USA in the 1994 World Cup and by Brazil the previous year. There were also bids from Qatar, Japan, the USA and Thailand.

The same day
US Department of Justice
950 Pennsylvania Avenue NW
Washington DC

At the same time as the FIFA Council sat down to announce the result of the bidding round for the 2022 World Cup, the US and world press had gathered in the Press Suite at the Department of Justice. Washington DC was five hours behind European time.

At 9am, Attorney-General Lorraine Hightower emerged and took her place at a lectern mounted centrally.

Hightower, now 50 years old, was the first African-American woman to hold the post of Attorney-General and had been in post for 12 months. Hailing from the mid-Western city of Cincinnati, Hightower had once been a talented track sprinter and had been close to being selected for the US athletics squads for the 1984 and 1988 Olympics. However, she was exceptionally bright and ambitious and she ploughed her efforts into obtaining legal qualifications and a law career instead.

Her appointment had been controversial as it was alleged that President Lamar Brackley had chosen her for both her gender and race. However, during her first year in office, she had impressed both Congress and the FBI with her grasp of detail.

Hightower began her speech.

"Ladies and gentlemen, good morning to you.

"The reason I have invited you to attend this morning is to hear the outcome of an investigation that the Federal Bureau of Investigation has been carrying out for the past three years and what action I as Attorney-General will be taking forward in response.

"Three years ago, the Department of Justice was in receipt of serious allegations of malfeasance in the governance of world soccer. These allegations related to the award of Copa America, which is due to be held in Miami next year, by the Confederación Sudamericana de Fútbol (CONMEBOL), and the Confederation of North, Central America and Caribbean Association Football (CONCACAF). It was alleged that members of both organisations' governing bodies accepted bribes in relation to the award of media rights.

"The FBI also discovered evidence that bribes had been offered to the governing bodies of the Fédération Internationale de Football Association (FIFA) in relation to the award of the 2018 World Cup and the Union of European Football Associations (UEFA) in relation to the award of the 2016 European Championship.

"Under US law, offering or receiving a bribe of favour is a felony, irrespective of where it takes place. The FBI has found evidence that members of the governing bodies of FIFA, CONMEBOL, CONCACAF and UEFA have all committed felonies through the acceptance of bribes and favours and in issuing corrupt decisions relating to the offer of media rights for Copa America and in the award of both the European Football Championship in 2016 and the World Cup in 2018.

"The Department of Justice will therefore be commencing criminal proceedings against the following persons. From CONMEBOL, the President, Hector Immobile, Vice-Presidents Nelson Braga, Roberto Mas and Rodrigo Sanchez, and Secretary-General Manuel Ortega. From CONCACAF, the President, Lionel Duarte, Vice-President Bob Kennedy and Secretary-General Harrell Walcott."

There were gasps from the audience. Bob Kennedy had been a former Secretary to the US Football Federation. It showed that Hightower was taking no prisoners.

"From FIFA, the President, Joao da Costa, Vice-Presidents Amadou N'Konte, Sergei Lavotchkin, Orville McKenzie and Secretary-General François Picard. And from UEFA, the President, Franz-Josef Sonnenberg and former Vice-Presidents Marc Hermans and Giancarlo Langarotti.

"I will be asking for arrest warrants to be issued in respect of these individuals."

Later that day
FIFA Headquarters
FIFA-Strasse 20
Zurich
Switzerland

Voting for the 2022 World Cup had proceeded to five rounds. Australia had maintained a lead in all four previous rounds but the main surprise was that the expected challenge from Asia did not come from Japan or Thailand but from Qatar. The Gulf kingdom was one of the world's weaker football-playing nations and they did not have either the stadiums in place, nor the hotels required to accommodate all the visitors expected. But they had money. They had used their oil revenues to create a wealth fund to protect the country's economy after the oil ran out and, in turn, had used the fund to purchase property, patents and intellectual property rights. For the ruling al-Thani family, securing the right to stage the World Cup would be a significant coup.

At 3:15pm, Joao da Costa signalled that he was ready to announce the result of the bidding round. At the end of Round 4, Australia were still favourites to win. However, their hopes were soon to be dashed.

"In the fifth round, Australia received ten votes. Qatar received twelve votes. I therefore declare that the 2022 World Cup will be staged in Qatar."

A massive cheer went up from the Qatari delegates. On the other hand, the Secretary of the Australian Soccer Federation, Joe Lukic, was furious.

"Have you got your sums right, mate?" shouted Lukic. "That's a complete fix."

"Come off it, Joe" shouted Orville McKenzie. "That was a fair vote and you lost."

Before the dust had settled, a detachment of the Zurich cantonal police under the command of Lieutenant-Colonel Hans Graber had burst into the Press Suite. Graber headed straight for Joao da Costa.

Da Costa was irritated that the police had disturbed what was FIFA business.

"Senhor, may I ask the nature of your business and why you did not have the courtesy to ask me for an appointment?"

Graber was an experienced policeman used to dealing with the high and mighty who wanted to exploit Switzerland's generous banking laws for squirrelling away ill-gotten gains. He was not prepared to back down.

"Herr da Costa, Lieutenant-Colonel Hans Graber, Zurich Cantonal Police. I am here to execute international arrest warrants for yourself, for Vice-Presidents Amadou N'Konte and Orville McKenzie and Secretary-General François Picard. I would suggest that you co-operate."

"What in God's name are we being charged with?" shouted Orville McKenzie.

"That you accepted bribes and favours connected to the award of the 2018 World Cup. Offences under the laws of the United States of America, no matter where they take place."

"You have no right to arrest us at the behest of the Americans" shouted Picard. "We are protected by the European Convention on Human Rights if you remember, Lieutenant-Colonel."

"Herr Picard, you appear to have forgotten something" replied Graber. "Both France and Switzerland intend to prosecute you as well and will take this forward if the Americans don't."

Two hours later
10 Downing Street
London

David Talbot was working his way through the red box of papers when his Principal Private Secretary, Rebecca Bonnington, phoned.

"Prime Minister, I've got the US Secretary of State on the line. He says it's urgent."

"Put him through, Rebecca" said Talbot.

"Prime Minister, Secretary of State Norbury here."

"Oliver, tell me what the problem is. What's the urgency?"

"I'm afraid I have to report there are serious criminal allegations against one of your Ministers."

Talbot was stunned.

"Who was it, Secretary of State? And what has he or she supposed to have done?"

"Mark Rudge."

"Mark? Are you being serious?"

"Very serious, Prime Minister. The FBI's obtained a record of a telephone call made to the Secretary-General of FIFA tipping him off that he and other members of FIFA's governing council were under an FBI investigation. This could have compromised a criminal investigation that the FBI was carrying out into corruption within FIFA and particularly relating to the 2018 World Cup."

"I don't believe it" said Talbot. "Tell me, what's going to happen?"

"Depends on what you are going to do. Attorney-General Hightower wants him to be prosecuted. But the President realises it won't look good if a Minister of State in a friendly country is dragged through the courts. However, it won't look good if your Government does nothing. Am I clear, Prime Minister?"

"I'm afraid you are."

4 December 2015
10 Downing Street
London

Mark Rudge was perplexed about the reason that the Prime Minister had summoned him for a 9am meeting.

"The Prime Minister will see you now, Mr Rudge" said Rebecca Bonnington.

As Rudge walked into the Prime Minister's office, he noticed that David Talbot had a severe expression on his face. This was uncharacteristic for a man renowned for being laid back.

"Good morning, Mark. If you are wondering why I've asked you to come in on a Friday, I'll now explain."

"Yesterday, I received a telephone call from US Secretary of State Norbury in which he told me that the FBI have evidence that you attempted to compromise a criminal investigation they were carrying out. It appears you tipped off the Secretary-General of FIFA, François Picard, about the FBI investigation."

Rudge's face dropped. He knew he had been found out.

"Prime Minister, I'm really sorry for what I did. All I wanted to do was to keep Picard out of jail so France would be able to stage Euro 2016."

"So, you're still pursuing your personal vendetta against Scotland and Wales holding it."

"Prime Minister, the Scotland and Wales bid has been a basket case from day one. Venues, accommodation and transport were all in need of improvement and, although they've got EU money to support them, the growing security issue means that the English taxpayer is subsidising a significant percentage of the cost. Other Ministers are unhappy with this, as are a significant proportion of Party members and the public. If we pulled the plug on Scotland and Wales and they had to drop the tournament, France would.............."

"Mark, you appear to underestimate the seriousness of what you've done" said Talbot. "By tipping off Picard, not only did you undermine a flagship investigation by the FBI, it nearly cost one of their agents his life."

"My God, what happened?"

"Your friend Picard apparently hired a hitman from the Paris underworld to try and bump off key witnesses. An FBI agent was interviewing one of the witnesses when the hitman broke in. He was very lucky to come out alive.

"The FBI and the Department of Justice were furious and wanted your extradition. I've managed to put them off. However, because of your conduct, I've lost all confidence in your ability to discharge your responsibilities within the Cabinet, Mark. I've got no choice but to ask for your resignation."

The same day
BBC News

"Hello, this is Mark Pitman with the lunchtime news on BBC.

"The fallout from the FIFA football corruption investigation continues to grow. Following yesterday's announcement by US Attorney-General, Lorraine Hightower, that criminal proceedings against FIFA and UEFA were to be carried out and the arrests yesterday by Swiss Police of FIFA President Joao da Costa, three Vice-Presidents and the Secretary-General, further arrest were made this morning. UEFA President Franz-Josef Sonnenberg was arrested at his Salzburg home, while former UEFA Vice-Presidents Marc Hermans and Giancarlo Langarotti have also been arrested.

"The arrests have brought into doubt whether the awards of the 2018 World Cup to Russia and the 2022 World Cup to Qatar will take place. Already, the Russian and Qatari football federations have threatened legal action if the World Cup is taken away from their country.

"Now for domestic news. The Secretary of State for Trade and Business, Mark Rudge, has resigned from the Cabinet. The reasons are undisclosed but it is believed that that there were differences of opinion between Mr Rudge and other Cabinet members. The Government has moved quickly to replace Mr Rudge, with Ben Richardson, previously Secretary of State for Employment, being appointed to the Trade and Business portfolio."

CHAPTER 15

12 January 2016
FIFA Headquarters
FIFA-Strasse 20
Zurich
Switzerland

The FIFA Council had assembled to discuss its response to the criminal prosecutions being launched by the USA. Any suspicion that Joao da Costa might be inclined to co-operate with the Americans was soon dispelled. The other FIFA delegates were like minded.

"Gentlemen, you will be pleased to hear that I have no intention of co-operating with the American authorities or surrendering to face these politically-motivated charges against me and yourselves" said da Costa. "The USA has been used to using the rest of the world as its personal fiefdom too long and doesn't like seeing what they consider vassal countries running events they consider to be their God-given right. Unfortunately, they've leaned on Switzerland to do their dirty work. Because our passports were taken away, we were unable to see our families over Christmas."

"You will have the support of my Government" replied Lavotchkin. "You will be aware, Mr President, that President Ivanov has praised the work you have done in helping underprivileged communities across the world. The Americans are now afraid of Russia again and, if they insist on extraditing me, they know they will face serious repercussions."

"That still leaves the rest of us vulnerable, Sergei" said N'Konte.

"There is one potential lever we've got" said Luis Arconada, the Argentinian FIFA representative. "Later this year, elections take place in Argentina, Chile, Ecuador, Nicaragua and Venezuela. All these countries have socialist or left-wing governments which are currently unpopular. On current forecasts, the conservative parties are expected to win these elections. However, South America has a deep-seated dislike of the USA because of what has happened over the past 200 years."

Arconada was referring to the Monroe Doctrine of 1823, introduced by the then President, James Monroe, as a means of securing US primacy over the whole American continent. The US had used the Monroe Doctrine to justify action ranging from supporting *coups d'etat* through to direct military intervention.

"If the American authorities proceed with prosecutions of yourself, Mr President, plus Amadou, Sergei, Orville and François, plus several members of CONMEBOL and CONCACAF, they will succeed in reminding everyone in Central and South America that the USA regards them as vassals, lesser beings. The conservative parties will be regarded as stooges of the USA."

"And the point is, Luis?" asked Orville McKenzie.

"The Americans are desperate to have conservative, pro-western governments back in power in the American continent. Particularly Venezuela, which has been a thorn in their side since Hugo Chavez came to power. If they proceed with these prosecutions, they will lose that."

There was one voice of dissent. David Rose, England's FIFA representative and a Vice-President indicated he wanted to speak.

"Gentlemen, have you considered the consequences of what you're proposing? You appear to have forgotten where FIFA gets most of its income from to finance tournaments."

Rose was referring to sponsorship from big business and income from broadcasting rights.

"Several companies which have previously sponsored World Cups and major sporting tournaments like the Olympics are starting to get cold feet about sponsoring the World Cup because of the corruption allegations made. Have a look at the business pages of yesterday's *Daily Telegraph*."

Under the headline that read **MAJOR SPONSORS RECONSIDERING SUPPORT FOR WORLD CUP FOLLOWING FIFA CORRUPTION PROBE**, the article explained that no less than seven major sponsors – Adidas, Budweiser, Coca-Cola, Ford, McDonald's, Sony and Visa – were all planning to review their sponsorship of the 2018 World Cup, and that other potential sponsors were planning to follow suit.

"David, sponsors have made threats like that before" said Picard. "They never get carried through because they stand to lose more than they would gain. And they don't want to risk letting a competitor grab a foothold."

Rose stood his ground.

"It is different this time round. This is the first time ever that representatives of a sporting body have faced prosecution. And I think that the markets are reacting accordingly.

"One thing more. You all appear to have forgotten that it is 2016, not the 1960s or 1970s. The USA has its first black president. The Attorney-General is a black woman. Lamar Brackley is hardly Richard Nixon or John Foster Dulles. He has offered the hand of co-operation with all countries in Central and South America. Attorney-General Hightower has not taken these prosecutions lightly. Indeed, one of the defendants is none less than Bob Kennedy."

Rose was referring to the USA's representative on CONCACAF.

"Are you seriously suggesting that we surrender to the Americans, David?" asked da Costa.

"Mr President, I am" replied Rose. "If you take them on, you will only damage FIFA. All the work you have done over the past thirty-five years will have been for nothing."

25 February 2016
Coca-Cola Company Headquarters
Atlanta
Georgia

The monthly meeting of the Board of Directors at Coca-Cola had one additional agenda item. It was about continuing sponsorship of sports events following the decision by the US Attorney-General to prosecute members of FIFA, CONMEBOL, CONCACAF and UEFA for corruption. Because of its importance, it had been elevated to the first item on the agenda.

Company Chairman and Chief Executive Officer, James Adams, signalled that the Board meeting was about to start. It was 9am.

Having formally welcomed attendees, examined the minutes of the previous month's meeting and followed up on progress against agreed action points, Adams moved to the first agenda item.

"Ladies and gentlemen, you will have the papers for the first agenda item on the table. An earlier summary of events was e-mailed to you last week. I hope you have read it.

"For almost ninety years, Coca-Cola has been a proud sponsor of sporting events. The first event was the 1928 Olympic Games in Amsterdam. Since then, we have sponsored football, baseball and basketball, along with speedway and automobile racing. Overseas, we have sponsored soccer and, since 1978, this has included the World Cup. During that time, we have struck up an excellent working relationship with the governing body for world soccer, FIFA.

"You will all be aware that, on 3 December, Attorney-General Hightower announced that she was launching criminal charges against several leading officials from FIFA, as well as officials from the European and the Central and South American soccer federations. This relates to allegations that officials received bribes that influenced their decisions to award broadcasting rights for the Copa America tournament taking place this year, and the award of the right to host the European soccer championships also taking place this year and the World Cup in both 2018 and 2022.

"Since it was founded 130 years ago, Coca-Cola has been rightly concerned about its reputation and integrity. The allegations made against FIFA and the other soccer federations referred to are extremely serious. There are real grounds for concern that decisions relating to the award of the aforesaid tournaments and of broadcasting rights were not because the merits of the successful bidders but was because who offered the most money.

"I recognise that it would be wrong to prejudge FIFA and the European and Central and South American soccer federations before court proceedings have been completed. But, as Chairman of Coca-Cola, I have real concerns about the impact on the company of being associated with bodies that are prepared to abandon all concepts of integrity and common decency in the conduct of their business.

"Fellow Board members, I am asking you if Coca-Cola should discontinue any association with sporting tournaments organised by FIFA, UEFA, CONMEBOL or CONCACAF."

First to speak was Mark Harland, Coca-Cola's Director of European Operations.

"Mr Chairman, thank you. Like you, I was most disturbed to hear the allegations made against FIFA and UEFA, both of whom with we have had a long and productive relationship. However, I would like to ask you and fellow Board members to exercise caution before deciding to remove any investment in tournaments run by either organisation. Firstly, there is no guarantee that the charges against FIFA and UEFA will be proven in court, or even proceeded with. As you all may know, the Department of Justice has a long track record of plea bargaining. We also have to consider whether any of our business rivals would take advantage of our withdrawal of sponsorship."

The Directors of Operations for Central and South America indicated their agreement with Harland.

Company Secretary Woodrow Harrison then spoke. Unlike other Board members, he was a native of Georgia.

"Ladies and gentlemen, I am grateful for the views of our Operational Directors for Europe and Central and South America. The Director of European Operations has a unique insight into market conditions in Europe which I and other colleagues do not have. However, I feel there is an important principle at stake. The Department of Justice does not take prosecutions lightly, particularly those as expensive as taking leading international sports federations to Court. Do you seriously want a great company like Coca-Cola to have its name and reputation tarnished by association with organisations where there is strong evidence of corruption having taken place? I certainly do not and I would imagine you think like me. Yes, there is a risk of us losing business to rivals. On the other hand, the damage to the global brand of Coca-Cola by association with corrupt organisations could far exceed the temporary loss of business.

"I would imagine that similar conversations are being held in the boardrooms of other companies who either sponsor sport or would like to. They are likely to draw similar conclusions to the evidence before them. I would therefore ask you to vote to withhold any sponsorship of sporting events until the organising bodies have proven their competence and integrity to govern."

Ten minutes later, the Coca-Cola board had made its decision. By fifteen votes to three, it had voted to withhold sponsorship of Euro 2016 and the 2018 World Cup.

1 March 2016
Sky News

"Good morning, this is Emma McGovern with the latest news on Sky TV.

"The crisis at FIFA surrounding the 2018 World Cup has continues to get worse following the decision by six of its sponsors to follow the lead of Coca-Cola and withdraw their sponsorship. Adidas, Budweiser, Ford, McDonald's, Sony and Visa have all confirmed that they will no longer be sponsoring the World Cup, and Diageo, Honda and HSBC have confirmed that they would not be applying to sponsor the World Cup in the event of any existing sponsors withdrawing.

"The financial implications for FIFA are potentially devastating. Sponsorship accounts for £30 million and, without it, FIFA might be forced to cancel the World Cup for the first time in its eighty-six-year history.

"The threat of withdrawal of sponsorship has also affected UEFA, which will be staging the European football championships later this year in Scotland and Wales. Vice-President Jose Maria Canizares is holding urgent talks with key sponsors to reassure them that UEFA has put its house in order following allegations of corruption and save the tournament. The impact of Euro 2016 being cancelled would be devastating for both Scotland and Wales who have staked on the tournament to give their domestic economies a boost."

3 March 2016
Russian Foreign Ministry
The Kremlin
Moscow

Russia's Foreign Minister, Alexei Primakov, looked extremely concerned.

"Sergei, how did you allow this to happen? Losing the World Cup will be a massive humiliation for the Motherland."

"I'm sorry, Foreign Minister" replied Sergei Lavotchkin. "Neither I, nor the fellow members of the FIFA Council, had any indication that sponsors were going to turn tail and run. I wonder if the Americans have brought pressure on their corporations to make sure the World Cup doesn't happen."

"You know you've got Tupitsin to thank for getting you here, Sergei."

Primakov was referring to the subterfuge that oligarch Vladimir Tupitsin had used to get Lavotchkin out of Switzerland. Tupitsin had sent his personal business jet to St Gallen airport in the east of Switzerland, supposedly for an internal flight to the Swiss capital, Berne. With no passport control, Lavotchkin had boarded without being challenged. Using bad weather as an excuse, the plane changed direction and flew directly to Moscow. The incident led to a major diplomatic row with the USA, who were furious because Lavotchkin was facing extradition to the USA to face serious felony charges.

"By the way, one bit of good news, Foreign Minister" said Russia's FIFA representative. "Elections are taking place in five Central and South American countries this year. Argentina, Chile, Ecuador, Nicaragua and Venezuela. Arconada reckons that the US decision to charge several of their nationals with corruption will rebound on the Americans."

"How?"

"Each of the five countries currently has socialist governments and are friendly to us. Until recently, there was a strong likelihood of a change of government in all countries. Not anymore. The USA has awakened the long-standing sense of injustice in Latin America by their action. The conservative parties will be regarded as stooges of the Americans. The socialists could hang on."

Primakov asked for FSB Director, General Grigoriy Tereschkov, to join the meeting. Five minutes later, the tall figure of Tereschkov was sitting opposite the Foreign Minister.

"Grigoriy, I understand there are elections in South America this year."

"That's right, Foreign Minister" replied the FSB head. "First one is in Argentina later this month."

"What's the situation like?"

"Two weeks ago, it looked a no-hoper for the Socialists. They were fifteen points behind the opposition. But the decision by the Americans to charge Hector Immobile with corruption has reawakened the old anti-Americanism that had laid dormant for years. And Julia Rodriguez has aroused nationalist feelings by promising to retake the Malvinas."

Immobile was Chairman of the Argentinian Football Federation and a member of the General Council of CONMEBOL. He was also a former international footballer and had represented his country 33 times, including in the World Cup winning side in 1986.

The "Malvinas" were better known as the Falkland Islands and were one of the United Kingdom's last colonial possessions. For years, Argentina had laid claim to them and had fought an unsuccessful war against the United Kingdom in 1982 in a vain bid to annex them. Julia Rodriguez, Argentina's President, had been vociferous in her support for Argentina's claims to the islands.

"That's just what Sergei said. Grigoriy, can you do what you can to ensure that Rodriguez gets re-elected."

"Leave it to me, Foreign Minister."

31 March 2016
BBC News

Mark Pitman had already covered the main news items of the evening bulletin before moving onto secondary topics. The next issue to cover was the Argentinian Presidential Election.

"There were scenes of jubilation in the centre of Buenos Aires last night as Julia Rodriguez defied recent polls and secured re-election as Argentina's President. The controversial President, who has made herself unpopular over the last year with tax increases

and has presided over a faltering economy with fifty per cent inflation, defied opinion polls which indicated that her conservative challenger, Martin Picon, was on course to win.

"It is believed that several bellicose speeches by Ms Rodriguez, in which she threatened military action to re-take the Falkland Islands, and the recent indictment of football legend Hector Immobile on corruption charges by the US authorities were factors which aided her."

1 April 2016
US Department of State
Harry S Truman Building
2201 C Street NW
Washington DC

Secretary of State Oliver Norbury had commissioned an urgent meeting of the Department's Executive Secretariat to discuss the implications of the re-election of Julia Rodriguez as President of Argentina. Sitting opposite Norbury were the two Deputy Secretaries, Sarah Haley and Tony Reynolds, Executive Secretary Janet Fearon, Director of Foreign Assistance Daniel Russell and Chief of Staff Lawrence O'Malley.

Norbury was not best pleased that forecasts of an easy win for Martin Picon had not happened and that Rodriguez, something of a *bête noire* for the US Government was back in power. He had spent the previous day explaining to the President the reason why State Department had got their forecasts so wrong.

"Well, ladies and gentlemen. As Oliver Hardy would have put it, 'another fine mess'. How come all your forecasts that Picon was as good as home and dry never came off? The President is somewhat pissed off, to put it mildly."

"Did you see some of Rodriguez's speeches, Secretary of State?" asked Haley. "Rabble-rousing would have been an understatement. Ranting on about the *Yanquis* and how she was going to re-take the Malvinas – sorry, the Falklands."

Haley had suddenly remembered that the US Government recognised the United Kingdom's claim to the Falkland Islands.

"Sarah, everyone knows Rodriguez's a blowhard. There was real anger about how the economy's been stuffed and the tax increases she brought in. Furthermore, there's been rumours about her extravagant lifestyle."

"Secretary of State, I wonder if our decision to charge Immobile with corruption had any effect?" asked Russell.

"Who's Immobile?" asked O'Malley.

"Ex-Argentina soccer international, more recently Chairman of their soccer federation and a member of the General Council of CONMEBOL. He's one of several soccer officials being indicted for corruption by the Justice Department, including one of our own. He played in the Argentina side that won the World Cup thirty years ago and is a national hero."

"So, Daniel, are you suggesting that Rodriguez made the forthcoming corruption trial an election issue?" asked Norbury.

"I am, Secretary of State" replied the Director of Foreign Assistance. "What everyone needs to be aware of is that Latin countries like Argentina have a ferocious sense of national pride. They revere their sporting heroes and see any attempt to put them on trial abroad as an insult to their country. In addition, the proposed indictment of Immobile has re-awakened old resentments about US interference in their domestic affairs."

"Have we got any further elections coming up in Central and South America this year?" asked Norbury.

"Four more, Secretary of State" replied Reynolds. "Chile, Ecuador, Nicaragua and Venezuela. And significantly all ruled by Socialists or left of centre governments."

Norbury then pondered the next steps and turned to his colleagues.

"Daniel, can you obtain details of all the soccer officials facing prosecution by Department of Justice and copy in all members of the Executive Committee. Sarah, can you carry out a risk assessment of the forthcoming elections in Chile, Ecuador, Nicaragua and Venezuela. Lawrence, can you arrange a new meeting in two weeks' time. And can you also contact Lorraine Hightower's Chief of Staff as I would like to meet her, sooner rather than later."

7 April 2016
US Department of Justice
950 Pennsylvania Avenue NW
Washington DC

"Good afternoon, Oliver. I understand you want to talk about the proposed prosecutions of FIFA officials." Lorraine Hightower was seated at a large oak desk in her office as she welcomed Oliver Norbury in.

"That's right, Lorraine" replied the Secretary of State. "But not just FIFA. I understand you also intend to prosecute officials from the Central and South American soccer federations too."

"May I ask the reason behind your query, Oliver?" asked Hightower.

"To cut a long story short, Lorraine, your proposals to prosecute several overseas officials of soccer federations is having and adverse impact upon US relationships with countries in Central and South America and the Caribbean. And, more importantly, adverse outcomes in terms of US interests."

"Can you explain what you mean by 'adverse outcomes'?"

"This year, Presidential and parliamentary elections are taking place in five countries in Central and South America. They have already taken place in Argentina and are due to follow in Chile, Ecuador, Nicaragua and Venezuela. All five countries have had socialist governments and have not been very co-operative with us. You will be aware that Nicaragua and Venezuela have given military assistance to Russia and that Argentina was considering buying Russian equipment. Up to a month ago, there was a strong likelihood that there would be a change of government in all five countries as the socialists had become unpopular. This would clearly be in the interests of US foreign policy."

"However, in the Argentinian presidential election which took place two weeks ago, President Rodriguez was re-elected. Reports I have received from our Embassy suggest that your decision to charge Hector Immobile with corruption has not been well received there. Immobile may indeed be guilty of accepting bribes in relation to media rights for Copa America. But remember that he was a former World Cup-winning soccer international and is a national hero in Argentina. The decision to charge him is regarded as an insult to the country and made us look like interfering Yankee imperialists. Rodriguez exploited this during her election campaign and the Embassy thinks this contributed towards her unexpected victory.

"State Department was hoping that Martin Picon would win, sort out Argentina's economic problems and bring it back into the US sphere of influence. Instead, we're left with an economic basket case that's getting too cosy with Russia. You are aware that Foreign Minister Primakov was in Buenos Aires today?

"I'm worried that if we go ahead with the prosecutions of Duarte, Mas, Ortega and Sanchez, we would end up with similar results in Chile, Ecuador, Nicaragua and Venezuela. That would be a disaster for the USA and would be a gift horse for the Republicans when we go to the polls later this year."

Hightower was unmoved.

"Oliver, I recognise you've a job to do in projecting the country's influence overseas. But the thought of abandoning prosecutions for reasons of convenience or political expediency revolts me. Department of Justice has material evidence that all the men we have charged have breached US law by corruptly accepting bribes for favours. I am not, under any circumstances, prepared to let any of the parties off the hook just because it might be politically expedient. I firmly believe that justice must see its course and I am prepared to put that to the President if necessary."

"Very well, Lorraine. I'll let the President know where you stand."

CHAPTER 16

19 April 2016
FIFA Headquarters
FIFA-Strasse 20
Zurich
Switzerland

Joao da Costa had convened an emergency meeting of the FIFA Council in response to the shock news that UEFA President, Franz-Josef Sonnenberg, and the entire Executive Committee had resigned the previous week. There was increasing pressure from FIFA delegates for da Costa, Picard and the Vice-Presidents facing indictment in the USA to follow suit to assure sponsors that FIFA was cleaning up its act.

Da Costa opened the meeting at 9am.

"Gentlemen, thank you for attending this meeting at such short notice. You will be aware from the recent news that the UEFA President and the entire Executive Committee resigned last Friday. I think you will all agree with me that the loss of Franz-Josef Sonnenberg to football is a grievous one. Franz-Josef spent all his life trying to promote the game he loved and it is sad to see him forced out because of malicious speculation in the media. We have also lost the services of other good men – Jose Maria Canizares, Giancarlo Langarotti, Henri Marcel and Florin Nastase – for the same reason.

"The impact of these resignations is serious for FIFA too. Like UEFA, they have been subject of malicious misrepresentation in the media which has led to a politically-motivated series of prosecutions being launched against myself and several fellow members present. There is pressure from certain politicians and from some FIFA delegates for the entire FIFA Council to resign and for a new administration to take its place. They believe this is the only way FIFA will restore its reputation for honesty and integrity.

"I see no reason why any of the Vice-Presidents, the Secretary-General and myself should resign. This would be an admission of wrongdoing which I strongly deny ever took place. As for those people who say that we must appease sponsors, may I remind them that all the sponsors are in the Western world and share Western values. They all believe that only prosperous Western countries should be permitted to stage major tournaments and that countries outside their inner circle are incompetent and corrupt. You will all know that I have spent the past thirty-six years fighting this nonsense.

"I repeat what I said earlier. The powers-that-be in the West wanted one of their own to stage the next two World Cups. It was our democratic decision that Russia should hold the 2018 World Cup and Qatar should hold it in 2022. I stand by that decision and consider that FIFA's decision was fair and objective. For these reasons, I see no need for any of us to resign."

"I totally agree, Mr President" added Luis Arconada. "I've heard that the reason for the prosecutions is to boost the reputation of the US Attorney-General, Lorraine Hightower. Because she's black and female and a controversial appointment, she's got to look good. Apparently, other members of Brackley's cabinet think the prosecutions will be prohibitively expensive and will achieve very little benefit, and they're pressing her to let the matter drop. And, by the way, this will be Hightower's last year in post as the USA will have a new President next year.

"If we stand our ground, Mr President, the prosecutions will be dropped and business can return to normal."

Next to speak was Prince Hamed, the Jordanian delegate and a recently-appointed Vice-President. He was a brother of King Abdullah II.

"Mr President, fellow Members, what has been said here today betrays a complete lack of self-awareness and awareness of how we are seen. Firstly, the statement that the proposed action by the United States of America being politically motivated is ridiculous. The USA has made bribery and corruption anywhere in the world a criminal offence and it should perhaps make it clear that they are prosecuting amongst others their own delegate to CONCACAF. That is hardly the act of a partisan administration. Furthermore, there are serious questions to be asked about the awards of the 2018 and 2022 World Cups as there was a serious lack of transparency. I want to see a Middle Eastern nation stage the World Cup in my lifetime, but not if it is secured by illegal and nefarious means.

"I also think you have shown a complete misunderstanding of the Brackley administration. I have had the pleasure of dealing directly with

Secretary of State Norbury and they have been more willing than any other US Government I have experienced to treat other countries as partners. I do not believe that Attorney-General Hightower took her decision to seek prosecutions lightly and any thoughts that a new Attorney-General might let the matter drop is naïvety in the extreme."

"Everyone here must accept that FIFA has a serious image problem and radical action is needed to restore its credibility. I am afraid to say that the appointment of a new Council might be the first step to repairing its reputation."

25 April 2016
UEFA Headquarters
Route de Genève 46
Nyon
Switzerland

The new Executive Committee of UEFA had wasted little time in inviting representatives of sponsors to a meeting to assure them that UEFA had reformed its governance and to obtain assurance that sponsorship of Euro 2016 would be guaranteed.

Barely five days had passed since an emergency congress of UEFA had elected a new President and Executive Council. Gerard Basquet, the former French football international who had resigned from the Executive Council six years previously after France failed to secure Euro 2016 and had earned much credit in exposing corruption within football's governing bodies, had been elected President. Amongst the new Vice-Presidents elected were Gordon Hunter and Alun Williams. Both men had earned a lot of respect for turning the 'no-hoper' bid from Scotland and Wales for Euro 2016 into reality.

There was one remaining hurdle to clear, and that was to obtain assurance from sponsors that they were content with the standards of governance within UEFA.

Not all the prospective sponsors were world leading corporations. Euro 2016 was an opportunity for smaller businesses to get noticed. Along with major players like Coca-Cola, Adidas and McDonald's were Carlsberg, a brewing corporation with Europe as its main market, Orange, a telecommunications company, Hyundai, a Korean car manufacturer and Turkish Airlines.

Basquet opened the meeting.

"Ladies and gentlemen, good morning to you and thank you for attending today.

"You will be aware that, within the past week, the Union of European Football Associations, otherwise known as UEFA, has elected a new President, in myself, and a new Executive Council, all of whom are present today. It is my aim that UEFA will return to its core function of supporting the development of the game of association football within Europe and will bring a complete end to corruption within both this organisation and the game which has damaged its reputation.

"The purpose of this meeting will be to outline the changes to our constitution and financial accountability which will assure the world that UEFA has put its house in order since the unfortunate turn of events which has led to criminal charges being proffered against my predecessor and two former Vice-Presidents. As your organisations are all prospective sponsors of the forthcoming European Football Championships, which start in little more than six weeks' time, I want to assure you that the reputation of your organisation will not be prejudiced by association with us.

"Vice-President Alun Williams will therefore outline constitutional changes that will safeguard UEFA's reputation for good governance while Vice-President Gordon Hunter will outline changes to financial procedures which will prevent further incidences of corruption taking place. Alun, over to you."

Alun Williams walked over to the lectern.

"Ladies and gentlemen, last Friday, UEFA's new Executive Committee as its first act endorsed a new constitution. You will have a copy.

"Please turn to Article 15 which deals with personal conduct of all UEFA officials and employees. This clearly states that all officials and employees have a duty to decide and execute the organisation's business impartially and without due favour or prejudice. It also makes clear that any conduct amounting to the acceptance or offer of money or reward is a breach of their employment or terms of office and that anyone found guilty of such practice will have their employment or term of office ended. To enforce this commitment to sound governance, UEFA will be strengthening its Compliance Office, which will be staffed by former police officers, along with trained lawyers and accountants. It will be headed by Lieutenant-Colonel Hans Graber from the Zurich Cantonal Police who has kindly accepted the offer. May I now hand over to Gordon Hunter."

Hunter then replaced Williams at the lectern.

"Ladies and gentlemen, my colleague, Alun Williams, has just explained the increased profile UEFA has given to compliance. I will now summarise changes to financial procedures that have taken effect. Once again, you have copies in front of you.

"You will see that UEFA has modified its existing guidance on approval of expenditure and the placing of contracts. Existing guidance covers low and medium-level expenditure and arrangements for compliance have proved effective. But it is the higher-level expenditure and the award of contracts where there has been cause for concern. From now on, any expenditure of over one million euros or the placing of a contract for the similar value will require the written approval of the Vice-President responsible for finance. That happens to be me. Expenditure or contracts worth over five million euros will require written approval of the President and the Vice-President responsible for finance. Once the ten million euros mark has been exceeded, the written approval of the entire Executive Committee will be required. In addition, copies of all contracts and expenditure records will be shared with the Compliance Office."

Basquet returned to the lectern as Hunter took his seat.

"Ladies and gentlemen, any questions please."

Woodrow Harrison, Company Secretary for Coca-Cola signalled that he would like to speak.

"Mr Basquet, thank you for outlining the changes to governance that UEFA will be putting in place. I would like to ask how it will work in practice. My company was most concerned that previous examples of corruption have taken place at the highest level and that it was not just one, but several officials involved. I am aware that when corruption occurs at the highest levels, there is often collusion between the perpetrators and that any staff with responsibility for monitoring honesty and integrity lack the authority to challenge any wrongdoing. Can you assure me and my colleagues that the new arrangements are nothing more than a smokescreen and that, in reality, nothing will change."

"Monsieur Harrison, I understand your concerns. But I can assure you that the new arrangements are intended to work. Firstly, I as President want to see them work. I was a professional footballer for fifteen years and I do not want to see the game I love sullied by unethical behaviour. Secondly, as Vice-President Williams explained earlier, our Compliance Office will be headed up by a senior Swiss police officer. He will have the authority to question decisions made by the Executive Council and to demand evidence. And there is no point in us dismissing him as he would return to work for the police and, dare I say it, be capable of investigating us."

"May I ask other guests what they think?"

"You have certainly moved in the right direction, Herr Basquet" said Helmut Vogt, Chief Executive of Adidas. "Indeed, your new procedures are not dissimilar to those adopted by Adidas after a case ten years ago when senior company representatives were found guilty of accepting bribes."

Similar views were offered by Lucy Moro of McDonald's and Carsten Olsen of Carlsberg.

"May I take it, therefore, that you are content with UEFA's new governance arrangements and that we can count on your support for Euro 2016?" asked Basquet.

There was universal agreement.

3 May 2016
Scottish Football Association
Hampden Park
Glasgow

The mood of Gareth John, the Chief Executive of the Euro 2016 Organising Committee, matched the weather. Outside the offices of the Scottish Football Association, steady rain had been falling all day from leaden skies.

John, a former Welsh rugby international who had gone on to enjoy a successful business career, was having the penultimate monthly review meeting with the Chairmen of the Scottish and Welsh football federations before Euro 2016 started.

On paper, the mood should have been one of jubilation. All the new stadiums were ready for use. The new Swansea International Airport had been opened by the Queen a month earlier. New rolling stock for Scotrail and Arriva Trains Wales had been delivered on time and the enhanced rail service during Euro 2016 was ready to start. The improvements to the A96, A470 and A483 had been completed. Sponsors had been satisfied about UEFA's standards of governance. Finally, arrangements for security and policing were in place.

John had been aware that prospective visitors might be attracted by other events and he had successfully negotiated for two rock festivals, T in the Park and the Green Man, to be moved to coincide with Euro 2016.

However, there was one element that the Organising Committee had no control over, and that was the weather. During the opening months of 2016, the United Kingdom had suffered a long and cold winter which extended through March into the first week of April. There had been a brief warm, sunny spell which was over in three days, which had been followed by three weeks of rain.

John gave his latest situation report to Gordon Hunter and Alun Williams.

"Gordon, Alun, I've got both good news and bad news. The good news is negotiations with the Home Office and the Scottish Government for policing and security during Euro 2016 have been successfully concluded. Police Scotland and South and North Wales Police are all confident that they have the manpower to police the tournament without the need for mutual aid from English or other Welsh forces. Officers from English forces, and the Dyfed-Powys and Gwent forces will be on standby in case they are needed. The Organising Committee has set up a link to COBRA so they are aware of any potential terrorist threats to the tournament or if any organised gangs of football hooligans intend to travel. Banning orders on hooligans from England, Scotland, Wales and Northern Ireland are being implemented during Euro 2016 under which they will be prevented from travel to any of the tournament locations. Finally, we've successfully negotiated with the Ministry of Defence for the army to provide security at the grounds. The 2012 Olympics was a lesson."

John was referring to the failure of G4S, the company contracted to provide security, to recruit sufficient staff. At the last minute, the army was asked to provide security, and successfully provided it.

John then turned to the issue concerning him.

"There is one thing that, unfortunately, we cannot control, and that is the weather. You can see for yourselves."

John pointed to the window which showed the gloom and pouring rain.

"Gareth, one thing anyone from Scotland and Wales is used to is rain" joked Hunter. "Has it had any impact?"

"I'm afraid it has, Gordon" replied John. "Bookings for tickets, flights and hotels are well down on what might be expected. According to the press, the prospect of bad weather during Euro 2016 is putting off people from making bookings. There's a real prospect that we might end up making a loss."

"Gareth, you need to remember that the English press will always report negatively on anything that Wales or Scotland does" said Williams. "Their sole interest is if an event takes place in England and, particularly, London and the South East. One thing I can assure you is that football fans will travel to follow their country. And don't worry about the weather. In a month's time, the sun could be out."

"Have you made any arrangements for indoor attractions while Euro 2016 is on?" asked Hunter.

"Plenty, Gordon. Here are the details."

John handed Hunter a thick sheaf of papers.

"Mmmmmmm. Quite impressive, Gareth. Looks like the Organising Committee has covered every contingency possible. Alun, like to have a look?"

Hunter passed the papers to Williams.

"One thing more, gentlemen. You know that elections for the Scottish Government and Welsh Assembly Government are due on Thursday."

"Actually, I didn't" said Williams. "Is there anything we should be aware of?"

"Have a look at this."

John slapped down on the table copies of the previous day's *Western Mail* and the current edition of the *Scotsman*.

Both papers gave prominence to the opinion polls for the elections. The Scottish National Party was on course to retain its overall majority in the Scottish Parliament and to form its third successive administration. This was no surprise in the light of their performance in the previous year's General Election. But the major shock was in Wales where Plaid Cymru was on course to become the largest party in the Senedd. There was speculation that they might secure an overall majority.

"Gareth, how is the business world taking the prospect of having two nationalist governments to deal with?" asked Hunter.

"Not very well, Gordon" replied John. "Both the SNP and Plaid are regarded as both profligate taxers and spenders, and hostile to business. Furthermore, both their leaders have got a reputation for being outspoken. Many companies are reconsidering whether they want to invest in Scotland and Wales."

"That could blow our strategy of using Euro 2016 to attract inward investment out of the water" said Hunter.

"One person will probably be pleased with such an outcome" added Williams. "President Ivanov."

6 May 2016
BBC News

"Good morning, this is Mark Pitman with the latest news on BBC.

"Nationalist parties have taken control of both the Scottish Government and the Welsh Assembly Government following yesterday's elections to the devolved administrations. The Scottish National Party increased their overall majority in the Scottish Parliament to twelve after winning three more seats, two from the Conservatives and one from Labour. In Wales, Plaid Cymru fulfilled the prediction shown by the polls by winning thirty-two seats in the Welsh Assembly. For the first time ever, they won seats in Cardiff, Newport, the Valleys and in Wrexham.

"The leaders of the SNP and Plaid Cymru, Amy MacDougall and Rachel Norris, have hailed the results as a vindication of their policies on seeking independence for Scotland and Wales.

The election of nationalist administrations in Scotland and Wales will be a setback to the Government and will once again bring into question the constitutional future of the United Kingdom.

"In Northern Ireland, the Democratic Unionists have maintained their position as the largest party, although the main nationalist party, Sinn Fein, gained two seats. The power-sharing arrangement reached under the Good Friday Agreement will therefore continue. However, it is predicted that, within the next ten to twenty years, demographic changes will make the nationalists the largest community in Northern Ireland and that Sinn Fein could be on course to become the governing party. As with the SNP and Plaid Cymru, they are committed to leaving the United Kingdom.

"A spokesman for the Prime Minister said that the Government respects the results and seeks to maintain working relationships with the existing Governments in Scotland and Northern Ireland and with the new Government in Wales for the benefit of its residents."

17 May 2016
Russian Foreign Ministry
The Kremlin
Moscow

Alexei Primakov, the Russian Foreign Minister, had just emerged from a bruising Cabinet meeting. President Ivanov was not pleased to find out that the entire FIFA Executive Council, including the President, Joao da Costa and the Secretary-General, François Picard, had just resigned *en masse*. He fully understood the implications of this act. FIFA would be electing a new Executive Council, along with a new President and Secretary-General, who would be acceptable to Western sponsors, and one of their first acts would be to review the awards of the 2018 and 2022 World Cups. Russia faced losing the right to stage the 2018 World Cup and the likely beneficiary was England.

Primakov summoned FSB Director, General Grigoriy Tereschkov, to his office.

"Grigoriy, take a seat please. You will be aware why I've asked to see you."

"Is it about FIFA, Foreign Minister?" asked the head of the secret services.

"It is. We had several friends on the old Executive Council. Da Costa, Picard, Arconada, McKenzie and N'Konte. The new Council will almost certainly have friends of the USA and Britain and one of their first acts will be to review the award of the World Cup. Because of the lies printed in the Western media, Russia now faces the possibility of losing the World Cup in two years' time."

"So where do I fit in?" asked Tereschkov.

"Grigoriy, in just under a month's time, Euro 2016 kicks off in Britain. In Scotland and Wales, to be precise. The British Government and the English Football Association will be hoping for a successful tournament because it will strengthen England's bid to stage the next World Cup if FIFA decides to reconsider their decision to give it to us."

"I understand that the FSB has cultivated links with some of the so-called football 'ultras'. Football fans, inludng many from CSKA Moscow and Zenit St Petersburg."

"That is right, Foreign Minister" replied Tereschkov. "They have been very useful to us in intimidating opponents of the Government. And unlike their British equivalents, they are extremely fit and disciplined. It's almost like having a second army."

"Grigoriy, I want you to arrange for some of these 'ultras' to travel to Britain with the official Russian supporters' party for Euro 2016. England are due to play Russia in Edinburgh on 15 June. Imagine the impact of clashes between the two sets of supporters."

"They'll be hoovering up the remains of the England supporters after our boys get hold of them" said Tereschkov.

"That's not the main point, Grigoriy" replied Primakov. "England has a history of football hooliganism over the past fifty years that is known across the world. And it has damaged the country's interests. Thirty years ago, English clubs were banned from participating in European football competitions after Heysel. Remember that?"

Tereschkov indicated that he did.

"Furthermore, Grigoriy, England's failure to eradicate hooliganism cost them the 2006 World Cup.

"All it will take is for clashes to break out involving England supporters to rekindle the bogey of football hooliganism. No one will care who started them. All they will focus on is that English fans were involved. If that happens, England can forget any idea of staging the next World Cup."

"Leave the details to me, Foreign Minister. I'll arrange for our 'ultras' to be in Edinburgh next month."

CHAPTER 17

10 June 2016
Hampden Park
Glasgow

The opening ceremony of Euro 2016 was underway. Dancers were performing their pre-planned routines to the backdrop of techno music in a show which was intended to represent 'modern Scotland'. They would be followed on stage by four well-known rock bands, 1980s post-New Wave survivors, Big Country, 1990s Britpop-era bands Travis and Teenage Fanclub and leading hard rock band Biffy Clyro before the climax in which rock legend Rod Stewart would headline.

The opening match was due to start at 7:30pm. The joint hosts, Scotland, were due to take on World champions Germany. The match was a total sell-out with all 70,000 seats in Hampden Park taken. The two main fan zones in Glasgow, Glasgow Green and Kelvingrove Park, were packed out with Scottish and German fans who were soaking up the late afternoon sunshine.

Up in the Royal Box, the Duke of Cambridge was representing the Royal Family. Also seated were UEFA President, Gerard Basquet, the Prime Minister, David Talbot, the First Ministers of Scotland and Wales, Amy MacDougall and Rachel Norris, and the Chairmen of the Scottish and Welsh Football Federations, Gordon Hunter and Alun Williams. Talbot was slightly miffed that Amy MacDougall had a more prestigious front row seat next to the Duke and Basquet as she was the Head of Government in Scotland.

MacDougall turned to Hunter.

"Gordon, how are bookings going? I heard things were rather slow."

"That's right, First Minister. A month ago, I was worried that no one was going to come. But since the weather's changed, we've been inundated with interest. Alun met the Head of the Organising Committee earlier in the week and will be able to let you have an update."

"Gordon's right, First Minister" said Williams. "Hotel bookings have gone through the roof, and campsites are having trouble in keeping up with the demand. All campervans here and in Wales have been booked out and English operators are running short on capacity. All matches have been sold out and T in the Park and the Green Man Festival are experiencing higher demand than in previous years."

Talbot overheard the conversation.

"Mr Hunter, are you saying that Euro 2016 is on course to be a financial success?"

"You are right, Prime Minister. We expect to more than cover our costs and run up a surplus. On top of that, there's been interest from businesses to invest here and in Wales."

Talbot made a mental note to raise the issue with Ben Richardson.

13 June 2016
Premier Inn
Edinburgh Airport

Oleg Malenkov led his party of supporters to the reception desk to book them into the hotel. At first sight, there was nothing to suggest they were amongst some of Europe's most notorious football hooligans. All were smartly, if casually dressed. The only noticeable feature was that they all looked muscular, which was a result of the hours of work they put in the gym.

"Good afternoon, madam. Booking in the name of Oleg Malenkov please."

Eilidh Robertson, the pretty, blonde-haired receptionist, called up Malenkov's booking on the hotel computer.

"Ah yes, Mr Malenkov, we've got your booking. Thirty people, all travelling with the official Russian Federation football supporters party. I presume you are here for Euro 2016."

"We are. We couldn't make the opening game but we will be here for the England game and all the others. And hope Russia wins this time."

Robertson distributed plastic cards to Malenkov and his party which would enable them to access their rooms.

"I hope you enjoy yourselves while you are here in Scotland" said Robertson.

We have every thought of doing that, thought Malenkov.

The same day
UK Football Policing Unit
Canterbury Court
Lambeth Road
London

Julie Benson was preparing to go home when the phone rang. As she was the last but one member of staff in the office, she took the call.

"Hello Julie, Neil Yates here, British Transport Police, Heathrow. Have you got a minute?"

Benson knew Yates well. He was a Detective Inspector based at London's main airport and was responsible for liaising with Border Force about suspect immigrants and had responsibility during Euro 2016 for focusing on attempts by foreign football hooligans to enter the country.

"Julie, we've got a positive match on twelve Russians who entered the country today on an official tour party. Europol has got records of convictions for violent offences in Germany, the Netherlands and Italy. I'm almost a hundred per cent certain they're here for the England game on Wednesday. Can you make sure that COBRA and Police Scotland are notified."

"Will do, Neil" replied Benson. "By the way, how come we've let them in if they had previous convictions?"

"They're on an officially-sanctioned tour party, Julie. All granted tourist visas following applications on their behalf by the Russian Foreign Ministry. When they came in, they all looked bona fide. Problem with Russian nationals is that we don't get much co-operation from their Government. Consequently, we had to go through Europol. And their records take time to obtain. As these guys had a connecting flight to catch and there was nothing immediately to hand that identified them as potential troublemakers, we had to let them go."

The Deputy Director of the Football Policing Unit, Tom Somerville, was still in the office.

"Tom, can I have a quick word?"

"Sure, Julie. I assume it was about the phone call you just took."

"Tom, that was Neil Yates. Apparently, twelve hardcore Russian hooligans have slipped into the country. Sounds like they're planning to cause trouble at the England match. He wants COBRA and Police Scotland to be contacted."

"Jesus Christ!" swore Somerville. "That's all we need – Russkie hoolies here for a ruck. Julie, how the hell did Borders let them in?"

"From what Neil told me, they were all part of an officially-sanctioned party. It was only when their names were run through Europol that anything suspicious came up."

"Thanks, Julie. I'll get in touch with COBRA. You can go home now – it's getting late."

Somerville then dialled in an encrypted number for COBRA. It was an acronym for the Cabinet Office Briefing Room and was brought into use whenever there was a national emergency or a highly sensitive public event where there was a risk of disorder. Membership was drawn from the Cabinet Office, Prime Minister's Office, Home Office, MI5, the police and other Government departments with an interest. It had previously been use during the 1984 Miners Strike and the London terrorist bombings in July 2005.

"COBRA, can I help?" A female voice was on the other end of the line.

"Tom Somerville, UK Football Policing Unit here. Just received some intelligence about football hooligans travelling to Euro 2016."

"Go ahead."

"Twelve Russian nationals, all with previous records for violence across Europe, entered the country earlier today. I've got the full details of their names, dates of birth and passport numbers. All are staying at the Premier Inn at Edinburgh Airport."

"How come they got in? I thought we could refuse entry to any foreign national with a criminal record."

"All were travelling with a tour party officially sanctioned by the Russian authorities. The criminal records only came up after we ran their names past Europol."

Somerville then realised there were potentially more serious implications for the country than he initially thought.

"Can I speak to someone from the Foreign and Commonwealth Office?"

Ten seconds later, Rebecca Vallance was on the other end of the line. She was a high-flying official who had been seconded to COBRA during Euro 2016."

"Hello Tom, I believe you've got some intel on Russian hooligans. How can I help?"

"Rebecca, the twelve guys reported are all with an official tour party. Sounds like they've got some ulterior motive for coming here. Anything I should know of?"

"Tom, it might be related to the World Cup" said Vallance. "FIFA has just replaced its Executive Council following a corruption scandal and they are going to revisit the award of the 2018 World Cup. There's a chance that England might be awarded it. But you will understand that any hooliganism involving England supporters, could undermine its case to stage the World Cup."

"So, you reckon this mob are here to deliberately start some aggro with the England supporters to stop them getting the World Cup?" asked Somerville.

"Can't be sure, Tom" replied Vallance. "But we're going to let Police Scotland have the details of these guys once you send them."

"Rebecca, you are aware that these guys are on an official party, don't you? Sounds like they've got the official backing of the Russian Foreign Ministry."

"Tom, it's well known that the police and the FSB use many of the football hooligans as an unofficial militia to intimidate opponents of President Ivanov. That's why they've managed to get official backing for their trip."

"What will happen if the police lift them?" asked Somerville.

"I doubt that will happen yet, Tom" replied Vallance. "But if they start any trouble, that will be a different matter. By the way, one thing both the Home Secretary and Foreign Secretary have made clear is that they will refuse to be bullied by the Russian Government if any of their nationals are arrested during Euro 2016."

"Thank God for that."

15 June 2016
Murrayfield Stadium
Edinburgh

Murrayfield had been built over ninety years earlier and had served as the headquarters of the Scottish Rugby Union. It had been used for football only once before but because it could hold 67,000 spectators, it had been selected as one of the venues for Euro 2016.

The match between England and Russia was now in the 69th minute and England were holding a 1-0 lead, courtesy of a goal in the twenty-fifth minute from Spurs midfielder Nathaniel Dyer. England had won their opening match against Wales four days earlier 2-1 and victory would ensure their passage to the second round.

Chief Superintendent Doug Murray of Police Scotland was also relieved as there had been no trouble all day. Earlier in the day, English and Russian supporters had been mingling and drinking together in the pubs of the Old Town and Rose Street and there was a sense that the scourge of football hooliganism had been consigned to the history books for all time.

The North, West and most of the East Stands were occupied by England supporters. The Russians had the South Stand and a part of the East Stand. A metal fence, hastily erected in the East Stand, segregated the English and Russian supporters.

Earlier that day, Oleg Malenkov had met up with Pavel Bobrov, leader of the Zenit St Petersburg Ultras, to discuss their plans to ambush the England supporters. In Russia, the CSKA and Zenit fans had a history of bloody clashes. But this time, they would be on the same side. Fighting for Mother Russia.

As the 70th minute of the match approached, Malenkov and Bobrov gave a three-finger sign to their fellow supporters. That was the sign to go into battle.

Within seconds, over thirty Russian ultras had scaled the metal fence separating them from the England supporters and stormed into the enclosure where the England supporters were sitting, throwing punches and kicks.

Pre-emptive action by the Home Office and the police had prevented all of England's most notorious football hooligans from travelling to Euro 2016. They had been required to report to the nearest local police station daily to prevent them from travelling. But there were still many England supporters who were ready for a fight and, with a bellyful of alcohol inside them, needed little encouragement.

Within a minute, a full-scale pitched battle was taking place in the East Stand.

16 June 2016
Home Office
2 Marsham Street
London

"Get me the First Minister. I want to speak to her. Now!"

Sarah Crosby was furious. Home Office officials had acted promptly to an intelligence report about the arrival of known hooligans from Russia and shared it with Police Scotland, only for the Scots to apparently ignore it.

The headlines on the newspapers pled on her desk told the full story of the violent clashes between English and Russian football supporters in

Edinburgh the previous day. **SHAMEFUL** read the headline in the *Sun*. The *Daily Mirror's* headline was **WARZONE**. **DRAGGED THROUGH THE MUD** greeted readers of the *Daily Mail*. **ENGLAND FACING EXPULSION FROM EURO 2016** was the headline in the *Guardian*.

Clashes between the two groups of supporters continued after the match had finished. Running battles between English and Russian supporters took place down the full length of Princes Street and the Royal Mile. Shop windows were smashed and a tram was derailed after a metal street sign was thrown into its path. Over 100 supporters were in police custody and the Sheriff Court was holding an all-night session to deal with all the miscreants brought before it.

The implications of the disorder were serious. UEFA had voiced its displeasure at the hooliganism that had occurred and they were considering sanctions against both Russia and England. However, FIFA were also sighted and it would have implications for their review of the decision to hold the 2018 World Cup in Russia. If Russia was to lose the right to hold the World Cup, it now looked unlikely that England would take its place after the previous night's disorder.

"First Minister here." Amy MacDougall was on the other end of the line.

"Well, First Minister. You haven't covered yourself in much glory."

MacDougall recognised the voice of Sarah Crosby.

"What the hell do you mean, Home Secretary?" snapped MacDougall. "And I need to remind you about protocol. If you want to speak to me, you go through the Prime Minister or Jason Berry. You do no' speak to me direct."

"Don't bandy words with me, First Minister" shouted Crosby. "Two days ago, my officials notified Police Scotland that several high-risk football hooligans had arrived from Russia, hell-bent on causing trouble at the England match. And what does Police Scotland do? Sweet F.A. if you ask me."

"May I point out, Home Secretary, that the law does not permit us to arrest people who might commit an offence. I believe that is the law in England and Wales as well as Scotland. We've not yet reached Minority Report."

MacDougall was referring to the Hollywood film in which the police could predicy which people would commit crimes in the future and arrest them before they had the opportunity.

"That is not the point, First Minister" spat Crosby. "Police Scotland, for whom you are responsible, knew that potential troublemakers were planning to attend the England v Russia match with the intent of causing violent disorder, yet nothing was done until trouble had broken out."

"If you keep up with the news, Home Secretary, you will find that all the Russian perpetrators are in police custody." MacDougall was referring to the mass arrests that morning of the entire groups of Russian supporters at their hotels.

"Too late, First Minister. I am less than impressed in the way both the Scottish Government and Police Scotland have performed. I will be recommending that the Home Office takes over full responsibility for policing of Euro 2016."

17 June 2016
UEFA Headquarters
Route de Genève 46
Nyon
Switzerland

"Re-run the video, Mr President. You will see the point I'm trying to make."

Greg Day, Deputy Chairman of the Football Association and England's delegate on UEFA, had spent the previous hour trying to convince UEFA's Executive Council that England's supporters had not instigated the violence that had broken out at the Euro 2016 Group match between England and Russia two days earlier. Gerard Basquet, UEFA's President had been at Murrayfield that day and, appalled by the scenes of violence in the city known as the "Athens of the North", had convened an extraordinary meeting of the Executive Council to decide what sanctions to take.

Day was aware that, even though the last serious outbreak of violence involving England supporters had taken place sixteen years previously, many UEFA delegates still remembered the dark days of the 1980s when repeated violence and vandalism by English football fans earned them a six-year ban from all UEFA competitions. Some delegates were talking about expelling both Russia and England from Euro 2016.

Basquet's Executive Assistant, Elke Muller, reset the video taken from CCTV coverage to the sixty-ninth minute of the game and pressed "Play".

The video was not focusing on the game. Instead, it replayed coverage of what was happening in the East Stand at Murrayfield and, particularly, the southern section where the England and Russia supporters stood divided by a barrier. As the seventieth minute of the match approached, it clearly showed several Russian supporters getting up from their seats. Two men, one tall, the other much shorter, gave three-finger signs. Barely a split second later, the Russians are seen charging towards the barriers and climbing over them before launching into the England supporters.

"Stop it there!" shouted Day. "You can all see that the Russian supporters were the clear aggressors."

"Objection!" shouted Oleg Grishin, Russia's UEFA delegate. "What that video does not show was the outrageous provocation that our supporters received from the English. They were singing obscene songs about our dear President and the unfortunate seamen who died when the *Kaliningrad* sunk."

Grishin was referring to the tragedy which took place the previous year when a submarine from the Russian Navy sank in the North Atlantic with the loss of all its crew.

"I suggest you replay that clip with the sound turned up."

"Very well, Oleg, we'll do that to see if your claim has any grounds. Elke, please run the video back to the 69th minute and, this time, turn the volume up."

Muller pressed the reset button on the console, then pressed "Play" again.

With the volume turned up, it was possible to hear the noise from the two sets of supporters. The England supporters were in good voice and they were singing a song to the tune of "The Grand Old Duke of York".

When you're up, you're up.

When you're down, you're down.

And when you're flying Aeroflot, you're never off the ground.

The England supporters were making fun of the Russian flag carrier's poor reputation for reliability and safety. Several members of the Executive Council could not help sniggering like schoolboys at what they considered to be an innocuous, if funny, chant.

Two minutes later, Basquet signalled that he and fellow Executive Council members wished to retire to the boardroom to make their deliberation.

"Well, gentlemen, what do you make of it?" asked Basquet.

"There was definitely provocation by the English supporters" said Greece's delegate Andreas Stylianou. "You heard the chants they were making. If we punish Russia, we have to punish England as well."

"Sorry Andreas, I don't agree" said Martin Ekstrom, Sweden's delegate. "I've heard a lot more offensive chants in domestic matches so it's stretching a bit far to blame England's supporters for provoking the Russians."

Next to speak was Gordon Hunter, Scotland's delegate.

"What you've all seem to have forgotten is that those Russian supporters had every intention to attack. You can see it from the body language, the signals given. It was planned, not spontaneous and would have taken place even if England's supporters had been silent. Sure, England's supporters are no angels and have many in their number looking for an excuse to fight. But the same could go for any country. Believe me, I have seen Old Firm matches that have turned into bloodbaths."

Hunter was referring to matches between Glasgow Celtic and Glasgow Rangers where animosity between Roman Catholics and Protestants going back over 300 years fuelled violence between the supporters of the rival clubs.

"It would be unjust to punish England" said Alun Williams, Wales delegate. "I have seen for myself the considerable efforts to rein in the hooligan problem they used to have. However, we need to take action against Russia. The supporters who caused the trouble were on a Government-sanctioned tour party and, as the video showed, they were the clear aggressors."

"You are not suggesting that we throw Russia out of Euro 2016, are you?" shouted the Bulgarian delegate, Georgi Bonev. "Remember, they are holding the next World Cup."

"I think we would all want to avoid that, Georgi" replied Hunter. "But you saw from the video that supporters from an officially-sanctioned party caused serous disorder. The implications for the game are huge. We've only recently managed to regain the confidence of sponsors."

"Doing nothing's not an option" added Williams.

"Gentlemen, I think we've spent sufficiently long discussing who was responsible for the trouble and what action to take" said Basquet. "We should decide what action should be taken."

Basquet then presented the options.

"First option. To expel Russia from Euro 2016."

Only one hand went up. It was from Predrag Boban of Croatia.

"Not carried."

"Second option. To expel England from Euro 2016."

No hands went up.

"Not carried."

"Third option. To fine the Russian Football Federation the sum of 150,000 euros and to issue a formal warning about the future conduct of their supporters."

Eleven hands went up.

"Carried."

"Fourth option. To fine the English Football Association the sum of 100,000 euros and to issue a formal warning about the future conduct of their supporters."

Only three hands were raised.

"Not carried."

"Fifth option. To give the English Football Association a formal warning about the future conduct of their supporters."

Nine hands were raised.

"Carried."

"Thank you, gentlemen" said Basquet. Let us return to the main chamber."

The same day
Scottish Government
St Andrew's House
Regent Road
Edinburgh

"Come in, Stuart. Take a seat please."

Sir Stuart Rankin, Chief Constable of Police Scotland, knew he was in for a grilling from Scotland's First Minister. The newspapers on both sides of the border had lambasted Police Scotland for their perceived incompetence in failing to control violence between English and Russian football supporters two days earlier. Amongst the stories in the press was a rumour that the Home Secretary, Sarah Crosby, was planning to exercise exceptional powers to take control of policing of Euro 2016 from the Scottish Government.

"Stuart, what happened two days' ago was totally unacceptable" rasped Amy MacDougall. "Euro 2016 was going to be an opportunity to showcase Scotland to the world. Instead, all that foreign visitors see are smashed up property and violent brawling. Does wonders for our image. On top of that,

I've just been on the end of a lecture from Sarah Crosby about how to run my country."

Rankin was determined to stand his ground.

"First Minister, I should point out that over one hundred arrests have been made and, already, forty Russians have been deported from the country."

"Great, but the fact remains that Police Scotland failed to act on intelligence supplied by the UK Football Policing Unit through COBRA. Why was that?"

"I'm afraid I can't explain yet, First Minister" replied Rankin. "But I can assure you that I am taking this dereliction of duty most seriously and there will be severe disciplinary implications for any of my officers found responsible. Furthermore, I've just put into place a new policing strategy for the remaining matches in Scotland which will focus on segregating different groups of supporters and using greater intelligence on planned hooligan activity. Already, seconded police officers from France, Germany, Italy and Turkey will be arriving later today and they will receive briefing from the respective Borough Commanders."

"Stuart, I hope for your sake that this works" said MacDougall. "If it doesn't, you might find yourself reporting to Sarah Crosby."

11 July 2016
Principality Stadium
Cardiff

Ninety minutes of play had already taken place in the final of Euro 2016 at Wales' national stadium which had been renamed earlier that year following sponsorship from the Principality Building Society. Spain, the holders, were leading France by three goals to two.

The indicator board came on. There were another six minutes of time added on to play.

Even though the sun had just sunk below the western horizon, the temperature was still in the low seventies. Players from both sides were feeling exhausted and both managers, José Marquez of Spain and Thierry Coquelin of France, knew the risk of a player making a mistake was high. Both managers shouted exhortations at their teams; Marquez wanted his side to pull back in numbers and retain possession, Coquelin emphasised the need to look for a third goal that would take the match to extra time.

By the ninety-fifth minute, Marquez's tactics appeared to have won the game for Spain. They had successfully contained France's final attacks and had denied them possession. It would be their third successive victory in the European Football Championships.

However, as the final minute of the match started, France had a gilt-edged opportunity. Midfielder Moussa Hamdaoui saw striker Patrice Auriol unmarked and rifled an inch-perfect pass which split open the Spanish defence.

"There's less than a minute to go here in the final of Euro 2016 and Spain are just holding onto their lead...........Hamdaoui's found Auriol and he's clear. Is this the goal that takes the match to extra time?"

Spain's goalkeeper, Daniel Comaneci was a Romanian by birth and had gone to live in Spain with his parents from the age of ten. He was the first of Spain's large Romanian community to represent his adopted country. Seeing Auriol advancing on his goal, he advanced adopting a wide stance to narrow the angles available to the French striker. At six feet four inches, he was almost a foot taller than the dimunitive Frenchman. If he could dive and smother the ball, all would be safe. The risk was that, if Auriol was brought down, France would have a penalty.

"Comaneçi's off his line and he's saved. That could have won Euro 2016 for Spain."

Fifteen seconds later, referee Mark Catling, blew for full-time. The jubilant Spanish players leapt for joy and embraced Comaneci.

The closing ceremony for Euro 2016 was already underway and ex-punk rockers, the Alarm, were on stage. They were to be followed by emerging band Catfish and the Bottlemen, the Manic Street Preachers, the Stereophonics before legendary singer Tom Jones took to the stage.

Inside the main hospitality suite, the VIPs gathered to discuss how the tournament had gone. UEFA President, Gerard Basquet, was present, as were vice-Presidents Gordon Hunter and Alun Williams. Prime Minister David Talbot was also present, as were his French and Spanish counterparts, Manuel Betancourt and Francisco Rodriguez. They were joined by the First Ministers of Scotland and Wales, Amy MacDougall and Rachel Norris who were representing the devolved Governments of the countries which hosted the tournament.

There were considerable grounds for optimism about the impact of Euro 2016. Both Scotland and Wales had been blessed with five weeks of uncharacteristically hot, sunny weather and overseas supporters turned up in record numbers to see the matches. All matches were sell-outs. In addition, pubs, restaurants and tourist venues all reported significant upturns in their income, while the T in the Park and Green Man rock festivals also reported the highest attendances on record.

The tournament had been a good-natured one, with the only incidence of trouble being in the England v Russia match in Edinburgh on 15 June. Following that match, Police Scotland and the North Wales and South Wales forces expanded their intelligence-gathering operations and brought in seconded police officers from other European countries to identify potential troublemakers. The remainder of the tournament had passed off without incident and Hunter and Williams were delighted to hear Basquet praise the behaviour of the Scottish and Welsh supporters and the welcome the public had given to visitors.

The icing on the cake had been the performance of the two host nations, both of whom progressed to the semi-final stage. Both David Talbot and Football Association chairman Richard Bentley reflected ruefully on England's performance. England had made it to the second stage of Euro 2016, but were beaten by Iceland. It had been one of the most humiliating defeats in the country's history and brought into question the commitment of what many people considered to be their overpaid footballers.

Euro 2016 had been a personal triumph, not only for Gordon Hunter and Alun Williams who had persevered in making Euro 2016 happen when many people saw it as a car crash waiting to happen, but also for Amy MacDougall and Rachel Norris. Euro 2016 had raised the profile of Scotland and Wales. Not only had income from tourism risen but, also, the Scottish Government and Welsh Assembly Government had used Euro 2016 as an opportunity to promote their countries' food and drinks industries and to attract inward investment. Already, HSBC and Samsung had promised to make inward investment in Scotland and Wales, and other multinational corporations were showing interest.

Noting the presence of Talbot, MacDougall and Norris made their move.

"Prime Minister, may Rachel and I have a wee word with you" asked MacDougall.

"Very well, Amy. But please make it short as I've got to go back to London tonight."

"We will" said Norris.

"Prime Minister, I think that, excepting for a wee bit of 'bother' in Edinburgh last month, Euro 2016 has shown that Scotland and Wales can manage their affairs very well."

"I certainly don't deny that, ladies" replied Talbot. "I've been most impressed in the way that Euro 2016 has been run."

"Then why has the Government been stalling on proposals for extending devolution to Scotland and Wales?" asked MacDougall.

"I think 'stalling' is a bit unfair, Amy" replied Talbot. "HMG has got a lot on its plate at present. We're having to prepare the ground for the referendum on EU membership later this year and, in addition, we are having to enact further legislation to combat terrorism. We simply don't have the Parliamentary time at present for other legislation, but I can assure you that we've not rowed back on our commitment to consider further devolution."

"Only 'consider', Prime Minister? You've had the reports of the Macpherson and Williams commissions for over a year now."

Norris was referring to reviews commissioned by the Government on further devolution of powers to Scotland and Wales. They had recommended full devolution of taxation and spending to the Scottish Government and the partial devolution of tax-raising powers and the full devolution of crime and policing to the Welsh Assembly Government.

"I recognise that." Talbot was getting rather flustered. "As I said before, the Government will get round to it once we've got the EU referendum out of the way."

"We'll hold you to that, Prime Minister" said Norris.

13 July 2016
Rue Perronet
Neuilly-sur-Seine
Paris

François Picard had not bothered to watch the final of Euro 2016. The fact that tournament had taken place in countries other than France and had been a resounding success brought home the enormity of what he had done six years earlier. The only reason he had backed the Scotland and Wales bid was to undermine England's bid for the 2018 World Cup. He had not expected Scotland and Wales to follow through and run a successful tournament. And to make matters worse, Gerard Basquet was lording it over the proceedings as President of UEFA.

At 1:30pm, the doorbell rang. Cècile Picard went to answer it. A blonde American woman was at the door. Sarah Friedman was a prosecutor from the Department of Justice in Washington DC and had come to discuss with François Picard the impending criminal prosecution for corruption that the US authorities were pursuing.

"Madame Picard? My name is Sarah Friedman and I'm from the Department of Justice in the USA. Is your husband there?"

"He is. Come this way." Cècile Picard led Friedman into the lounge.

"François. Sarah Friedman. I understand you were expecting her."

Picard got up and shook the hand of the American prosecutor.

"Mademoiselle Friedman. Shall we go to my study? We'll have a bit more privacy there."

Once in the study, Picard pulled out a chair for Friedman and sat down opposite her.

"Monsieur Picard, I'm here to discuss your forthcoming court case. The charges against you are extremely serious. If you are found guilty, you will be looking to face a sentence of thirty years in prison."

Picard gasped.

"I thought that would be your reaction. However, I'm willing to discuss options that may result in more lenient treatment. Or possibly no action being taken."

"What are they, Mademoiselle?" asked Picard.

"We could offer a plea bargain which could result in a lesser sentence. The most you would get is six months in an open prison. Or you could offer to turn State evidence."

"You mean give evidence for the prosecution?" asked Picard.

"That's right" replied Friedman.

Picard stopped in his tracks to give some thought to what Friedman had just said. Turning State evidence would get him out of this predicament. He would be a free man. But he also thought what future would he face. He was already a figure of hate in his own country for stitching them up over Euro 2016 and in sullying their reputation by accepting bribes. His career at FIFA was certainly over. But betraying men like Joao da Costa who had supported his promotion to the position of Secretary-General, and Orville McKenzie and Amadou N'Konte, who had done so much work for promoting football in developing countries, would gain him even more enemies than he had already. And how would the Russians react? They were not known as good losers.

Picard also took time to eye up Friedman. Her large nose, which betrayed her Jewish origin, spoiled an otherwise attractive face but she had a nice figure and her short skirt showed a shapely pair of legs. If she hadn't been there on official business about his prosecution, Picard might have been tempted to ask her out.

One thought which crossed his mind was whether France or Switzerland would seek to prosecute him if the Americans dropped all charges.

"One question I've got, Mademoiselle. If I decide to turn State evidence and you decide to drop charges, will the French or Swiss authorities still seek to prosecute me?"

"I can't confirm that at present, Monsieur Picard" replied Friedman. "But in previous cases of this kind, other jurisdictions have generally not proceeded with prosecutions against people who have co-operated with the prosecution."

"If you can obtain confirmation from the French and Swiss authorities that I will not be prosecuted, I am content to provide evidence for the prosecution."

CHAPTER 18

9 November 2016
Cabinet Room
10 Downing Street
London

Sarah Crosby, the new Prime Minister, was preparing to chair her first Cabinet meeting in her new role. Her two Chiefs of Staff, Fiona Gilchrist and Greg Nicholas, whom she had brought with her from the Home Office, were giving directions to civil servants about the seating plan, the agenda and timings and the additional papers that the Cabinet would require.

It is said that a week in politics is a long time. For David Talbot, the last three weeks seemed like a lifetime. Only a month earlier, he had been delivering the leader's speech at the Conservative Party Conference. Just over a week later, the country held the referendum on whether to remain in or leave the European Union that Talbot had promised in the party's Election Manifesto back in 2015. Most people expected that, despite the grumbles that people had about the European Union and its lack of accountability, the country would vote to remain.

What happened on 13 October was a cataclysmic shock. The United Kingdom had voted, albeit by the narrow margin of fifty-one per cent to forty-nine per cent, to leave the European Union.

The overriding reason behind people voting to leave had been immigration. There had been two sources. One had been the formerly Communist countries of Eastern Europe which had been joining the European Union from 2004 onwards. There had been high volumes of migrants from Poland, Lithuania, Bulgaria and Romania, many of whom were highly skilled. Employers could offer them lower wages than British workers would expect and they had taken jobs that would have otherwise been filled from the domestic labour market. In addition, many brought families with them and it put pressure on housing, schools, the National Health Service and public transport.

The other source of immigration was North Africa and the Middle East. Nearly all were Muslim and many people felt they were failing to integrate with the indigenous community and were forming ghettoes which were 'no-go' areas for white people. Hostility had been reinforced by several incidents of terrorism in the name of Islam over the previous decade.

For Talbot, who had campaigned vigorously for the United Kingdom to remain, it represented a total loss of personal credibility. The day after the referendum, he resigned as Prime Minister.

The campaign to appoint a new leader was relatively short. The early front runner for the leadership was the flamboyant former Mayor of London, Hugo Fentiman, but he withdrew his bid early on following a series of embarrassing disclosures about his past. Eventually, it ended up as a contest between two women, Sarah Crosby, the Home Secretary and Angela Lawrence, Secretary of State for National Heritage. Crosby, who had been in the Cabinet since 2010 and in by far the most difficult post, won easily and had been declared leader on 3 November.

Crosby had been ruthless in taking an axe to the Cabinet that had served under Talbot. Two very high-profile dismissals were James Hamilton, the Chancellor of the Exchequer and Martin Vine, Secretary of State for Education. Caroline Russell became the new Chancellor of the Exchequer while Ben Richardson took Crosby's former post of Home Secretary.

Two appointments which raised eyebrows were Hugo Fentiman as Foreign Secretary and Mark Rudge as Secretary of State for Brexit. Fentiman, despite his excellent record in office as Mayor of London, was regarded as something of a loose cannon with the potential to embarrass the Government. Rudge's recall to the Cabinet was however controversial as he had been dismissed the previous year for a breach of Cabinet discipline. Although nothing had been said publicly, it was no secret that Rudge had leaked details of the FBI's investigation into corruption within FIFA to its Secretary-General.

Crosby's priorities were to get on with taking the United Kingdom out of the European Union and to use the departure to secure advantageous trade deals. She was however aware how divisive the referendum had been. There was a clear split on age, with the numbers voting to leave the European Union increasing amongst older voters. Nowhere more had this been demonstrated by comparing the 18-24 age group, where sixty-four per cent voted to remain against the 65 and over age group, where fifty-eight per cent had voted to leave.

There was also a significant difference between the way England voted and the Celtic countries. Apart from London, where sixty per cent voted to remain in the European Union, the rest of England voted to leave and, in parts of the country, over seventy per cent voted to leave. In contrast, Scotland, Northern Ireland and Wales all voted to remain. Crosby had already been on the receiving end of demands from the Scottish First Minister, Amy MacDougall and the Welsh First Minister, Rachel Norris, for Scotland and Wales to be exempted from leaving the single market, while Northern Ireland's Deputy First Minister, Gerry Doherty, had been calling for a referendum on Irish unification.

At 10am, Crosby signalled that the meeting was ready to start.

"Good morning, everyone. You should have in front of you the papers that were distributed last Friday. I addition, there are some further supplementary papers. Fiona, Greg, have they been distributed?"

She pointed to her Chiefs of Staff.

"They have, Prime Minister" replied Nicholas.

"Excellent. We can start."

Crosby then went on to set the scene for the new Cabinet.

"You will be aware that there has been a lot of uncertainty about the Government's direction following the vote to leave the European Union. That uncertainty will end forthwith. This Government intends to fulfil the obligations imposed by the result of the referendum. In short, we will be leaving the European Union without fail. I do not anticipate a radical change of direction for this Government. However, I want to make it clear that it will be a Government for the people of Britain so some of our policies may need to change.

"As a first step, I want you to summarise your Department's key policies and priorities, where we stand at present and our intended future direction. Caroline, can you start."

Crosby pointed to Caroline Russell, the first ever female Chancellor of the Exchequer.

Russell was followed by the Secretaries of State for the most important Departments of State, namely Ben Richardson, the Home Secretary, Hugo

Fentiman, the Foreign Secretary, Bob Anderson, the Attorney-General and Noel O'Brien, the Secretary of State for Defence. There were no surprises with the policy priorities. For the Chancellor of the Exchequer, it was maintaining tight control over the public purse strings and a further round of public expenditure cuts were planned. For the Home Secretary, it was strengthening the surveillance powers of the police and security services to combat the terrorist threat posed by Al-Q'aida and Islamic State. For the Foreign Secretary, it was pursuing new trade agreements following the vote to leave the European Union. For the Attorney-General, it was accelerating plans for reform of the criminal justice system while, for the Secretary of State for Defence, it was modernising the Royal Navy and Royal Air Force to deal with the growing threat from Russia and China.

Next to speak was Jason Berry, Secretary of State for the Environment, Communities and Local Government.

"Prime Minister, members of the Cabinet, here are the Departmental priorities for the Department for the Environment, Communities and Local Government. Firstly, housing. The issue of affordability has now become a problem which potentially has a negative impact on the future prosperity of the country. With the average price of a property in London and the South East being over ten times the average national salary, people are unable to get on the property ladder and employers are finding it increasingly difficult to recruit and retain skilled staff. This is impacting on the country's prosperity at a critical time. With the United Kingdom leaving the European Union, it is essential that we hold onto skilled and able workers.

"We are therefore planning to introduce legislation to remove much of the red tape that applies to planning and to encourage new development. A Bill will be introduced early in 2017."

"Jason, do you anticipate any contentious issues?" asked Crosby.

"Only that some of the protections under the Green Belt will be relaxed. The Green Belt has been a perennial obstacle to new development, but I think the overall housing situation has become so serious that action is needed. It was introduced during the 1930s. Conditions have changed considerably since then."

There were a few murmurs of discontent. Several Cabinet members represented constituencies where the Green Belt was located and they knew the potential reaction of their constituents to plans to build on the Green Belt.

"Secondly, electoral reform. You will be aware that, shortly after being re-elected, we commissioned Lord Bridgeman to carry out a review of voting practice and procedure. This was a result of the disgraceful events that took place in Tower Hamlets."

In 2014, the London Borough of Tower Hamlets held its first election for the post of Mayor. Although the Conservative, Labour and Liberal Democrat parties all fielded candidates, the election was won by an independent, Habibur Choudhury, who had been expelled from the Labour Party the previous year. Serious allegations of electoral malpractice were made, including the abuse of postal voting, use of false identity to vote, intimidation of voters by supporters of Choudhury who were milling outside polling stations and pressure being brought on the large Muslim community in the borough by local imams. The Labour Party and Conservative Party both lodged complaints with the Electoral Commissioner about the conduct of the election and the Commissioner found in their favour. The election had to be re-run and court proceedings were taken against Choudhury, resulting in his disqualification in running for electoral office.

The Government's response was to appoint Lord Bridgeman, a former Cabinet Minister who had retired as an MP in 2015, to chair a review of electoral practice and procedure. It had issued its report two months previously.

Berry continued.

"Lord Bridgeman's report was received in September and we have been considering its recommendations. We are planning to pilot a scheme whereby voters are required to produce evidence of their identity, such as a passport or photographic driving licence. This will be piloted in the following local government areas: Tower Hamlets, Newham, Lambeth, Greenwich, Brent, Hounslow, Slough, Luton, Birmingham, Leicester, Bradford, Oldham, Burnley and Blackburn. In addition, we will be piloting the restriction of postal voting to people who are unable to travel to polling stations because of age, infirmity or disability."

"Jason, don't you think those proposals seem rather contentious?" asked Fentiman. "All the areas targeted have sizeable ethnic minority populations. It will convey the impression that this Government regards minority communities as untrustworthy and will undo our efforts to reach out to them."

"I accept they are likely to be contentious, Hugo" replied Berry. "But there is real concern across the country about electoral fraud. If we do nothing, it will lead to a greater divide between the indigenous community and migrants as it will give the impression that migrant communities are being allowed special privileges."

"I'm with Jason on this one, Hugo" said the Prime Minister.

"Finally, the Scotland and Wales Bills have been prepared for a first reading in January" continued Berry. "The Scotland Bill will give the Scottish Government full tax-raising powers. The Wales Bill will give the Welsh Assembly Government partial tax-raising powers and will devolve crime and policing. However, before proceeding, I want the Cabinet to consider whether further devolution remains a Government priority. Prime Minister, I know your views about devolution and would not wish to proceed if the Cabinet is like-minded."

"Thank you for referring this matter, Jason" said Crosby. "You are quite right in saying that I have reservations about devolving further powers to Scotland and Wales. Can you stay on at the end of Cabinet to discuss this matter further."

The last Minister to speak before the agenda moved onto the second item, which was Brexit, was Seb Mitchell, newly appointed to the Cabinet as Secretary of State for National Heritage. Having first explained that his Department would be scaling down proposals to regulate the media, Mitchell then turned to the 2018 World Cup.

"Prime Minister, members of the Cabinet, you should be aware that, next month, FIFA will be announcing the result of the re-bidding for the 2018 World Cup. The Football Association has submitted a new bid and, now that FIFA has changed its rules and is allowing a vote of all member countries rather than by its Council, I am optimistic that England will be chosen to stage the next World Cup. Can I assume that the Government will be in support?"

There was unanimous agreement round the table.

Once the Cabinet meeting had finished, the Prime Minister and Jason Berry retreated to the Prime Minister's personal office.

"Jason, I was most grateful for you bringing up the issue of the Scotland and Wales Bills. You are quite right about how I feel. I do not want to see further devolution to either country. Frankly, both First Ministers are a complete pain in the backside."

"I know, Prime Minister. I have to deal with them regularly."

"Jason, you will be aware that our forthcoming departure from the European Union will be an event of great magnitude. I can see potential opportunity for the United Kingdom to be a great trading nation once again. But there are also dangers ahead. The European Union will have a vested interest in us failing as it will deter other countries from leaving. Russia and China will be seeking to exploit divisions, as will terrorist organisations such as Al-Q'aida and Islamic State."

Crosby continued.

"The United Kingdom has got to present a united front over the next few years if it is to make a success of its departure from Europe. That is not going to be achieved if the Scottish and Welsh Governments continue making noisy demands for separate treatment. You will have heard MacDougall and Norris asking to be allowed to stay within the single market."

"I therefore want you to suspend all further action on the Scotland and Wales Bills."

"Consider that done, Prime Minister."

"One more thing, Jason" said Crosby. "I want you to start a study into reclaiming powers from the devolved Governments. Specifically, tax-raising, criminal justice and policing in Scotland and health and education in both Scotland and Wales."

There was a sharp intake of breath from Berry. He knew that the Prime Minister had been a long-standing opponent of devolution ever since it had been introduced under the Labour government in 1999, but he did not think that she would go as far as clawing back powers.

"Prime Minister, are you serious?" asked Berry.

"Yes, I am, Jason" replied Crosby. "The performance of Police Scotland, and the NHS and education services in Scotland and Wales is quite frankly dreadful. Police Scotland failed to act on intelligence about Russian football hooligans at Euro 2016, and there have been other operational shortcomings. Health and education are also performing poorly under devolution, Jason. Why is it that patients feel it necessary to travel to England for treatment? And have you seen their exam results? More money per head than England and their performance in is almost the worst in the Western world. I can't think why David ever countenanced the idea of giving them more powers."

"I think he was worried about the possible break-up of the United Kingdom, Prime Minister. He thought that, by giving Scotland and Wales more powers, they would choose to stay."

"Just what Labour thought twenty years ago" said Crosby. "And look what's happened."

"When do you want me to start, Prime Minister?" asked Berry.

"Immediately, Jason."

"One further question, Prime Minister. What about Northern Ireland?"

"Hold off Northern Ireland for the time being, Jason. The Unionists are still in power there and are on our side over Europe. However, I've got long-term concerns about Northern Ireland. The nationalists are on the brink of becoming the majority community and it's only a matter of time before Sinn Fein is in power. Already, their leader's calling for a referendum on unification with the Republic of Ireland in the wake of the Brexit vote."

"I assume you are going to tell Gerry Doherty that there is no chance of such a referendum taking place."

Doherty was the leader of Sinn Fein and, under the power-sharing agreement reached in 1998, the Deputy First Minister of Northern Ireland.

"I most definitely am, Jason."

11 November 2016
Department for the Environment, Communities
and Local Government
Marsham Street
London

Sam Tarrant was devastated. Earlier that day, he had received a letter from Human Resources Department advising him that he was going to be made redundant.

Compulsory redundancy was one of several initiatives that DECLoG had adopted to reduce its costs. Two years previously, it vacated its headquarters at Eland House and moved into part of the Marsham Street buildings in which the Home Office had been the sole occupant. The previous year, DECLoG had reduced its staff headcount through a voluntary exit scheme which resulted in the departure of 400 staff. But further cuts were now demanded to reduce the burden on the public purse and, this time, it was necessary to make compulsory redundancies. The criteria were to select 200 staff who had the lowest comparative ranking in the previous year's annual staff appraisals.

Very few staff who fell in this category were poor performers. Previous staff reduction exercises had removed most of the so-called "dead wood" from DECLoG's ranks. Instead, the staff selected had, in most cases, performed reasonably well in their posts but had the misfortune of being compared against highly capable staff. And staff like Tarrant, who worked in humdrum business as usual roles had little chance of outshining staff working on high-profile policy or legislative development roles.

Tarrant's line manager, Victoria Summers, was sympathetic. She had high regard for his work and commitment. However, she pointed out that Tarrant needed to up his game to move from the good category to very good. She also advised Tarrant to contact Human Resources for advice on finding a new job.

Tarrant was not convinced that Human Resources would help. It was common knowledge that a Civil Service background was regarded as more of a hindrance than a help in finding equivalent work in the private sector. The stereotype of the lazy, clock-watching, tea-drinking, risk averse civil servant was perpetuated and he suspected that job applications from former civil servants ended up in the wastepaper basket.

For Sam Tarrant, the future looked grim. He was twenty-six years old and had only had five years' service behind him. The compensation payout would be tiny. Over half of his Executive Officer salary went on renting a shared property in Tulse Hill, and he would no longer be able to afford the rent. He had not paid off the debts he had acquired as a student and the only job opportunities available were zero-hours jobs in the retail or hospitality trade. Returning to live with his parents was not an option. His parents had divorced ten years' previously. His father was working in Australia and his mother had remarried and was living in Marbella for most of the year with her new husband, a property developer.

Later that day
Leigham Vale
Tulse Hill
London

"Sam, you're joking, man" shouted Mo Shabbir, one of Sam Tarrant's flatmates. "Civil Service's a job for life."

"Not any more, Mo. See the letter."

"You'll get a job, easy Sam" said Dan Betts, another flatmate. "You've got a degree after all."

"It's not as easy as you think, guys" cried Tarrant. "Yes, I've got a degree. An upper second in Politics. Half the country's graduates have got 2.1s. And no one wants to take on a Politics graduate. You've seen what some businessmen and Government Ministers have said about useless qualifications?"

"Sam, you've been shafted by the Government" said Ashley Rivers. "Shaft them back."

"How, Ash?" replied Tarrant.

"You must have access to sensitive information. Bound to interest someone like Wikileaks. Do what Edward Snowden did." Rivers was a member of the Socialist Workers Party and saw his life's mission to undermine the Government and its agencies.

"Are you out of your fucking mind, Ash?" shouted Tarrant. "Do that and I'll be spending the next 20 years in Belmarsh."

"Not if you encrypt documents, Ash" replied Shabbir. He worked in the IT industry and knew how to format documents so they could not be opened or traced. "What's more, there's part of the internet where the authorities don't know how to access or monitor. They call it the 'Dark Web'. I'll show you how."

"Jesus Christ, guys, you're asking me to break the law." Tarrant was becoming exasperated. "Don't you understand. The Government takes no prisoners when someone leaks information. The cops and MI5 get involved and they're willing to break down doors to bust anyone involved. On top of that, they'll use the law to demand that any media outlet tells them the source of the leak. And anyone done for leaking information goes before a hardline judge and a vetted jury that's most likely to convict."

"We were only trying to help, Sam" replied Rivers.

18 November 2016
Department for the Environment, Communities and Local Government
Marsham Street
London

"One more thing, Sam. You will remain subject to the provisions of the Official Secrets Act indefinitely. Resist the temptation disclose any information and knowledge you have obtained from working here. And remember to exercise discretion when on social media. We won't hesitate to prosecute anyone who breaches the law."

Sam Tarrant had just been interviewed by the Director of Human Resources, Simon Marshall. It had not been a pleasant experience; Marshall was magisterial in approach and made no attempt to offer condolences for being made redundant or thanks for his service and instead gave a lecture on his responsibilities after leaving the service.

On arriving back at his desk, Victoria Summers asked him how the interview went.

"I could have done without that, Vicki" replied Tarrant. "It was like being back in school. Marshall did not bother to thank me for my service or offer any support. Instead, he lectured me about my conduct when I leave the service and basically said that, if I don't keep my mouth shut, I'll be prosecuted. He seems to think that everyone working here is a potential traitor."

"I know how you feel, Sam" replied Summers. "Simon Marshall's not the most tactful person. Problem is that Ministers think highly of him and that's why he's got to where he is now."

Later that day
Leigham Vale
Tulse Hill
London

Sam Tarrant reached his shared house at 7pm. Delays on South Eastern Trains had added 25 minutes to his journey time.

Dan Betts, Ashley Rivers and Mo Shabbir were all watching the television. "Hi Sam. How was today?"

"Absolute shit" replied Tarrant. "The HR Director gave me a lecture about what I'm allowed or not allowed to do after leaving the service."

"As I've said before, that shows the contempt employers have for their staff these days" said Rivers.

"You know something, Ash. I'm inclined to agree."

Tarrant then turned to Shabbir.

"Mo, could you show me how to encrypt documents. Might be useful."

21 November 2016
Department for the Environment, Communities
and Local Government
Marsham Street
London

The malfunctioning of the printer closest to the Local Government Finance Unit had forced Sam Tarrant to use one of the printers at the other end of the building. The introduction of new printers two months previously had enabled staff to route printing requests to any printer in the building if their normal printer had broken down.

Tarrant had run off a spreadsheet on local government finance and minutes of a meeting, and did not think to check that the papers he had picked up were all his. There had already been several cases where people had printed papers and had been unable to find them because a colleague had inadvertently picked them up and walked off with them. It was common courtesy for staff to notify colleagues if they had accidentally walked off with their papers.

When Tarrant thumbed through the papers, he soon realised that he had mistakenly picked up those belonging to someone else. But what drew his attention was the contents and the security marking. The papers were marked SECRET so they were not run of the mill documents. He then noticed that they were a policy submission from the Devolution Unit to the Secretary of State and were about options for reclaiming powers from the Scottish Government and Welsh Assembly Government.

Tarrant recognised the magnitude of the proposals and the impact of unauthorised disclosure. Relations between the UK Government and the devolved administrations in Scotland and Wales had been fractious at the best of times, and had got worse since the vote to leave the European Union. Plans to return Scotland and Wales to direct rule from Westminster could potentially result in a break-up of the United Kingdom. Many of the country's adversaries would welcome such developments. The European Union. Russia. China.

A month earlier, Tarrant would have been on the phone to the Devolution Unit immediately to arrange for the return of the papers he had picked up by mistake. But he was now seething with anger because of his forthcoming redundancy.

Tarrant thought about possible outlets. The *Guardian* was one. *New Statesman*, the *Morning Star, Socialist Worker* were other possibilities. But all were based in the United Kingdom and had to comply with the law to operate. They would almost certainly be required to disclose their source if they were not to be prosecuted. Or worse, shut down. However, there was one site which had none of these constraints. Wikileaks. They operated clandestinely and, if the document was encrypted and sent through the 'dark web' the authorities would have no idea who was responsible for the leak.

CHAPTER 19

24 November 2016
Cureton Street
Pimlico
London

"Secretary of State. Thank goodness I've managed to contact you."

Jason Berry had been woken up to the sound of his telephone ringing. It was 5am and would still be dark for another two hours. He recognised the voice on the other end of the line. It was Stephen Knight, Permanent Secretary at the Department for the Environment, Communities and Local Government.

"Stephen, do you know what time this is? It better be important."

"I'm afraid it is, Secretary of State" replied Knight. "There's been a leak."

The mention that an unauthorised disclosure had taken place aroused Berry from his slumbers. With the country now in the process of taking forward the mandate from the electorate to leave the European Union, the Government had become paranoid about information security.

"You better tell me the details now, Stephen" replied the Secretary of State for the Environment, Communities and Local Government. "How bad is it?"

"Details of proposals to reclaim powers from the devolved Governments in Scotland and Wales have appeared on Wikileaks."

"Oh my God" sighed Berry. He didn't need an explanation of the impact. He could envisage an enraged Amy MacDougall and Rachel Norris screaming like demented banshees at him. Not to mention a glacial interrogation from the Prime Minister. Sarah Crosby was notorious for getting rid of anyone who messed up in office. His ascent up the so-called 'greasy pole' looked doomed.

Berry collected his thoughts.

"Stephen, what has happened has serious consequences for the trustworthiness of the Department and everyone who works there. I want a high-level investigation into how this information ended up in the hands of Wikileaks. If necessary, I want the police and MI5 brought in. And when the culprit is found, I want a full criminal prosecution to go ahead. A prison sentence will be a lesson to others not to try anything similar on."

"Yes, Secretary of State. I'll keep you posted on developments. By the way, the Prime Minister wants to see you. Nine o'clock sharp."

The same morning
Prime Minister's Office
10 Downing Street
London

Sarah Crosby was not in the best of moods. She had just got back from Dublin where she had emerged from three days of bruising talks with her Irish counterpart, Donal O'Grady, about the impact of the United Kingdom's departure from the European Union on the Republic of Ireland.

Ireland was the United Kingdom's biggest trading partner and would be most heavily affected by a British withdrawal from the European Union. O'Grady was concerned that the reintroduction of tariffs between the United Kingdom and the European Union would have adverse economic repercussions for his country. They were only just emerging from almost a decade of austerity imposed after recession hit their economy, and O'Grady was concerned that Ireland would be plunged back into recession.

Another concern was the possibility of customs and immigration posts reappearing on the border between the Republic of Ireland and Northern Ireland. These had been removed in 1998 following the signing of the peace agreement that ended almost 30 years of terrorism and strife in Northern Ireland. Crosby was not herself enthusiastic about their reinstatement but she was aware that a large proportion of Conservative MPs wanted the United Kingdom to withdraw from the Single European Market, which would make the reappearance of the customs and immigration posts unavoidable.

O'Grady had been nicknamed "The Quiet Man" in Ireland for his low-key and unspectacular style of leadership and many republican supporters instinctively felt that his party, Fine Gael, was too favourably inclined towards the United Kingdom. But, during the talks, O'Grady had been robust in insisting that Ireland should not be disadvantaged by the United

Kingdom's departure from the European Union and made it clear that the Irish Government would oppose the reintroduction of a 'hard' border with Northern Ireland.

What particularly irked Crosby was O'Grady's suggestion that a further Irish recession and the reintroduction of border posts might lead to a Sinn Fein government in Dublin. She felt it was blackmail.

The last thing Crosby needed was to be woken in the early hours of the morning to be told that sensitive Government policy proposals had been leaked to a highly subversive website.

At 9am, Jason Berry was in the outer office.

"Prime Minister, the Secretary of State for the Environment, Communities and Local Government to see you" said Joe Halliwell, her Assistant Private Secretary.

Berry took a seat opposite the Prime Minister's desk.

"Well, Jason, can I have an explanation."

"I was only made aware of this leak four hours ago, Prime Minister. In response, I have asked my Permanent Secretary to set up a full investigation and to call in the police and MI5 if they are needed. I also spoke to Ben Richardson to ensure that police and security service support is ready and to Bob Anderson to ensure that Court time is available for a trial once the perpetrator is identified."

"That's all very well, Jason" replied Crosby. "But there's two unanswered questions. Firstly, how in hell did someone manage to get hold of sensitive Government papers in the first place? With Brexit now happening, every Government proposal is of interest to our adversaries, whether domestic or overseas. Looks like there's questions about your Department's internal security arrangements. And secondly, what have you done to manage the fallout? In case you've missed it, have a look at this."

Crosby pointed to a copy of the *Daily Mail* on her desk. It was open at Page 2.

MacDougall and Norris renew demands for independence

The First Ministers of Scotland and Wales, Amy MacDougall and Rachel Norris, have called for immediate referendums on independence following the leak of Government proposals to reduce the powers of the Scottish and Welsh Governments.

SNP leader MacDougall said that the proposals to claw back devolved powers were an act of bad faith by Westminster and repeated her view that Scotland's best interests would be served by remaining part of the European Union and that could only be achieved by independence. Plaid Cymru leader Norris said that the British Government had never respected the will of the Welsh people and that full independence was the only solution.

The provocative stance taken by the First Ministers will only add to the problems that Prime Minister, Sarah Crosby, is facing in taking forward Britain's departure from the European Union. She has just returned from three days of talks in Dublin with Irish Prime Minister, Donal O'Grady, in which she failed to reach agreement about the post-Brexit trading arrangements between Britain and the Republic of Ireland and the possible reappearance of border controls between the Republic and Northern Ireland, which may put the 1998 Good Friday Agreement at risk.

"We tightened up our internal security arrangements a year ago after a previous leak, Prime Minister" said Berry. "Information is now shared on a 'need to know' basis, our internal security can now audit all outgoing telephone conversations and e-mails as well as monitor social media posts by our staff, we've introduced new printers which only print when someone swipes their building pass against the printer and we've introduced a whistleblower helpline so someone can report any allegations of wrongdoing anonymously. Obviously, what happened recently has revealed new weaknesses in our security so I will be asking for a report on how these can be tightened, once we find out the source of the leak.

"As for managing the fallout, I think we may have to bin the proposals to claw back powers from the devolved Governments for the timebeing. That at least may keep MacDougall and Norris quiet for a while. At the same time, we should make it clear that the Government has no intention of allowing either Scotland or Wales to have a referendum on independence. This will make clear that the British Government is firmly in charge of Brexit."

"Very well, Jason. I hope for all our sakes this is going to work. Can you keep me informed about progress on the investigation into the leak? This has already derailed Government policy once too often. I want to see no repetition. Hope you understand."

30 November 2016
Crowne Plaza Hotel
Badenerstrasse
Zurich
Switzerland

"Good evening, fellas. How are you doing? Fancy a beer?"

Eamonn Mulvaney, the Republic of Ireland's FIFA representative and recently voted onto the organisation's Council, recognised Andrew Telfer and Emlyn Rees, the FIFA representatives from Scotland and Wales. Both men had recently been appointed Chairmen of their respective country's football federations following the appointment of their predecessors, Gordon Hunter and Alun Williams, as Vice-Presidents at UEFA.

The bar at the Crowne Plaza had Guinness on tap and both Telfer and Rees indicated they would like the well-known Irish stout. They joined Mulvaney at his table.

"You must be well pleased with the outcome of Euro 2016" said Mulvaney. "I heard it was a roaring success."

"It certainly was, Eamonn" replied Telfer. "The financial report that's due out next year suggests that Euro 2016 benefited our economies by over two billion pounds. If you remember, when we first got the tournament, most people thought we'd never deliver it. We've also managed to secure inward investment from HSBC and Samsung although the Brexit vote has put off other would-be investors. But I think we've sent England the message that Scotland and Wales are pulling their weight."

"That should change the British Government's view of your economic value" said Mulvaney.

"Fat chance of that, Eamonn" said Rees. "You've heard what the British Government were going to do?"

"Don't think I did" replied Mulvaney.

"They were planning to claw back powers from us. Crime, policing, health and education. That would have left us in control of virtually nothing. Next steps would almost certainly be to close us down."

"The Brits haven't changed their mentality in over a century" said Mulvaney. "Good job we got out when we did."

Mulvaney was referring to the independence of the Irish Free State in 1922.

"When is this going to happen?"

"The British Government's called it off, Eamonn" said Telfer. "Someone gave WikiLeaks a copy. Probably a disgruntled civil servant. But I wouldn't rule out them trying again in a few years' time."

"Crosby's never liked the idea of Scotland and Wales running their own affairs" added Rees. "Same with a lot of the Tories. They don't like the idea that we spend our money on ordinary people rather than the rich. They've still got the Empire mentality and see Scotland and Wales as vassal nations. It's got even worse since the Brexit vote. How's it affected Ireland?"

"We're very worried about the impact of Brexit, Emlyn" replied Mulvaney. "Britain's our biggest trading partner. If tariffs on our goods and services are brought in, it will hit our economy just as we are emerging from recession."

"I believe Crosby was over for talks with your Prime Minister, Eamonn" said Telfer.

"She was, Andrew. The talks didn't go well. Crosby's demanding that we introduce immigration controls on our borders to stop people entering who might be on their way to Britain. That's an infringement on our sovereignty. She's also tried to warn us off poaching business from companies who require access to the EU."

"How did your Prime Minister react, Eamonn?" asked Rees.

"O'Grady's not the most forceful of people at the best of times. But he told Crosby in no uncertain terms that what she was proposing was unacceptable."

"I don't suppose Crosby was too impressed with being told to bugger off" said Telfer.

"That's an understatement" replied Mulvaney. "She's threatened to reintroduce customs and immigration controls on the border with Northern Ireland."

"Doesn't that stupid woman understand that would sink the Good Friday Agreement and lead to the return of the Troubles?" said Telfer.

"That's what I fear might happen, Andrew" said Mulvaney. "Turning to a different subject, how's Brexit impacting on yourselves. I understand that Scotland and Wales both voted to remain in the EU."

"We did, Eamonn" replied Rees. "In Wales's case, only just. But there was a clear majority in Scotland. And Northern Ireland."

"Both Scotland and Wales face losing EU funding" said Telfer. "A lot of the infrastructure improvements that made Euro 2016 possible were paid for by Europe. I don't see Westminster making up the difference. They're willing to spend big bucks on London and the South East as if there was no tomorrow. But any expenditure in Scotland, Wales or indeed the North of England, has to be justified with a platinum-plated business case. They've just stopped work the electrification of the railway lines from Edinburgh to Dundee and Aberdeen and from London to Cardiff and Swansea. Also, they've dropped plans for improving broadband access in Scotland and Wales. Meanwhile, they're proceeding with a second Crossrail line in London while the South East's getting an upgrade to broadband systems put in just six years ago. So, I'm not hopeful."

"Is there any chance that Britain might secure a trade deal with the EU and retain access to the open market?" asked Mulvaney.

"Very doubtful" replied Rees. "Crosby's made it clear that the UK will be leaving the EU totally and without exception. She's already charged Fentiman with securing trade deals with other countries. Notably the USA, Australia, Canada and New Zealand but also Malaysia, Thailand, Singapore and Brazil."

Telfer and Rees then turned to the issue of the forthcoming recall vote for the 2018 and 2022 World Cups. Following the appointment of a new President, Secretary-General and Council earlier in the year, FIFA had made a radical change to their constitution. Instead of the FIFA Council taking the final decision on awards of tournaments, responsibility was to be devolved to all 211 delegates from member nations. The first exercise of the new rules would take place the following day when they would be voting on whether their previous decision to award the World Cup to Russia in 2018 and Qatar in 2022 would still stand. All members of FIFA were fully aware that any decision to leave the awards unchanged would be controversial and would have reputational implications. But equally they were aware of the negative implications of taking the award away from emerging countries, particularly if they awarded it to a first world country. The two front runners to take over responsibility for staging the two World Cups, England and Australia, were such countries.

"How are you intending to vote tomorrow, Eamonn?" asked Rees.

"Haven't decided yet on 2018. For 2022, Australia should have it. They've got all the infrastructure in place and their international record is good. But for 2018, I'm going to stick with Russia. I know the previous decision was tarnished by corruption and there's real and justified concern about their Government's commitment to freedom and democracy. But they've done nothing to harm Ireland. Unlike England. So, I'm going to vote for Russia. How about you?"

"Like you, Eamonn, I'm voting for Russia" said Telfer.

"Russia" added Rees. "And for the same reason."

1 December 2016
Department for National Heritage
Cockspur Street
London

"I don't believe it. I just don't fucking believe it."

Seb Mitchell, Secretary of State for National Heritage, had just seen Sky News on the telescreen in his department's Press Suite. The banner headline could not have been any clearer: **ENGLAND WORLD CUP BID FAILS**.

Less than an hour previously, all 211 FIFA delegates had participated in a recall vote for the 2018 and 2022 World Cups. The 2022 World Cup went, as expected, to Australia by a clear majority. But expectations that England would be staging its first World Cup since 1966 were extinguished as Russia retained the 2018 World Cup by a majority of seven votes.

Seated alongside Mitchell were the Sports Minister, Tim Brazier and the Department's Permanent Secretary, Sally Robbins.

"Tim, Sally, I thought we had the bid in the bag. What the hell were those idiots thinking by voting for Russia again?"

"The Russians have a lot of influence with emerging countries, Secretary of State" said Brazier. "And money. That's how they got the World Cup in the first place."

"Yes, I recognise that, Tim" replied Mitchell. "But last week, you assured me that if European countries voted for us, we would win the bid. Looks like some of them voted for Russia."

"It's possible that Brexit might be a factor, Secretary of State" said Robbins.

They were interrupted by the presence of Suzanne Dudley, Mitchell's Private Secretary.

"Secretary of State, David Rose is on the phone for you." The Chairman of the Football Association had gone to Zurich for the vote.

A minute later, Mitchell was back in his office.

"David, can you explain to me what happened. What in God's name persuaded FIFA to give the World Cup back to Russia?"

"I'm trying to work that one out myself, Secretary of State" replied Rose. "Russia's done little to assure the world that they've cleaned up their act. There's still justified concerns about corruption, the Government if anything is becoming even more authoritarian than before and evidence that the hooliganism at Euro 2016 was state-sanctioned is on the table. Yet they've managed to hold onto the World Cup."

"How?" asked Mitchell. "Who the hell voted for Russia?"

"The usual suspects" replied Rose. "Traditional allies like China, Serbia, Belarus and Iran. And countries hostile to Britain like Argentina. However, quite a few emerging countries voted for Russia as they have been beneficiaries. But I was surprised that some Western European countries voted for Russia."

"Which countries?" asked Mitchell.

"France, Germany, Belgium, Spain and the Republic of Ireland for starters. I've asked for the full list of votes cast and will let you have details when available."

Mitchell was stunned and was trying to control his temper. "Any reason why, David?"

"Brexit was the main reason" replied Rose. "It has not gone down well with our European partners. And I understand that the Prime Minister had a rather stormy meeting with the Irish Prime Minister a week ago. This could have influenced the way they voted."

"So, it looks like we're going to be subject to vindictive acts of spite and pettiness from the EU from now on" replied Mitchell.

"One thing more, Secretary of State. Scotland and Wales also both voted for Russia."

EPILOGUE

13 June 2018
Hotel Ritz Carlton
Place Vendôme
Paris

"Monsieur Picard. So glad we could meet."

The pretty blonde escort that François Picard had arranged to meet was no more than thirty years old and young enough to be Picard's daughter. However, it raised no comment in the Ritz Carlton where it was common to see attractive young women on the arm of much older men. In all cases, their wealth and power were the attraction.

Picard had come through a traumatic year that would have tested the constitution of a less robust man. The previous year, he had been the chief prosecution witness in the trials of the former President of FIFA Joao da Costa and two former Executive Council members, Orville McKenzie and Amadou N'Konte which took place in the USA. Da Costa had died before the verdicts were announced but McKenzie was sentenced to thirty years' imprisonment and N'Konte received twenty-five years. Picard had secured immunity from prosecution from the US Department of Justice, but the personal fallout for him was considerable. His decision to turn state evidence had earned the enmity of friends and families of the four men prosecuted, as well as former colleagues on FIFA.

Picard's act in undermining France's bid for Euro 2016 had also made him a pariah in his own country. Although the French authorities agreed to drop their plans to prosecute Picard, he was declared *persona non grata* by the French Football Federation and his life Presidency was revoked. He was also expelled from Les Republicains, the main centre-right political party whom he had served as a Minister.

Finally, Picard's marriage had collapsed and his wife, Cècile, was suing for divorce. He would be facing a sizeable settlement.

"Your name, my dear?"

"Olga" replied the escort.

"Would you like to come through for a drink?"

"I would. Thank you so much."

In normal circumstances, Picard would have been extremely wary of entertaining a stranger. He had already made many enemies by turning State evidence in the trial of his former FIFA colleagues. There were already rumours that Joao da Costa's son was hiring a hitman to extract revenge upon Picard. But, more seriously, he had upset several Russian oligarchs. The Russians did not take prisoners. Anyone from intrusive journalists through to business rivals who had crossed them had met a grisly end.

But Picard's personal vanity had got the better of him. He couldn't care less that he was one of the most loathed men in France. By having a beautiful young woman on his arm, he was effectively sending a gigantic V-sign to his adversaries.

Picard and his escort received many admiring glances as they strode into the cocktail bar at the Ritz Carlton. He bought a Napoleon brandy for himself and a Bloody Mary for his escort. For the next hour, they were talking. Then Picard made a proposition.

"I have an apartment here, Olga. Would you like to join me there? It's a bit more private."

"Not just yet, François. In another half-hour, maybe. Oh, I must go to the ladies. Won't be a minute and I'll be back."

Olga Karpova had no intention of going to the ladies' rest room. She was a former FSB agent who was now employed by Vladimir Tupitsin and had been sent on a mission to assassinate Picard. Although Tupitsin had avoided facing trial for his part in bribing FIFA delegates to give Russia the 2018 World Cup, all his assets in Western banks had been impounded, along with properties he owned in London, New York and Zurich. Picard had given the US authorities details of how FIFA had been bribed. Tupitsin wanted revenge.

Karpova removed her smartphone from her handbag and rang an encrypted number. Tupitsin was on the other end.

"Olga, how are things going?" asked Tupitsin.

"Couldn't be better, Mr Tupitsin" replied Karpova. "Picard suspects nothing and he's even invited me up to his apartment. I'll phone back later."

"Excellent work, Olga. Once you've disposed of Picard, a car will be waiting to take you to Le Bourget. A white Peugeot 408, registration AO 358 TB. At Le Bourget, I've arranged for a private jet to take you back to Russia."

"What about the police, Mr Tupitsin? Once they find Picard's body, won't they close all the airports?"

"I've made sure they won't, my dear. Don't worry."

A minute later, Karpova was back in the cocktail bar.

"François, I would like to accept your kind offer. Shall we go up?"

"My pleasure" replied Picard.

Picard and Karpova took the lift to Picard's penthouse apartment. Once inside, they sat down on the large leather sofa in the middle of the room. For Picard, he anticipated a night of passion in the air. It had been years since he had made love to his wife and Olga seemed so much better than any of the previous mistresses he had been associated with.

The couple were soon kissing each other. Karpova was impressed with Picard's lovemaking. He might have been in his sixties but what they said about French men being great lovers was correct.

"Darling, let's get a bit more intimate" said Karpova. "How about your bedroom?"

"I'm up for that" replied Picard.

"Can I go in first, François? I'll call when I'm ready."

Two minutes later, Karpova indicated she was ready. Picard opened the bedroom door. He did not notice that Karpova was holding a GSh-18 pistol, which was the current standard sidearm for the Russian security forces. As Picard walked in, Karpova opened fire twice. Picard fell to the ground, bleeding and mortally wounded.

Karpova's FSB training had taught her of the importance of making sure that a target was dead. She pointed the GSh-18 to Picard's left temple and opened fire.

"Sorry, my darling. Orders."

She then changed out of the expensive cocktail dress she had been wearing into a white blouse and black skirt which was the standard uniform of the Ritz Carlton's staff. This meant she would look inconspicuous as she left the building.

14 June 2018
Sky News

"This is Sam Broadbent with today's headlines from Sky News.

"François Picard, the former Secretary-General of FIFA, was found dead in his Paris apartment earlier today. Staff at the Ritz Carlton Hotel found his body earlier this morning. He had been shot three times. A spokesman for the police said they had no idea of the motive for M. Picard's murder but that enquiries were in process."

"M. Picard's ten-year spell as Secretary-General of FIFA was highly controversial and dogged by allegations of bribery and corruption which led to the former FIFA President, Joao da Costa and two Vice-Presidents being tried in the United States. It is believed that M. Picard's decision to turn state evidence against his former colleagues may be a factor."

"Over to our Paris correspondent, Emma Robertson....................."

The same day
Olympic Stadium
Moscow

The opening ceremony for the 2018 World Cup was underway. The Russians had spared no expense on the ceremony and were desperate to prove to the rest of the world that they were fit and ready to stage one of the world's most prestigious sporting events. The first part of the ceremony was given over to traditional Russian musicians and dancers. Later on, the legendary German rock band, the Scorpions, were scheduled to appear. The audience was keenly anticipating them playing their iconic hit record from 1991, "Wind of Change".

Russia's President, Dimitriy Ivanov, smiled as he looked back on a successful two years. Against all odds, Russia had managed to hold onto the right to stage the World Cup after a reconstituted FIFA had held a re-run of the bidding process in November 2016. The vote by the United Kingdom to leave the European Union and the election of a belligerently right-wing business tycoon, Mark Judd, as US President in the same year had reopened divisions within the Western world, and arguments over trade and defence had blunted their ability to present a united stand against Russia.

The Presidential Box was already full. Ivanov had invited favoured leaders from across the world. The Presidents of China, Iran and North Korea, Li Zhang, Mohammed Alizadeh and Park Ryeung-Chee, were present, as was Daniel Gallardo, Julia Rodriguez and Roberto Valenzuela, the Presidents of Cuba, Argentina and Venezuela. The Russian Football Federation was represented by Sergei Lavotchkin and FIFA's new President, Sepp Müller, sat beside him.

There was no official representation from either the USA or the United Kingdom. Although both the USA and England had qualified for the Wold Cup and were taking part, both the US and British Governments refused the invitation to attend to show their disapproval towards the Russian Government for domestic human rights transgressions towards political opponents, economic and military aggression towards neighbouring countries including NATO members and officially-sanctioned corruption in securing the right to stage the World Cup.

However, there was an unofficial US and British presence in the Presidential box. The Reverend Jesse Ferguson, an outspoken and militant black rights activist from the USA who was frequently in conflict with the Judd administration, had accepted an offer from President Ivanov to attend. As had the leader of the Labour Party in the United Kingdom, Philip Rutland. Both men had been fiercely castigated by the conservative media in their respective countries for giving aid and comfort to a hostile regime and many of their countrymen and women regarded what they had done as treason.

Vladimir Tupitsin had also been invited into the Presidential box. The powerful oligarch had been primarily responsible for Russia winning the original vote by FIFA to stage the 2018 World Cup. He had put up over half the money that was used to bribe key members of the FIFA Executive Council. He had also made available the additional money to bribe UEFA's leaders so that Scotland and Wales would win the right to stage Euro 2016. The fact that they eventually ran a highly successful tournament was irrelevant. The damage had been done five years earlier when the early problems faced by Scotland and Wales helped cast doubt on England's capacity to stage the World Cup.

Having met all the foreign dignitaries, Ivanov made a beeline to meet Tupitsin. He had every reason to thank the oligarch for helping secure the World Cup for Russia.

Tupitsin was a tall man and towered over the short- stocky President.

"Vladimir, a pleasure to meet you again. I must thank you for your services in helping the Motherland secure its first major international tournament for nearly forty years." Ivanov was referring to the 1980 Olympic Games, at which time he was a trainee agent in the former KGB.

"Not at all, Mr President" replied Tupitsin. "It was my pleasure that I could be of service to the Motherland."

"What an excellent job you did, Vladimir. Have a look at it. An opening ceremony fitting for a great country and showing the world that Russia means business. Sorry to hear about what happened to your overseas assets. Has there been any progress in unlocking them?"

"None so far, Mr President."

"I'm afraid that the current US President wants conflict rather than peace" replied Ivanov. "It may take time to recover your assets, Vladimir. But you'll get them back in the end. By the way, did you hear about François Picard?"

"I did. Most regrettable. But Monsieur Picard was the architect of his own demise."

"How come, Vladimir?"

"He was a vain, greedy man. Obsessed by power, money and status. And lacking courage when the shit hit the fan. He tried to hunt with the hounds and run with the fox. It never works – eventually, you get caught. He took our money with no sense of shame and, when found out, changed sides. He made a lot of enemies as a result. Any one of them could be responsible."

"That's all in the past, Vladimir" said Ivanov. "The present is out there. And above."

As Ivanov spoke, everyone was deafened as six Sukhoi SU30s of the "Russian Knights" aerobatic team overflew the Olympic Stadium, streaming red, white and blue smoke.

Tupitsin allowed himself a wry smile as he thought of the now deceased Picard.

ROB MURPHY

KINGDOM COME

2015. The United Kingdom's just discovered enough oil to guarantee prosperity for the next 100 years. The Government sees this as the final cog in its project to make the United Kingdom the enterprise capital of the world and to restore the country's greatness.

The only problem is that most of the oil lies off Scotland and Wales. And the Scots and Welsh want their share of the bonanza.

Over the next six years, the United Kingdom descends into a spiral of conflict in which old nationalisms re-emerge and threaten to drag in European neighbours and the United States as the violence spills over beyond the country's boundaries.